EVERY LAST DROP

I blow some smoke at the ceiling.

—I feel like I'm forgetting something. Vyrus. Clans. Zombies. Stay out of the sun. Don't get shot. Abandon your life. Drink blood to survive.

I shake my head.

—No. Guess that pretty much covers it.

I flick my cigarette butt away.

—So, question is, can you take it? I lay it out like that, do you think you're the kind who can take it?

She wipes at the drying tear tracks in the grit on her cheeks. She sticks a finger in her mouth and touches her healing tongue, takes her fingers out of her mouth and looks at me.

Says nothing.

I nod, point up at the barred window at ground level, the night sky above.

—Look up there.

She looks.

I pull out my gun and use my last three bullets.

BY CHARLIE HUSTON

Already Dead

No Dominion

Half the Blood of Brooklyn

Every Last Drop

EVERY LAST DROP

CHARLIE HUSTON

www.orbitbooks.net

ORBIT

First published in the United States in 2008 by Del Rey Books,
an imprint of The Random House Publishing Group,
a division of Random House, Inc., New York.
First published in Great Britain in 2008 by Orbit
This paperback edition published in 2008 by Orbit

A CIP catalogue record for this book is available from the British Library.

ISBN 978-1-84149-681-8

Typeset in Fairfield LH Light by Palimpsest Book Production Limited,
Grangemouth, Stirlingshire

Papers used by Orbit are natural, renewable and recyclable products,
made from wood grown in sustainable forests and certified in accordance
with the rules of the Forest Stewardship Council.

Mixed Sources
Product group from well-managed
forests and other controlled sources
www.fsc.org Cert no. SGS-COC-004081
© 1996 Forest Stewardship Council

Orbit
An imprint of
Little, Brown Book Group
100 Victoria Embankment
London EC4Y 0DY

An Hachette Livre UK Company
www.hachettelivre.co.uk

www.orbitbooks.net

To New York City,
with thanks for everything.

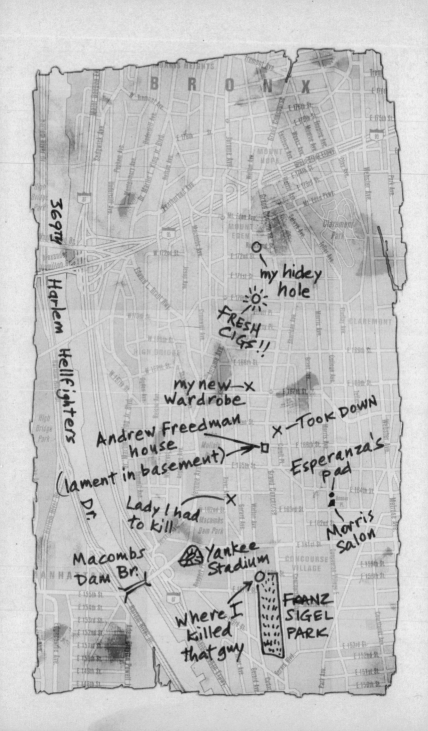

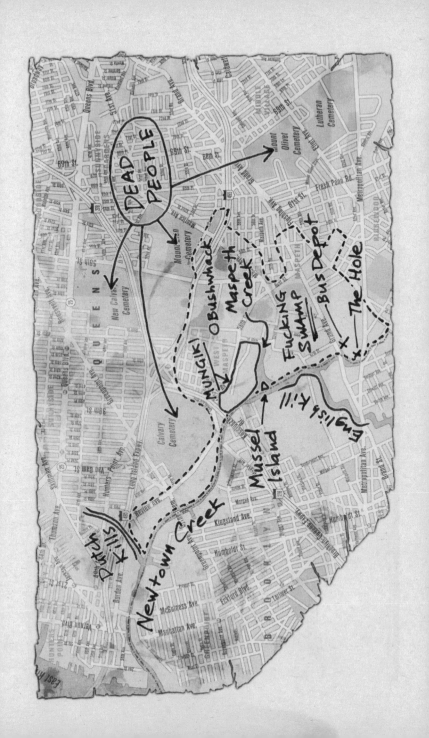

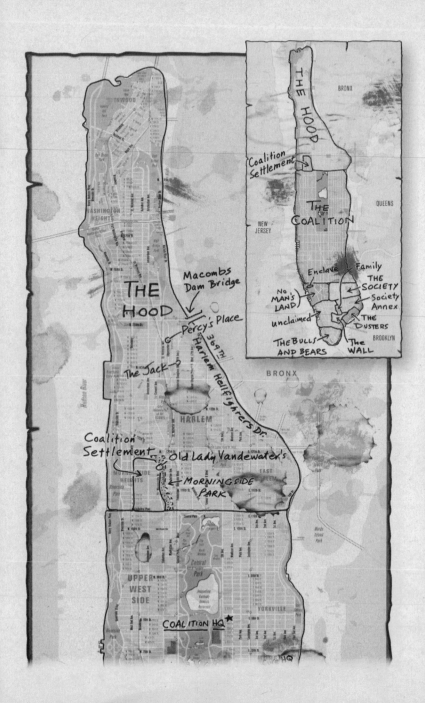

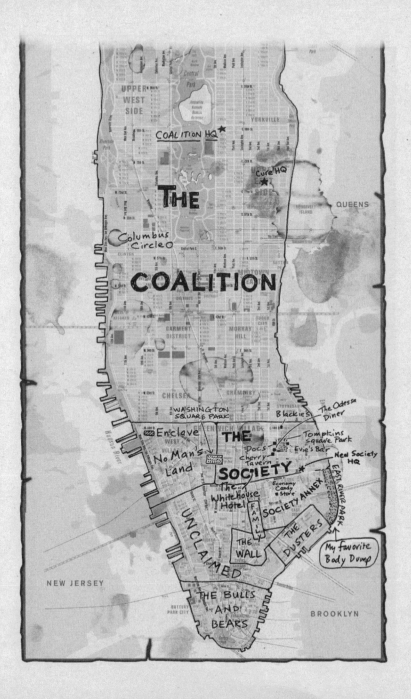

RIPE FOR THE TAKING.

That's all I can think as I watch them.

The crowd pouring out of the Stadium, tens of thousands cramming out onto River and the Concourse, flooding the street under the 4-train tracks as the trains screech in and out overhead, more people packing the cars sardine tight, tripping up the steps, cascading down into the tunnels, mashing into Stan the Man's, northbound traffic making for the Cross Bronx Expressway and the Triborough stalled out from all the people wandering the street. Drunk and half drunk, ecstatic from a win or enraged from a loss, a blue-and-white pinstriped mass of thousands.

All of them full up.

Each of them enough to keep some sad son of a bitch on his feet for weeks. For months if he has some self-control and knows how to go about his business. Most of them strangers to the South Bronx, never seen more of it than this one subway station or the parking lot and the Stadium itself. Each one full to their pumping heart with quarts of blood.

Any wonder every fucking game brings trouble?

Sure, no big secret. That's why the cops are out there. Cops keep the traffic moving in fits and starts. Cops keep the Bleacher Creatures from chewing the ears off any Sox fans stupid enough to stay through the ninth inning on a night their team came to town and won. Cops keep an eye out for pickpockets and for drunks falling under the buses and for snatch-and-grab artists.

If I gave a shit about any of that stuff I'd give them a hearty pat on the back and maybe buy a boy in blue a beer sometime.

But I don't care.

What I do care about are poachers. What I care about are starvelings. I care about the greedy and the weak, the foundering and the lost and the plain stone stupid. I care about them so much that I try to show my face around here after every night game. Just to make it plain and clear.

Clear that they should get off this turf before I come up behind them in an alley one night and put two in the back of their fucking skull before they even know I'm there.

The halt and the lame. They got no place. Not as long as I'm stuck up here.

Up here.

Stand up top long after a game, well before sunrise. Stand on the 4 platform and look south and you can see it. You can see the City right there. One stop over the river.

Fucking China to me.

Coming down to the street, iron bars walling stairs and turnstiles and platforms, arching overhead, meeting the steel undercarriage of the tracks, like walking circles in a cage.

My cage.

No one shits in my cage.

So after a game I make the scene. Truth to tell, figure I'd make it even if I didn't have practical concerns. Figure I'd be out there on River just to take advantage of pretty much the only time I can stick my face out of doors in the neighborhood and not pique someone's curiosity.

A white face in the South Bronx after dark, it draws a little attention. During the day, around the courthouses on One Sixty-one, you see plenty of them. Cops and lawyers and the occasional plaintiff. But they all go home come night. Closest any of them live to One Sixty-one and the Concourse might be Riverdale. More likely Jersey or Queens.

Still, during the day I could blend in real easy eating a Cuban from Havanna Sandwich Queen on one of the benches next to a statue of Moses bringing the Ten Commandments down the hill. Look at my build, my face, my black boots and black Dickies on a summer day, with my leather jacket draped over the warm stone bench, and someone might naturally think *undercover*. Think I'm some cop up here to testify.

But that would require I was out during the day.

Which isn't on my agenda. Ever.

Not until I develop a serious taste for dying from instantaneous eruptions of bloody pustules on my eyes.

So if I desire to take the air, my promenades must come betimes at night. And, man, there just ain't no other fucking white people in these parts after the sun goes down. And drawing eyes is not something I have much desire to do.

Who that guy?

Seen him around?

Gotta be Five-0.

Naw, see him for months. Never make a move on no one.

He ain't livin' up here.

Don't know, could be he is.

What block? What building?

Next thing you know, go down a block on a hot night: Old guys got their card table and their wives' favorite kitchen chairs out on the sidewalk to play dominoes; young guys standing around someone's leased Escalade, bass beats rippling their baggy shorts, shooting texts to the shorties looking down from a fire escape across the street; windows open, rice and beans and stewed chicken smells coming out, mothers and grandmothers and pregnant girls inside laughing and sipping sangria made from jug red and 7Up; someone catches sight of me and the party just shuts down. Hear nothing but my boots on the pavement, see nothing but sideways eyes scoping me out all the way to the end of the street until I turn the corner and they all look at one another.

Who the fuckin' white guy?

Figure a question like that can drive some people crazy. Figure some people got to know. Figure sooner or later someone gets in my face. Figure that doesn't end well.

Figure that isn't the real fucking problem anyway.

The real fucking problem is when that question circulates too far, rumors start, people tell stories, stories spread.

The river, I can't cross it, but any of these people can. And they can take questions and rumors and stories with them. And once that kind of shit is over there on the Island, no telling where it ends up. Ends up in the wrong place, maybe someone hears it. Someone hears it, maybe someone decides to look into it. Someone looks into it, maybe someone sees me. Someone finds me. And once I'm found by someone from the Island, figure my game is played out. Figure me dead.

Well, that's on the agenda, but I'm trying to see if I can't attend to that matter at a later date. More pressing business at the moment.

Places to go. People to see.

And kill.

Goals. Ambitions. They keep a man going.

Any case, all the restrictions my new neighborhood puts on me, figure I'd stroll over after the games just to mix with the crowd. Just to be out. Anonymous. *Free* is a word you could use if you like. If you like a good laugh, that is.

And while I'm there stretching my legs, I take a look around, take a sniff of the air, see if I maybe smell something I don't like. I smell something I don't like, I can make a point of finding who it is. Maybe find an intimate moment when the crowd eddies around us, lean close and make myself clear.

I had such an opportunity tonight.

Waiting on the last couple outs of the ninth inning inside

Billy's, nursing a plastic cup of tap beer, mentally adding the last of the singles and change in my pocket to see if I could make it come out to enough for a real drink before I wrapped up. I smelled something waft in from the street. I knocked the bottom of my cup against the bar and watched the foam rise, watched it boil down, drank the last of it lukewarm and headed out to the street where the crowd from a not very close loss was already pouring surly out of the Stadium.

Want to smell rank? Smell a few thousand baseball fans on a hell-humid night after a bad loss. Sweat-soaked jerseys, urine-soaked sneakers, dribbled pump-cheese, a cloud of exhaled peanut breath and hot dog farts.

Unpleasant.

And still, I can smell it.

Scent like slightly diluted acid, cutting my nasal passages. Hard sharp poison. Venom.

Vyrus.

I start cutting the crowd, working my way back and forth across the street on sharp diagonals, looking for the scent. And finding it. Finding it over and over.

The dildo somewhere up ahead of me must be following a similar path, but cutting for signs of different prey. Looking for a mark. Someone who will cull themselves drunk from the herd and wander down the wrong long street, into an absence of light where any old bad shit can take place.

I can be patient. Wait till he starts moving in a straight line. That will be the sign, when he stops blundering back and forth leaving trail after trail, that'll be the sign he's found what he wants. The idiot, out here making a spectacle of himself, hunting in the open like a bag-snatcher.

Or.

Oh, shit.

Yeah, who's the idiot now?

Right. Me.

It's not a single trail zigzagging the crowd.

It's *trails.*

A pack. A fucking pack in the crowd. A fucking pack of young-bloods working the crowd after a game. Cocky in numbers, ignorant of fear, dumber than dirt.

Christ, does that ring a bell.

Like my own bell tolling away before I learned a thing or two.

I can't tell how many. Their lines are all stirred together in the dead air by the shuffling herd. But the scent is strong. So make it three. Maybe make it four. No more than that. Four together is pushing any kind of balance. Four can't last together for long. Tear each other apart.

No more than four. More likely three. Two?

That's wishful thinking.

But Christ, let it be no more than three.

More than three and I just won't have enough bullets. Three bullets being all I have at the moment. Three bullets, a likewise amount of dollars, and maybe that many days I can get through healthy before I need to get my hands on some more blood of my own.

Well, not blood of my own. More like blood of someone who can maybe spare a couple pints. Those people, they tend to be a rare commodity. Most people need all they got. And some of us, some of us need all we can get our damn hands on.

Every last drop.

—Now! Now! Clear the fuck off now!

—Fuck you!

—Yeah, fuck you!

—Not your fuckin' street!

—Gonna meet the street in a second. Gonna be assumin' the position gangsta style, face in the gutter in a second.

—Man, fuck you!

I swing round and watch some cops dealing with four kids whipping through the crowd on bright little pocket bikes, knees jutting high from the two-foot-tall cycles, engines rising and falling as they give little pulses of gas to keep themselves in motion.

The cop on point adjusts his gun belt.

—Say that word to me again! Say it again! Taser your ass right off that bike. Know what happens I hit you with a Taser? Make you shit your pants, kid. Lie there crying *mami, mami* and your pants full of shit just like when you were a baby.

One of the kids guns his bike, the tails of his do-rag flapping behind him.

—Man, Taser you mama.

—What? Say what?

The kids cut back and forth between cars and pedestrians, never losing balance, staying just far enough from the cops that if the officers get serious the kids know they can get away.

—Say you mama need a Taser for her stinky pussy.

The cops are half smiling as they walk slowly, herding the kids away from the heart of the Stadium outflow. Enjoying the distraction. But clearly not above busting a little skull if they can get their hands on the fuckers.

The point cop fingers the handle of his baton and tilts his chin at his partner.

—Kid's clearly never met your mama, Olivera, otherwise he'd know how sweet her pussy smells.

Olivera hoists a middle finger at him.

—Not as sweet as your mama says my dick is.

Do-rag rises on his pegs.

—Cops be all in each other mama's pussies. I wait till you at it and fuck you daughters.

The point cop's fingers curl on his baton.

—That ain't fuckin' funny, you little shit.

Olivera adjusts his hat.

—I ain't even got a daughter and I don't think it's funny.

Do-rag shrugs, weaves around a clot of baseball fans watching the scene play.

—No problems, man. I fuck you wifey instead.

And the two cops run at the kids and the two other cops that had been working their way over from the north end of the street where the new Stadium is going up run at the kids and the kids hit the gas, the tiny 49cc engines whining and the crowd scatters and the cops scream and when the dust settles the backs of the kids flick out of sight around the corner, one of them waving the cap he snatched from the head of one of the cops.

The crowd rustles back into its former rhythm and shape, everyone avoiding eye contact with the cursing cops. The cops stand in a circle and ask one another if they've ever seen those kids before, what block they maybe live on, what building they maybe live in, discussing how much ass they're gonna kick when they catch up to them.

I wander across the street, crossing the path the kids took as they rode off, knowing the cops will be lucky if they never see that particular group of little shits ever again.

Poison in the air.

Poison left hanging by that pack.

Kids no older than thirteen. Could they be older? Sure they could. If they were heavy feeders they could be old men on the inside. But they're not. Old men wouldn't make a spectacle like that. Old men wouldn't bait cops. No, they're new.

New to the life.

Jesus, thirteen, they're new to everything there is. And destined to never get old to it. Not the signs they're flashing. Big signs, neon and bright: *KILL ME NOW!*

I cross to Gerrard, the crowd thinner, the traffic for the CBE and the Triborough heavy, past the long low bunker of the parking garage.

Thinking.

Yeah, I'm thinking about the kids. But I got other things on my mind as well. Like I'm thinking about who made them that way. Who bled into them. And how many must have died ugly on the way to infecting those four.

And I'm thinking how life isn't an easy thing. Nasty, brutish and short, so they say. And how you got to take your pleasures where and when you find them. Because they may not come again.

And I'm thinking just how much pleasure I'm gonna take from scalping the guy who infected those kids. How much fun it's going to be to peel his skull and shove the rag of skin and hair down his throat to muffle the screams while I figure ways to make him live as long as possible as I yank his ribs out.

Any wonder I'm so distracted I don't register the stink of them as I pass the gated mouth of an alley until I'm twenty feet past it?

I pull up and walk back. The alley is right next to Cassisi and Cassisi Accident Cases. *Se habla español.* Like any of the ambulance chasers in these parts don't *habla español.*

I look between the red-painted bars of the gate, down the narrow space between buildings where old stone walls topped by curls of razor wire separate good neighbors. There's a concrete staircase climbing to the backs of buildings that face on Walton. A splash of red much brighter than the paint on the gate at the foot of those stairs.

I push the gate open, the chain that's meant to keep it closed dangles, links snapped clean. At the end of the alley, a sound. Reminds me of a cat I saw once, had its hindquarters run over by a bus. Cat's forelegs kept reaching out, claws rasping the asphalt, trying to get purchase, pull itself away from the pain. People stood on the sidewalk, stared at the mutilated cat. I stepped on its neck and it stopped moving. Way people reacted, you'd have thought I did the wrong thing.

She's where they left her, on the pavement, blood bubbling from her lips, red fake fingernails raking the ground. Her eyes roll as my shadow falls across her. Looks at me, wheezes, says something.

—Ee iunt aigh ee.

It takes a second, but I get it.

She's right. They didn't rape her. A hard thing for her to fathom about a gang of rabid kids who just bit her tongue out.

Her eyes roll again, up into her head this time, and she's out.

I look around. Lights in the back windows of the tenements. A collection of overfull garbage cans with a chain running through their handles. The kind of alley where people steal fucking garbage cans. Up the stairs it's darker, a little alcove huddled at the bottom of one of the buildings, a door leading into a basement.

I pick her up and put her over my shoulder and go up the stairs and down into the alcove. The door is steel, the lock is cheap. It pops the second time I put my shoulder into it. I take her inside and dump her in a corner.

She's stopped bleeding. She's stopped bleeding for the same reason I'm not drinking her blood right now. The kids infected her. Could have been on purpose. Could have been an accident. Biting off someone's tongue, figure there's a good chance you might get your own lips bit. However it went down, she got some of the kids' blood in her.

And she liked it.

Or something in her liked it.

Or however it works.

If it hadn't worked, if she wasn't the kind can take the Vyrus, she'd be dead in a puddle of white spew already. As it is, the wound in her mouth and the various scratches and scrapes she got in the tussle are closed up. Vyrus going to work. So I settle in.

I could kill her.

I should kill her.

I don't and she'll either end up drawing attention to her new condition and making things harder for everyone else. Or she'll take to it and be another mouth that needs to feed. More competition for everyone. Not that I care about everyone. Still, fact that she's likely got no future that doesn't involve making my life harder in one way or another is enough that I should kill her now.

But I don't.

Someone had a chance to make that call on me way back and he passed on the option. I don't talk to that guy anymore. Not since I stuck a nail in his femoral artery, but he did right by me once.

Least I can do is try the same.

Give her the score.

Let her decide.

So I smoke. And wait. Wait for the Vyrus to finish working her over. Then we can have a talk.

Christ I hope she doesn't scream too much when I try to explain it to her.

—Here's how the rest of your life works. You're fucked. Your family, you don't get to see them ever again. Same with your friends. Your job is over. Wherever you live, you don't live there anymore. You see someone on the street that you used to know, you go the other way. You see those people, you get tempted to talk to them. Try to explain. What you try to explain is that you're sick. You try to explain it's not what they think. It's a virus. A thing living inside you. It makes you sicker than they can imagine. And there's only one way to treat it. To treat the symptoms. That's to feed it. And there's only one thing to feed it. That's blood. People blood. Know what happens when you tell them that? They get the same look on their face that you got on yours right now. Know the difference? They're not infected. They didn't just get jumped and beaten and have their tongue bitten out by a pack of wilders who proceeded to suck on their mouth like it was a water fountain. And because that didn't happen to them, they can't feel what you're feeling. That burn inside, the heat and tingle around your wounds. They can't look at the cuts on their bare arms and see they're already closed up, turning pink to white. They can't feel the scab grow over their stub of a tongue, feel it flaking away, feel how smooth and perfect it is now. Feel that it almost seems to be growing back. Unlike you, they hear a story like that, they got no reason to think you're anything but out of your fucking head, and get you locked up. And that's the happy ending. The unhappy ending is if they should believe you. If someone should somehow find out you're telling the truth. Because they sure as shit won't think you're sick, they'll think you're a goddamn monster. And won't it be fun to see *that* look on their faces. So, no more life. It's over. Other things are over too. You'll never see the sun again. Not unless you're about to die a horrible death. The virus in you goes crazy if it's hit with shortwave UVs from the sun. Your whole body becomes cancerous. Fast. Good news, none of the other crap is a problem. Crosses, holy water, garlic. That shit, it's shit. You're infected, not damned. Or maybe you are. I don't know. A stake through the heart will kill you, just like any asshole. But when it's fed, the Vyrus will crank up your system. Stronger, faster. Heightened senses. And tough. But keeping it fed is the thing. A pint a week. Blood. Human. More if possible. Think about drinking blood. Not a happy thought. Now think about getting it. The kids that attacked you, they're not the norm. Well, up here they may be a little more normal, but still pretty fucking baroque. The City, Manhattan, it's organized. Clans got it carved up. Coalition, Hood, Society, others. Each one's got an agenda. A Clan takes you in, they'll help you get settled. Adjusted. Not a joiner, you can go Rogue, stay the fuck off Clan turf. That means staying off the Island. Means getting blood on your own. Means hurting people, mostly. Means sometimes someone gets killed. But better if they don't. Better if you develop a system. Find a junkie on the nod you can tap him for a pint. Vyrus doesn't care about the junk. Doesn't care about any kind of illness or poison. Keep it healthy, it keeps you healthy. And maybe I'm wrong about your people. Maybe you're special close to someone. Could be your boyfriend. Could be your sister. Someone that's got a taste for being used. You know the type. Maybe they got it in them to let you cut into a vein every few weeks. That makes things a lot easier. Still need to make some moves, but you have someone like that, a Lucy like that, and things get easier. Not that easy is a word gets thrown around much in this life. What else? People know about us. Not a lot, but a few. Well, some know about us, others just hope we're real. Some, they want in on the game, want to make the scene. Fucking Renfields. Others, they got an axe to grind. Some of them got real axes. Van Helsings. A real one is bad news. Someone who can go around in the day, poke into things, has a credit rating to buy guns and bullets and stuff, and who also knows the real score on us, that's a serious danger. And? What? And there's some infecteds think the Vyrus isn't a virus. Like maybe it's something, I don't know, something supernatural. *Enclave.* They're crazy. And there's a bacteria. Kinda like the Vyrus, 'cept it turns people into brain eaters. Zombies. But that's pretty rare. So. I don't know what else. I don't usually talk this much.

I blow some smoke at the ceiling.

—I feel like I'm forgetting something. Vyrus. Clans. Zombies. Stay out of the sun. Don't get shot. Abandon your life. Drink blood to survive.

I shake my head.

—No. Guess that pretty much covers it.

I flick my cigarette butt away.

—So, question is, can you take it? I lay it out like that, do you think you're the kind who can take it?

She wipes at the drying tear tracks in the grit on her cheeks. She sticks a finger in her mouth and touches her healing tongue, takes her fingers out of her mouth and looks at me.

Says nothing.

I nod, point up at the barred window at ground level, the night sky above.

—Look up there.

She looks.

I pull out my gun and use my last three bullets.

Walking down the street, heading north, my ears ring loud from the shots fired in the basement.

I'm a good shot. But shooting from the hip, I didn't want to worry about the first bullet missing the middle of her brain and her having a couple seconds to think about it. To feel it. Better to put all three in her face as fast as possible. Leave nothing to chance.

She wasn't stupid, she'd never have been able to make that play herself.

Someone who knew me might say I was trying to make up for some kind of mistake I made in my past. Trying to do something like compensate for the mess I left behind on the Island. Trying to make right for a time when I moved too slow and let someone slip away from me.

But no one knows me here.

Any other reason to be in the Bronx, I don't know what it could be.

At the north end of Joyce Kilmer Park, a rust, primer and white station wagon that looks like it was recently firebombed cruises up next to me and a match flares inside.

—Tell me, Joe.

I put a hand on my gun, wishing I'd maybe used just two bullets instead of three.

The match flame touches the end of a cigarette between two red lips.

—Was doing that as unpleasant as it looked?

—You see who hit her?

—Yeah.

—Want to share?

—Know anything about tweens on pocket rockets, wilding for blood?

She looks at me, puts a tilt on her head, looks away.

—Yeah. I know that picture.

She leans her arm out the open window of the decaying station wagon, looking at the towering glass façade of the Bronx County Hall of Justice across One Sixty-one from the Concourse Plaza shopping center where she's parked us.

—Was it them?

I do my own head-tilt.

—Did the four spastics buzzing the Stadium crowd chew the chick's tongue out? Tell ya, Esperanza, I didn't witness the act, but I'm assuming they did the deed.

She flicks a spent cigarette butt out the window.

I blow rings at the windshield, watch them explode against the glass.

Not to be outdone, she lights a fresh Pall Mall and blows a ring of her own.

—That girl without the tongue. You made a lot of noise. Cops are already over there.

—I guess even around here someone is bound to call in shots fired in their basement.

—Well, we're not savages up here.

—Didn't say otherwise.

Smoke jets from her nostrils.

—Girl with her face shot off, gonna create some interest.

—Maybe. As much interest as another gun killing gets these days.

—Could get more than usual attention if anyone saw you. White guy in the Bronx murdering a Rican girl. Never know with a story like that. Turns out she was a college student, maybe supporting her grandma and her little sister, a story like that could end up with legs. Social outrage. *White men coming to the Bronx to hunt our Latina sisters.* End up with Reverend Sharpton doing interviews at the scene of the murder.

I peel a strip of fabric from the shredded headliner.

—Better give the *Post* a call. Give your exclusive before it's too late.

She blots some sweat from her temple with the back of her hand, a cross tattooed in the flesh where her thumb joins her hand glistens.

—I'm not arguing whether it was the thing to do, I'm just saying you could have been a little quieter.

—Sure. I could have left a nice quiet corpse of a woman with a broken neck. And they could have autopsied the body and found nothing else wrong, except that she had only half a tongue. Nice and pink and healed and looking like she'd been born that way.

And wouldn't that have provoked some interest when her family found out about it. *Half a tongue? What are you talking about?* Oh, and I imagine the M.E. might also have been intrigued by the way she was missing about half her blood with no fresh wounds through which it could have come out.

She pinches the butt of her cigarette between thumb and forefinger.

—And when you showed the fuck up here on my turf I could have cut a deal with the Mungiki and had you escorted into the fucking river. But you said you'd be cool. So if I want to talk to you about shit that doesn't play cool by me, you can listen and not talk hardcase. Yeah?

I flick some ash.

—Didn't know you had pull with the Mungiki.

She lights a fresh Pall Mall.

—Yeah, well, you don't mix enough to know shit up here, do you?

—Nope.

—No one has pull with the Mungiki. But since they moved to Queens they sometimes need a favor here.

—How you get that gig?

She sighs.

—I used to date one of them.

—Dated a Mungiki? Filed teeth and all?

She gives me that look again.

—Don't believe all the shit you hear, man. They don't file their teeth.

She watches as a handful of couples file out of the Multiplex from the last show.

—Not all of them, anyway. And he wasn't Mungiki when we were hooking up. Just a guy.

—Huh, well, fascinating stuff, but if we're done threatening each other, I thought I might get on. Maybe look into those kids.

She blows ash from the tip of her cigarette.

—Don't fuck with the kids.

I eye her.

—There a reason I shouldn't?

She eyes me back.

—Yeah. I just told you not to.

We do a stare-down while I chew it.

Lady looks twenty-one. Maybe younger. She older? Yeah, a few years, but not by much. You don't feed heavy in the Bronx, not heavy enough to keep the years at bay. Look at me, couple years back I looked maybe late twenties. Now I'd be pressed to pass for thirty-five. At this rate I'm gonna catch up with forty-eight in a hurry.

But she's got youth on her side. Real youth, not the borrowed kind.

Long in the legs. Khaki cargo pants, white retro Jordans, a black tank tucked at the waist, tight over a black sports bra. Tattooed shoulders, hands, neck, designs dark against brown skin. Black hair, short and greased back. Sinews running down long arms. Loping muscles built playing point guard with the boys at Rucker Park over the river.

Esperanza Lucretia Benjamin.

Closest thing the Concourse has to a boss. Only one up here seems to care if the lid ever blows off. Only one can talk to the Mungiki and come away with her head unsevered. One tough chick.

Warden.

Two ways you go to prison.

First way is keep your eyes down and suck up against the wall when the big dogs pass by, hope no one notices how harmless you are, how badly you just want to do your time and get back to your life on the outside. Spend your days counting the minutes till someone maybe decides you got a mighty pretty mouth.

Second way is go in and take a look around and find the chair in the day room with the best view of the TV, go up to the skin-head sitting in it, spit in his face, and shank him in the ear with the sharpened end of your toothbrush. Let everyone know you're not going anywhere. You're not a guest, you're fucking home. Do it that way, and when you get out of solitary you'll find that chair waiting for you to plop down in it and watch *General Hospital*.

Guess which was my approach.

Found a patch of Franz Sigel Park, a patch near the corner of Walton Avenue and Mabel Wayne Place where they got that cute red, white and blue sign. *The Bronx. All-American City*. A patch of trees and weeds and rock that reeked of some fucker doing his thing there for years.

Then I staked it out, waited till he dragged someone back into his favorite spot, came up on him as he was getting ready to put on the feedbag and I broke his spine in three places and let him lie there paralyzed and watch me while I dined out on his handi-work.

I peed all over his yard.

Then I killed him.

Soon enough, Esperanza called. Made it clear she was what passed for law around here. Made it clear what she was looking for in a neighbor. Made it clear that One Sixty-one and the Con-course being about as close to civilization as you get up here, she wanted to see it remain that way. Made it clear that the only kind of profile that would do in these parts was a low one. And I made it clear I couldn't agree with her more. Proved the point by show-ing her the corpse I'd made out of the guy who'd been living in Franz Sigel. A guy it turned out had been the source of *Monster in the Park* stories amongst the citizens. The kind of stories that attract undue attention.

She was pleased.

And I was home in the Bronx.

Again.

Not that I've strayed over to Hunt's Point to walk down memory lane and see the house I grew up in or anything. Do that and I might get inspired to burn it down. And I kind of doubt that my folks are still living there, so what would be the point?

Any case, not an easy woman to get on the right side of. And, once there, you don't want to circle round to the wrong side.

Not on her turf.

Our cigarettes go out and, in the interest of lighting new ones, we end our staring.

I inhale smoke, blow it out.

—OK. I'll stay away from the kids.

She looks me over, nods.

—*That* out of the way.

The tip of her finger touches the corner of her mouth.

—You got plans the rest of the night?

I wave my cigarette.

—Smoke this. Steal some money so I can get more cigarettes. Go hide from everybody.

—Very nice.

—Yeah, and I got a good book and a lovely bottle of chardonnay to curl up with later.

—Feel like company?

I look at her. I try to do it from the corner of my eye, but why bother? She knows I'm looking.

This one, pure hell on wheels, asking me if I want some company.

Do I.

I take a drag, chew on it, let it loose, and climb out of the car.

—I want company, I'll find a dog.

She keys the ignition and the wagon grinds to life.

—If that's what floats your boat, Joe, you have a good time.

She puts the car in gear, rolls to the drive, exhaust pouring from her tailpipe.

I stand there and watch till her lights are lost in traffic.

It ain't the first time she's asked. Not that I'm bragging. I'm just saying she's the kind of woman knows how to complicate a man's thinking.

A place like the South Bronx has a way of narrowing a person's focus. So you'd think my thinking would be pretty uncomplicated all the way around these days. That would be smart.

People having a conversation about me, that word, *smart*, it doesn't come up often. And I'm just smart enough to know there's a reason why.

But not smart enough to do anything about it.

What can I say? This old dog, he's still too busy chasing his own tail to bother learning any new tricks.

Across the river I had a life. Or a thing that I'd shaped into a semblance of a life. Had a face in the straight community. Folks downtown, citizens without know-how of this other life of ours, they knew me as a local fixer and rough hand. A guy could take some shifts when your bouncer got picked up by the cops for armed robbery and you needed a quick replacement. Guy you could come to when that deadbeat boyfriend still hadn't gotten out of your apartment four months after you dumped him. Guy you could slip a few bucks to escort said boyfriend to the curb. Trace a skip. Kick the vig loose from a welcher. No office, mind you, but a guy around that if you knew the right person I might get pointed out as the type could solve your problem.

Not what you'd call steady work, but I made my own hours. Kind of a key point, all things considered.

And some gigs for the Clans. Do some deeds in the cracks, unofficial and off the books. And toward the end, a real job with the Society. But that didn't go so well. Low job satisfaction. Engagement terminated by agreement between both parties. No references forthcoming from previous employer.

Guess it was that nail in the artery thing. That and maybe that I didn't give two weeks' notice. Not really sure which it was that queered the deal.

Any case, on the Island I was a face, and a face can make some money. Make moves. Get his hands on the necessities of life.

Food. Shelter. Clothing.

Blood. Bullets. Money.

Those kinds of things.

Blood is tricky. But blood is always tricky. Money can help you lay hands on blood but it's *always* tricky. No doubt it's trickier up here, you expect that. No local organization means no hustlers, no infrastructure to support a dealer who might be able to buy pints off the local junkies or something, act as a clearinghouse. Means no friendly faces at Bronx-Lebanon or St. Barnabas who you might slip some cash to and come away with a bag.

No, it's all pretty much smash and grab up here.

An uncomplicated life in the Bronx. By which a man means a predator's life. No job. No prospects. No permanent place of residence. No prospects. Prized possessions are best carried on one's person, as running may be required at any moment. And needs of the moment are the tasks of the moment.

So, after having Esperanza cloud my thinking, I work my way south. Toward a certain dead-end block of Carroll Place, just behind the Bronx Museum, where I recently clocked a rotating cast of young men receiving calls on their cells, soon after followed by slow-cruising cars that swept into the cul-de-sac, paused to pass handshakes out the window, and rolled back out the way they came in.

Blood. Money. Bullets.

I feel in my bones that the guy hanging on the stoop with his cell will have all three.

How fortunate, that vacant lot at Carroll and One Sixty-six. It invites privacy. Limits distractions. While I tend to business.

I should have broken into a couple cars on the way, scrounged a few bucks for a pack of smokes. That would have passed the time. Better, I should have done something to scratch *Bullets* off my to-do list before running this particular errand.

Who'd have thought the modern crack dealer went unarmed these days? Not that I expected his bullets to fit my gun. I'd assumed he'd be carrying the standard 9mm that's been all the rage for decades now. My own sidearm is a fusty .38. But, not being too attached to these things, I'd have happily tossed mine in favor of his. Seeing as I used mine to commit a homicide earlier this evening, I'd planned on leaving it on this guy after I knocked him out, took his cash and tapped him for a couple pints. With a bit of luck he might have kept it, *at least that mugger left me with a gun,* and gotten busted while it was in his possession. A long-odds bet, but worth putting some chips on.

But no gun.

Pity.

A gun would come in very handy when the hornet buzz of furious engines bounces from the sides of the buildings lining Carroll and I find myself pinned in four crossing headlight beams.

The engines drop to idles.

—What up with white guy?

—Yo, what up, white guy?

—He a funky-lookin' white guy.

—Like that jacket.

—You like that jacket, niggah?

—Like that jacket.

—Gonna bite off white guy's style?

—Just I like that jacket.

I shake my head.

—Kid, this jacket won't fit you.

The one who snagged the cop's cap outside the Stadium pulls the bill of that cap to the side.

—White guy talks.

The one with eyes for my jacket runs a finger over the thin shadow of a moustache that rims his upper lip.

—Don't worry, white guy, I grow into it.

The smallest one guns a bike forward into the light from the streetlamp, and I see she's a girl

She snaps her bubble gum.

—Don't know why you want that funky-lookin' jacket. Look stinky.

The last one, the one with the Dominican flag do-rag, drags on a Newport.

—Too hot for a jacket. He don't need no jacket.

Moustache holds out his hand.

—Gimme the fuckin' jacket, white guy.

The unconscious drug dealer in the dirt at my feet groans. I was just getting ready to slip the business end of an I.V. needle in his arm when the kids rode by and one of them caught a whiff of me and they veered onto the sidewalk and into the shadows behind the abandoned shed at the back of the vacant lot. With just me to worry about, the dealer would have been in pretty good shape. I'd have taken his bankroll, sure, that and whatever rock he's carrying, to make it look like a straight robbery. Other than his arm being a little sore and his head being a bit woozy, he might never have known about the blood I would have siphoned off.

But now it looks like he's gonna have a few more mouths to feed.

I look down at him as his eyes flutter open.

—Trust me, buddy, you don't want to see any of this.

I kick him in the head and he goes back to sleep.

—Said, *Gimme the fuckin' jacket, white guy.* Didn't say kick niggah in the head.

I look at him.

—Told you it's too big for you.

He rolls his shoulders.

—Told *you* I grow into it.

I stuff my hands in my jacket pockets. Gun, switchblade, blood works, lock picks, Zippo, last few dollar bills and some change fill those pockets. Those things I'm most reluctant to leave behind when the running starts.

Prized possessions?

Not really.

But the jacket itself.

That was a gift.

I take my hands out of my pockets; one holds the switchblade, the other the empty gun.

—Touch my jacket, you won't grow any more at all.

Gum Snapper pulls a gun as big as her head from the waistband of her skintight low riders and shoots me in the stomach. The clear advantage of having actual bullets being that you get to shoot people instead of just empty-threat them.

I fall on top of the dealer and bleed on him and point my gun at the four kids as they duck-walk their bikes over and look down at me. Moustache reaches for the gun and I pull the trigger a few times, hoping my math is off and that maybe there's a bullet in there I forgot about. But there isn't.

He takes the gun and looks at it.

—This a nappy fuckin' gun.

He chucks it over the fence behind the lot, down into the bushes at the back of the Museum.

Do-rag flicks ash from his Newport.

—You gonna rock his jacket, or what?

—Jacket got blood all over it now.

Gum Snapper climbs off her bike, tucks the massive piece back in her pants and comes over to me. I wave the switchblade at her and she kicks it from my hand.

—Bitch, don't even think 'bout cuttin' my ass. I stick that thing in you fuckin' dick.

She grabs the shoulders of my jacket and pulls me off the dealer.

I could make it harder for her. The pain is pretty bad, but I could definitely make it harder for her. Except that gun she shot me with, it was really, really fucking big. And just now I need to focus on holding the guts that want to spill out of my belly in their proper place. Right now I need to focus on not moving too much so the Vyrus can use all its energy to close up this goddamn hole and put my intestines back together. Whatever attention I can spare from that task, I can maybe use hoping the bullet didn't fragment inside me and rip up my liver and kidneys and spleen and such. Cause that much damage, I don't know if I can get better from that.

So I'm gonna lie here quiet in the dirt and try to bleed as little as possible while Gum Snapper breaks out a set of homemade works that consist of the sharpened needle from a bicycle pump, a length of junkie's rubber hose, and a few heavy-duty Ziploc freezer bags. She goes to work on the dealer, and Police Cap comes and looks at me.

—Think this him?

Do-rag takes a wire cutter from the pocket of the jeans that sag down past the top of his boxers.

—It him.

He climbs the fence and starts clipping lengths of barbwire, handing them to Moustache. When they have four long ones he climbs down and comes over.

—Got it all?

Gum Snapper pulls the needle from the dealer's neck and licks it.

—I got it.

Moustache kneels at my feet and starts wrapping barbwire around my ankles while Do-rag runs the ends to the bikes, twisting one strand each around the bikes' rear forks.

Police Cap helps Gum Snapper with the blood bags and they all saddle up.

Moustache looks over his shoulder at me.

—Fuck I want you shitty jacket anyway, white guy? Fuck you jacket.

Gum Snapper rises up on her pegs.

—Roll. Get this white guy to lament.

And they gun hard, rear tires roostertailing dirt all over me until they grab traction and burn out of the vacant lot and onto the street. Dragging me behind them, trailing blood and wondering why they think they need to take me to lament someplace special.

I can lament just fine here.

—Miserable. Pathetic. Meager. Low.

The four kids stop what they're doing and look at the man.

He bends a twisted finger at the bags of blood set on the rusted TV tray beside him.

—What is this?

The girl snaps her gum.

—S'blood.

He leans forward and peers at her.

—What is that in your mouth, Meager?

She shuffles her feet, looks elsewhere.

—Nothin'.

Something like a tongue snakes out from his mouth and leaves a slimy trace over dry lips.

—Is it? Is it nothing?

His arm snaps out and long spider fingers clutch her round cheeks and squeeze.

—Then you shall not mind opening wide for me to see.

Her throat works, trying to swallow, and he squeezes harder.

—Now, now, dear. Open wide.

He wrenches and her mouth opens and he thrusts the fingers of his other hand inside and comes out with the gnawed wad of gum.

—*Nothing.*

He grips her by the jaw, three fingers inside her mouth, his thumb digging under the chin, and pulls her close, holding the gum in front of her eyes.

—This is *nothing,* is it?

She makes a grunting noise.

He clacks his teeth twice.

—Chewing chewing chewing. Grotesque. Perhaps I will change your name. Grotesque. Would you like that? It would suit you.

Her throat hitches again, tears are coming out of her eyes.

The hand holding the gum is shaking.

—No? You would not like to be Grotesque? Well, to keep your name there will be a price. This, this is *nothing?* Then the price will be easily paid.

He shoves the gum into her left nostril, yanking her head down as she tries to pull back.

—This is *nothing,* child, *nothing* at all. Be still.

A long whine comes from her throat as he forces the gum farther inside, his index finger pushed in past the second knuckle, blood trickling out.

—Don't fret so, child, but a little farther and it will be back in your mouth.

She coughs and gags and he shoves her onto the floor.

—*Nothing*.

He holds out his saliva and mucous covered hands.

—Pathetic.

The boy with the police cap steps forward with a box of tissues, and the man plucks several and wipes his fingers.

—The ends I went to, the sacrifices I made, the labors endured to bring you here for your betterment. And yet here you are, even now, defying my most basic edicts and commands.

The girl hacks loud three times and the gum coughs out of her mouth, elongated and glossy.

He mashes the tissues and throws them at her.

—Wipe your spittle, child.

She takes the tissues, still hacking, picks up the gum and wipes her phlegm and spit and tears, creating wet trails in the grime on the filthy linoleum.

He lifts his chin high, looks down his nose.

—Disgusting. Foul. Those names, too, would be apt.

—You know, next time he sticks his fingers in your mouth, you should really bite them off.

The girl and the man and the three boys look at me in my dark corner of the room where I lie in my own blood, bound in the twisted lengths of barbwire.

—Seriously. You snap off a couple of those digits, I guarantee he'll be thinking twice before he goes mining for your gum again. Those things don't grow back too well. Makes a real impression when you bite one off.

—Low!

Moustache pushes the man's wheelchair forward, into the overhead light.

—Closer, boy, closer.

He rolls until his feet are inches from my face, the long gnarled nails almost poking me, reeking of toe jam and rot.

—A biter, are you? Like something to chew on, would you?

His foot lashes and the nail of his big toe cuts into my lips and he forces it inside.

—There. Tasty? How you most like it, is it?

I bare my teeth, the toe between them.

And he pulls a cap-and-ball .44 from the greasy bathrobe draped over his shoulders and puts it against my head.

—Yes, now bite. It will please me if you do.

So I bite.

But I don't think it pleases him much at all.

He doesn't shoot me. He just watches as I rip his toe off and spit it onto the floor. And he laughs as he has the three boys work together to keep me from thrashing too much while they take one of my boots off and the girl lifts my foot to the man and he shares with me just what it feels like to have a toe bitten off.

Me, if I had the gun, I'd definitely shoot him. A lot.

—You see, yes, you see how they task me, yes? This, this is what they bring me. This paltry offering. This soupçon. And out of this I am to feed us all? How, I ask you, how?

He takes one of the bags of blood from the TV tray and unzips the top a little, places his mouth over the opening and tilts his head back and sucks and swallows and the blood runs too fast and wells over his cheeks and down his chin and onto the collar of the robe and the pleated front of his wilted tuxedo shirt.

He finishes and tosses the bag aside and lifts his chin.

—Miserable.

Do-rag takes a crusted square of linen from the TV tray and wipes the man's mouth and chin and neck, careful not to pull on any of the long strands of oily reddish hair that hang to the man's shoulders.

—Yes, good, enough.

The boy steps back.

The man lifts the second swollen bag of blood.

—And this to last for how long? How long until they can find some other feeble and crippled runt that they might manage to bring down? Barely worth keeping. Pathetic.

Police Cap takes the bag from him, to a fridge wheezing in the corner, and slips it inside onto shelves loaded with bags of pig trotters and chicken feet.

The man picks up the last and smallest of the bags, the dregs of the dealer the girl drained in the vacant lot.

—Since you still resist the concept of industry, this will have to serve for all of you.

He holds the bag out at arm's length and the girl reaches for it.

—Not you, Meager.

He points at the empty bag on the floor.

—Scraps will serve for you.

He offers the bag to Moustache, a grin cracking around the teeth that still trap a bit of my toe between them.

—For you, Low, to share with Miserable and Pathetic.

The boy reaches for the bag and the man pulls it back.

—And you say what?

Low touches his moustache.

—Thanks, Mr. Lament.

Lament smiles again.

—Such a good boy.

He gives him the bag.

—And all of you?

The kids chorus.

—Thanks, Mr. Lament.

He nods.

—Yes, manners. When prompted, I know, but some manners, nonetheless.

He flicks his fingers at them.

—Away now. Go feed your disgusting faces away from me.

They scramble for the door, the boys clustered with their half-full bag, the girl trailing, looking at the red residue inside hers.

The door closes.

Lament's kinked neck bends toward me.

—Children. One can do little with them short of stuffing them in a sack and tossing them into the river like kittens.

I bleed, eyeing his scalp.

—It was a misstep on my part. I will admit to that much. But the blame is not entirely my own. If I had been listened to, left un-molested in my methodology, I might have avoided the conflict utterly. As it was I had no choice but to confront the rabble.

He wheels himself to the fridge and takes out one of the bags of trotters.

—I had operated in admirable discretion.

A gnarled finger pokes into the bag and comes out with a trot-ter. He holds it before milky eyes and studies it.

—Until *they* manifested.

He digs a bit of meat from between the pig toes and sucks it from his yellow nails.

—Mungiki savages.

He rotates the trotter, finds more sinew, tears it loose with his teeth.

—It would be almost comical. Their pretensions. That is to say, not only are they not from Kenya, but most of them are not even negroid.

He licks the trotter, sucks a last twist of gristle from it, and tosses it aside, plucking another from the bag.

—Skag Baron Menace.

He spits on the floor.

—Filthy child. He read about the Mungiki in a magazine article.

He waves the fresh trotter at the moldy magazines and newspapers heaped along the walls, barricading the windows.

—An article from my library, no less. Yes, this is ironic.

He pops the whole trotter in his mouth, rolls it about, the sound of cracking cartilage loud, then opens his mouth, dribbling the stripped foot onto his hand then dropping it to the floor.

—Kenyan gangs that thrive on kidnappings and protection rackets. Political party enforcers that cultivate legends of their own brutality. They keep oil drums of blood. And drink it. So the stories go in backwater Kenya. If it is not redundant to use the words *backwater* and *Kenya* together in a sentence.

He holds the bag up, shakes it, doesn't find what he wants and puts it back inside the fridge.

—Menace thought it was clever, naming his little litter of hyenas after the blood-drinking gangsters. Clever? As if cleverness is a thing that ever happened inside Menace's feeble head.

He rolls to a small shelf of books, pulls down a moisture-swollen Webster's and flaps it open in his lap.

—Not even his own name is his. Menace. *Something that threatens to cause evil, harm, injury, etc.* I gave him that name. I had hoped it might instill some sense of pride in him, some modicum of self-respect. Something for him to aspire to. Better if I had done as I originally planned and named him Insipid.

He slaps the dictionary closed.

—Perhaps it did inspire him. Sent him off to new territories.

Queens. Indeed. As if that was my fault. They act as if it was my fault. His adventurism of my making. But it was meddling in my methods that caused the problems. They have bred their own complications, not I. Little hairy monkey with dreams of his own empire. *Skag Baron*. The pretension of it. That little scrap of half-nigger and his delusions of nobility.

He places the book back on the shelf.

—*Skag* is a word I know not the meaning of. Nor do I deign to seek it out. So sure am I that it is some foul slang for vagina or penis.

His chair creaks close and he butts me with the wheels.

—And you, were you in my charge at an early age, what should I have named you?

His lips purse, dry flakes of blood, and grease from the trotters, mingle in the whiskers on his chin.

—Shiftless. Yes, Shiftless. Lazy and contemptible. Placing yourself outside the structure of things. Imagining yourself better than your place. Adding nothing to the common good and weal.

He reaches behind the chair and comes up with a short cat-o'-nine-tails and prods me with the wood handle.

—You are a burden on us all. We strivers, we reachers and dreamers, without us, without our mighty efforts at forward progress, you and your slovenly kind would perish in your own filth.

He dangles the knotted leather cords of the whip in front of my face; I can see the dry blood clotted thick.

—Parasites. Sucker fish. Tapeworms. Reveling in the bowels of the citizenry. Living off our wastes. Upsetting the smooth functions of the body politic that we nourish with hard labors.

He raises the whip and lashes it across my face.

—Shiftless. Useless. Leech.

I flinch, draw up my shoulders and duck my face into my chest.

He prods me again with the handle.

—Yes, huddle and hide from the light and truth, Shiftless. Is that shame? No, I think not. Fear. Simple fear of pain. Well, fear is a good forge. We can work many a useful tool with fear at hand. I have done so for years. In good service.

He shoves the end of the handle under my chin and forces my face up.

—Sharp tools I made. Even if they have never been appreciated. Good tools and able. Suited to their task. And I would have made more and better. But for interference.

He pulls the handle away and bangs it against the floor.

—Had I been left to my own methods, Menace would never have shunned his conditioning and reverted to his nature. Under my own auspices and left unmolested here, the Mungiki would never have manifested.

He throws the cat-o'-nine-tails, upsetting a pile of newspapers that sloughs to the floor.

—*Skag Baron Menace!* With no Mungiki he was nothing. I told them, *Leave off and let me attend, yes?* But they would not listen. Insisted in meddling. All but created the Mungiki with their own hands. Intrusions. Invasions.

He takes his hair in fistfuls.

—And who must then negotiate with the savages? Who must settle them in their place? And at what price?

He puts his hands on the arms of the wheelchair and pushes himself up on twisted legs; frozen at the waist, he stands cocked at nearly ninety degrees, waving arms as warped as his legs, all the bones of him corkscrewed.

—Mere seconds in the sun, yes? Cancers in my bones, yes? Mad growths, yes? All because I went out to negotiate, to compensate for failures and oversights that were none of my own.

He drops back into the chair, sending it rolling a few feet across the moldering room.

—Mr. Lament.

—A misstep, did I say? On my own part, yes? Surely it was a misstep. The misstep was loyalty. Listening to the simple caw and cries, yes? I should have followed truer stars. My own heart and mind I should have followed!

—Mr. Lament.

He heaves air in and out, wipes spittle from his mouth, fingering the blisters that pebble his cheeks.

—A life in service. For me, who should have been a prince in my own right. This is the price of sacrifice. This is the price of loyalty, Shiftless. The wages paid by an ignorant sovereign.

—Mr. Lament.

He turns to Low, the boy standing in the open door.

—You have something to say, idiot boy? Something that can't wait till your better concludes his business? Come here, thing.

Low doesn't move.

Lament crooks a finger.

—Come here now, Low. Or risk my displeasure.

Low comes slowly into the room, his tongue probing the ends of his moustache.

—Sure, Mr. Lament.

Lament's hand ducks into the pocket of his robe and comes out with a honed carpet knife. It flashes once as he uses it to hook the underside of Low's upper lip.

—Something to say? Something pressing, yes? Say it, boy! Say it while you still have lips to make human sounds! Say it before I cast you into your proper station as a maker of animals mewling!

—Honestly, Alistair, the boy is simply doing as I asked. You might try an ounce of civility just now and again. We are none of us above the use of good manners and simple kindness.

Lament and I look at the door where the old woman stands between an efficient-looking young man and woman in matching black suits, holding matching machine pistols that look every bit as efficient as they do.

—We are not savages, after all.

She takes a step into the room, into the light, luster on the single strand of pearls she wears at the neck of a white cardigan with buttons that match the necklace, a faint greasy sheen on the warty gray orb that's half grown from the scarred pit that used to be her right eye socket.

—Put the knife down, Alistair. Try to effect the gravity of your years.

Lament removes the blade from Low's mouth.

—This is my domain, Maureen. How I conduct affairs is my business.

She places a hand on Low's head and looks at his face.

—How you conduct your business has proven ineffectual. At best.

She shakes her head.

—A *dismal failure* is a far more accurate assessment of your affairs.

She pushes Low toward the door.

—Go out there with your friends.

Low looks at Lament.

Lament bares his teeth, snaps his fingers, and Low goes out the door.

He looks up at the old woman.

—A *dismal failure?* I think not.

She inclines her head at the two young people and they come farther into the room.

—Fear as a control is limited, Alistair. Your instrument is dulled by it. Incapable of independent actions. They will never serve as anything but your lackeys. Sad prison wards. A pathetic, if necessary, fate for them. Truly, it's as much as mongrel races can or should aspire to, but the added indignity of being lorded by your-self seems all but cruel.

He grunts, opens his mouth.

She shakes her head.

—No. No further comment is required.

She lifts a hand and the young man takes the handles of the wheelchair and pushes it to the door.

—Go join your protégés.

He twists about in the chair, looking back at her as he is wheeled out.

—This is my place, Maureen! This conclave is my doing and I should be present.

The old woman looks about for a place to sit.

—Yes, Alistair. Yes, yes.

His further comments cut off as the young man closes the door behind them.

The young woman finds a folding steel chair with a cracked plastic seat cushion, wipes dust off it with a few tissues from Lament's box, and places it for the old woman.

She takes a seat, runs her hands over the legs of her light wool slacks, then folds them in her lap and looks at me.

—And tell me, Mr. Pitt, how have you enjoyed Alistair Lament's hospitality?

I shrug as best I can.

—He's not quite up to your style, Mrs. Vandewater.

I glance at the door and then back at her.

—I mean, he only let me bite his toe off. You let me take a whole eye.

—He was, hard to imagine, a quite remarkable student. Attentive, frighteningly able, insightful in a manner quite unique. An eye for weakness. A sense, if you like, for frailty. Vulnerability.

Not a virtue, I admit, in the normal course of things, but essential to certain ends.

She looks at the floor, raises the glasses that hang by a chain from her neck, and brings the discarded pig's feet into focus.

—Over the years, obviously, he has rather deteriorated.

She lets the glasses hang free.

—His eye is no less keen, but he himself is blunted. Become vulgar.

She looks about the filthy backroom.

—The isolation. He seemed to have inward reservoirs. No lack of self-confidence, I'm sure you have noticed, but more than that. Or so I believed. A mind and spirit suited to independent action. Bold initiative. Yet still responsive to authority.

She allows a small sigh.

—Wrong on many counts it seems.

She rises, looks behind herself and brushes at the seat of her slacks.

—More willful than independent. When I dispatched him here to see if he might find suitable subjects for infection, I never dreamed how far he'd stray from my prescriptions. Recruiting, identifying those who might take most naturally to the Vyrus, has always required an acceptance of the fact that those most isolated from typical social supports are most likely to embrace an utter change in their circumstances. Offer the unwillingly solitary the opportunity to elevate themselves, to become a part of something larger than themselves, and they will find reserves of emotional and mental resilience they never knew existed. Resilience that can make them capable of the most basic of our compulsions.

She bends and picks up the cat-o'-nine-tails from where Lament had discarded it.

—After all, if a prospective recruit cannot come to terms with the implications of the Vyrus' thirst, what use can we possibly make of them?

She weighs the lash in her hand, shakes her head, places it on the TV tray.

—Crude.

She pulls a tissue from the box and wipes her hands.

—So like Alistair.

She looks at me, wound in barbwire, my clothes scabbed with my own dry blood, the marks of the whip on my face barely closed, a crust of tangled meat grown over the stump where my toe was.

—At this moment, you could serve as the perfect visual referent for Alistair's methods and mindset. Vulgar and base. And, truly, a fair indication of just how far he has strayed.

She places a hand at the high collar of her gray blouse.

—Set to find loners and outsiders, he went too far afield. These delinquents and hoodlums. What use can they come to? He enticed them with blunt offers of power and money. Suggested they were involving themselves in criminal enterprise.

She sniffs.

—Narcotics, no less. A context, so he claims, they could understand.

She opens the door of the fridge, the corners of her mouth pulling down.

—And he implied a dark rite of initiation. Evoked voodoo. Santería. Again, a context he thought they could embrace.

She pushes the door closed.

—And then he infected them. Or had one of his current miscreants infect them. And, if they survived that process, he began a program of abuse. *Reprogramming.* His word, not mine. But apt, I will admit. Whatever slight self-regard they might have, he removed it. Amputated it whole and cauterized the stump. The names he gives them. You've heard them? Failure. Distress. Encumbrance.

Her good eye blinks slowly, as if erasing something from the surface of its lens.

—My own fault. What I'd failed to account for was how he would respond to isolation himself. I'd forgotten that he'd been a foundling in his own right. Lost and adrift until I brought him to harbor and gave him a purpose. I esteemed the training I'd given him too greatly. And once here, once in this lonely outpost amongst the savages, he became very much a product of his environment.

A finger traces the edge of the mass of scar on her face.

—Not the last time, sadly, I was the victim of overconfidence and pride.

She looks at me.

—Was it, Mr. Pitt?

Something rustles in my gut. The skin has sealed over the wound, but the Vyrus is struggling inside to reknit my organs. I grunt, exhale, try not to move too much.

—If that's what you call pissing me off, then yeah, you were a little full of yourself that time.

A flutter, a twist, a sensation like sharp nails picking at a knot in my intestines. I grunt again.

She lifts her glasses, looks at me through the narrow lenses.

—Some discomfort, Mr. Pitt?

I nod.

—Yeah, yeah.

She nods.

—Something I could do for you?

I think for a second. Something the Coalition Clan's chief recruiter and trainer of their enforcers could do for me?

Sure there is.

—Yeah, lady, you could maybe just shoot me now instead of talking me to death.

She looks over her shoulder at the young woman with her efficient machine pistol.

—Shoot you?

She looks back at me.

—No, Mr. Pitt, I think not.

Slowly, she lowers herself into a graceful squat that someone who looks as old as her should have more trouble executing.

—Being shot is not in your immediate future.

She reaches out and places the tip of her index finger on my cheekbone.

—Other things are in your future, but not that.

She presses the finger gently into my cheek, drawing the skin down from the bottom of my eye.

—By the way, Mr. Pitt, you mentioned that I'd *let* you take my eye when we last met. In point of fact, and while I don't wish to be thought ungenerous, I never actually considered it a gift.

She lifts her finger.

—And I've always rather believed you owed me something in return.

She opens her mouth wide and goes to work, evening accounts between us.

There comes a time when you think there are no new territories of pain. After a certain number of stabbings, shootings, clubbings, whippings, beatings, thrashings, cuttings, slashings and eviscerations, you begin to assume you've had the worst of it and nothing of that nature can really surprise you very much.

And then someone comes along to show you that you're wrong.

And you can do little but scream your thanks and appreciation for the lesson.

So I scream. My eye being gnawed out by a crazed old woman,

I scream like I rarely have. Because some things, some things are truly horrifying.

But maybe you have to have them happen to you to get that.

—Because it was due me.

—I am not arguing whether you had grounds, Mrs. Vandewater. I am stating as fact that you were charged to bring him *unmolested*.

—Yes, so I was. And I abused that charge. And you have asked me why I abused that charge. And I have answered. *Because it was due me*. This seems to leave little enough to discuss. The only question seems to be, how will you discipline me for my failure to do as you *charged*?

I open my eyes.

Correction.

I open my *eye*.

Seeing as it's caked with the blood that spilled out of what used to be my other eye, it doesn't help much. Clotted darkness with a distant blur of light punctuated by two smaller clots of darkness that don't seem to be getting along all that well just now. I close my eye and let my ears do the work, still having two of those for the moment.

—Yes, how will I discipline you. Yet again we come around to the same topic. I am bemused, Mrs. Vandewater, as to how a person so wholly devoted to the concept of discipline can be entirely lacking in it herself.

—That is due entirely to your own lack of awareness.

—Indeed. Well. Illuminate me. If you are inclined.

Her footsteps sound down the long echoing room as she begins to pace.

—*Illuminate*. I have spent my life in that very effort. And no little part of it in a specific effort to illuminate *you*. Bright child. Such a bright child. With an utterly dim outlook. You still see no further than your dogma. Maintenance of status quo. This, despite all evidence of the erosion taking place under your feet. *Illuminate!*

The hard slap of a flat palm on a desktop.

—You fail to make sense of my actions, and you interpret them as disobedient and undisciplined, because you measure them against your own authority. You refuse again and again to see that I am in the service of a larger order of things. While your eyes continue to be on the path just before your feet, I am looking well ahead to where the path becomes lost and tangled in the woods.

Silence. The impression of contemplation. Then the man's voice.

—And yet I am still unclear as to what that has to do with biting his eye out.

Silence again. The impression of a stare-down. The woman's voice.

—I took his eye because I have no respect for your authority. Because I do not believe you are long for your position. Because in some few months' time I expect not to be forced to answer to you any longer.

A chair creaks as she sits.

—Does that clarify the matter?

Leather-soled shoes take a few steps. Another chair creaks.

—Yes. Yes it does.

—And so, after an unnecessary digression to *illuminate* you regarding the obvious, we can return to the matter at hand? I have disobeyed your charge. What cost must I pay? What is due to Caesar? What can you afford to extract with your power crumbling about you?

Papers being turned.

—You are still well regarded by some members of the council.

This hinders me somewhat. Limits the scope of what correction I might impose. Yes.

A folder being snapped shut.

—But you force my hand, and I must do something. If you can tolerate another question, let me ask, in similar circumstances, when I was in your care, what would you have done to me had I shown the same lack of regard for your commands?

Whisper of fabric.

—What a coward you are. Unable even to devise your own chastisement. I'd have killed you. There is no room for any lack of—

The sound of something sharp cutting the air, a clatter of furniture, breath whistling from a hole nature made no allowance for.

—No need to say anything further, Mrs. Vandewater. When you are right, you are right. And I can complete the thought for you. There is, indeed, no room for any lack of discipline in this life of ours.

The floorboards vibrate as a body thrashes against them. Thick fluid leaks onto wood.

—And you are, as ever, correct in most things. You were correct in thinking that you would soon be released from any obligation of answering to my authority.

Metal scraping on bone, sawing.

—But giving myself some credit, you were off by several months in your estimation of how soon your release might come.

And a sound not often heard in the natural course of things, but one I've had opportunities to hear on more than one occasion: the soft but solid thump of a human head being dropped to the floor.

—My only regret being that I cannot ask you how the view of the path appears from where you are now.

Footsteps striding down the room toward me, stopping.

I open my eye and look up as a lean, dark shadow leans over me. It kneels, whisking a handkerchief from its breast pocket and using it to ream the caul of blood from my eye.

—Open your eye, Pitt, I have a job for you.

I blink as he comes into focus: smooth-faced, a fall of glossy brown hair across his forehead, a painfully flawless bespoke suit splashed generously with blood.

—Hey, Mr. Predo.

I rest my head on the floor and sight down the room at the beheaded corpse lying in a spreading red pool.

—If it's her old job, I think I'll pass.

He's not going to kill me.

It's not that fact of him telling me he's not going to kill me that assures me I've got some time to breathe. Predo could look me in the eye and tell me whiskey's good and cigarettes are better and I'd still need a drink and a Lucky to believe he's not lying. The man breeds lies. He spawns them asexually, with no need for any assistance. He exhales and lies fill the air. Alone in a room, he mutters lies to himself to keep from falling into the trap of truth-telling. In the day, sleeping in his bed, deep in the safest heart of Coalition headquarters, he dreams in lies. The better to keep his left hand from knowing what betrayals his right has planned.

Stretched on the rack and burned with hot irons, Dexter Predo will be in no danger of revealing the truth. Living so far beyond its borders.

—I'm not going to kill you.

Said as we watch two of his own burly enforcers, black rubber aprons, galoshes and gloves protecting their suits, while they bag Mrs. Vandewater's remains and mop her blood from the floor of the rotting ballroom around us.

I finish the big bag of blood Mrs. Vandewater had taken from

Lament's fridge, and that Predo has given to me to speed the Vyrus through my wounds.

—I can't make the same promise, Mr. Predo.

I toss the empty bag into the bucket containing Mrs. Vandewater's head.

He finishes wiping the last of the blood from his hands and neck and drops the towel in a bag held open by one of his men.

—No, Pitt, nor would I expect you to. But seeing as you spent this evening being waylaid by teenage delinquents, and having your anatomy masticated by the crippled and the aged, you will understand my lack of alarm as regards your threat.

I feel my pockets for a smoke.

—Yeah, fuck you too.

He looks down at his blood-ruined suit.

—Would you excuse me for a moment, Pitt.

He starts for the door, the question not actually being a question.

I settle in my chair, feeling the drug dealer's blood slide deeper into my wounded guts, burning cold as the Vyrus colonizes it and recoups strength.

—Take your time.

I raise a hand.

—Hey, don't suppose you've started smoking since the last time I saw you?

The door closes, leaving me with the two button-lipped enforcers, the squeak of their rubber boots and the swish of their rags in the bloody mess.

Naw, he's not gonna kill me. He was gonna kill me, he wouldn't have given me the blood to put me right and get me on my feet. Not that he and his boys couldn't still gang me and take me down, but blooded up like this I'd be sure to make it hurt. Not like Predo to make a job harder than it has to be. He was gonna kill me, he would have done it while I was wrapped in barbwire and leaking all over the fucking place. Or at least he would have left me that way till it got to be daylight so they could pitch me easily out of doors and watch me blight in the sun.

The last of old Mrs. Vandewater goes into the bags and bucket and the enforcers take a look around for anything they might have missed before hauling the remains away.

Of course, figured another way, it would be just like Predo to fill me with blood and get me back to something like health and wellness. Figure he might play it that way if he wanted to keep me kicking while these cleaning laddies found what few bits I have left to hack off. But figure he'd only bother with that kind of production if he had questions to ask me.

The door opens and Predo comes back in, a suit, all but identical to the one he was wearing before, cinched into place on his narrow frame. Really, it is identical, just without an old lady's blood all over it.

He waits at the open door as the enforcers exit, closes it behind them, comes to the circle of light cast by the bright floor lamp set next to the desk and two chairs here in the middle of the ballroom, and settles into the chair on the boss side of the desk.
—So, Pitt.

He makes a slight adjustment to his silver tie bar.
—Let me ask you a few questions.

I wait for the arms to encircle me from behind, for the garrote to drop around my throat, the gun to be placed at my temple.

And when none of the above occurs, I let the knife Predo used to kill Vandewater slide from the sleeve where I'd tucked it after the enforcers clipped me from the barbwire and dragged me across the floor past where it had been dropped, and I throw it sharp and hard and straight and it wings past Predo by a good two feet and thunks into the wall outside the light.

He raises an eyebrow, turns, looks off at the gleam of the blade in darkness, and turns back to me.

—You'll find it, I believe, Pitt, somewhat of an adjustment now that your vision is no longer triangulated.

I scratch the side of my neck.

—Well, if you'll just sit there while I go fetch the blade, Mr. Predo, I'm pretty sure I can do better the second time around.

Just because he's not going to kill me right now doesn't mean he doesn't want me dead.

He wants me dead.

I'm not saying my name is at the top of his list, but it is in the upper ten percent. Yeah, he's the kind of guy who keeps a list. That comes with running the Coalition's security arm. An organization like that, they just love lists.

List of friends. List of enemies. List of subversives. List of agents. List of counteragents. List of those at the top. List of those at the bottom. List of people they can kill with impunity. List of people they need to take a little care with before they kill. List of those on the inside. List of those on the outside.

Being inside the coalition means buying the line. The line is secrecy. The line is *we don't exist*. The line is the people out there who don't know about the Vyrus, they should *never* know about the Vyrus because if they know about the Vyrus they'll build camps and open labs and start rewriting all kinds of laws and redefining what it means to be created equal.

Frankly, I think they got it pretty much right.

It's not the line I disagree with so much. It's that they got no room for anyone who *does* disagree with the line. Disagree with the line and you're on that outside list. That list, it's pretty much identical to the People to Kill as Soon as Possible List.

So while it's an interesting turn of events to be in Predo's presence without someone nearby stirring a pot of molten lead to be poured in my nostrils, I know the ultimate outcome to a scenario like this likely allows him to scratch my name off that list when all is said and done.

He opens a drawer and takes out a slim automatic with polished wood grips. One of those guns that looks designed by the same kind of people who dream up the hardwood and leather interiors of luxury sedans with obscure Italian names.

He sets it on the desk.

—In hopes I might make you a bit more attentive, Pitt.

I look at the floor around my chair.

Predo edges up a bit to peek over the front of his desk.

—Lose something?

I look up.

—No. Just checking to see if your flunkies left any other lethal weapons lying around. Seems I'm out of luck.

I fold my arms.

—Guess I may as well listen to you.

He flips open one of the folders on his desk.

—Gracious as ever. But just so we can be certain you don't grow bored with what I have to say, why don't I make it more interesting for you by including some visual aids?

He draws a photograph from the folder and slides it to the edge of the desk.

—Like a picture book. So that you may follow along more easily.

—I prefer a pop-up book.

He rotates the photo so that it faces me.

—I'm certain this will grab your attention.

Light gleams off the glossy finish, hiding the image from me. I scoot my chair forward, the feet grinding on the floor. I take the photo from the desk. I look at it.

I look at Predo.

He nods.

—We can dispense with wit now and speak of things concrete?

I look again at the photo.

A very young woman. Younger than you'd imagine a person has a right to be. And beautiful. The photo is tinted in a manner that hides the color of her hair, but it looks like she's not dyeing it anymore. The natural color would be a complex shade of blond, much like her mother's was. She is exiting one of those cars suggested by Predo's gun, the door held for her by another woman, older, black, muscled in a way that promises the clean and abrupt snapping of a neck. The tint is greenish. The photo taken through a night filter. The only thing missing is a crosshairs painted across the young woman's face.

I set the photo down.

—Yeah, tell me something concrete.

—She has gone quite out of control.

—Interesting. I never knew she was *ever* under control. Last I checked that was how I got involved in the first place.

Predo taps the end of a pen against a thumbnail.

—I am not talking about the delinquencies, teenage drinking and underage sex her parents fretted about. Her actions are on a new order of magnitude.

The hole where my eye was is throbbing. I knuckle it.

—Guess the new scale of troublemaking goes hand in hand with becoming filthy fucking rich at a young age.

He drops the pen.

—Do not pretend nonchalance, Pitt. If I was not certain you cared, we would not be having this conversation. Whether you would feel some responsibility for the girl had you not killed her parents, I cannot say. But you did. And I trust your year here among the uncivilized masses has not changed your nature so much that you can shrug off such things. However sentimental.

I look at my bare foot, rub the stump that used to be my big toe, flaking away scab.

—I only killed her mom.

He squints.

—So you've claimed before.

He leans back, his chair giving a little squeak.

—A persistent little lie, that.

—I only killed her mom.

—A lie I have some trouble penetrating. Why you should be reluctant to take credit for her father's death. Repugnant man.

—What can I say, I take credit where it's due. I only killed her mom.

I look out of the light, into the darkness, back into the light.

—The other *thing* got her dad.

He picks his pen back up.

—*Other thing*. Gullible as you are in so many things, I am still somehow disappointed that you embrace that particular bit of superstition.

Nothing else to say. Seeing as I'm not superstitious.

He puts the end of the pen to his chin.

—Another time then.

I peel an especially long and stringy bit of dead skin loose from my foot, look at it and drop it on the floor.

—The girl is out of control?

He grips the pen in both hands, flexes the shaft.

—Yes.

He bends it just to the breaking point, holds it there, relaxes, looks at it as it springs back into shape, and sets it aside.

—Yes. She is out of control.

—In what way?

He aligns the pen with the right-hand edge of the desk.

—She has declared a new Clan.

He shifts the angle of the gun, bringing the length of the barrel true with the top edge of the desk.

—Using her wealth to disseminate word through the community. Bribing otherwise loyal members of the Clans to help spread word of this new "Clan." She has made it clear that any and all are welcome in her . . .

He looks through the gloom to the ceiling.

—Her new *organization.*

He looks back at the desk, tapping the stack of folders flush with one another.

—Uninfected herself, she is enlisting other uninfecteds to carry word off the Island. Daylight travelers. Renfields and Lucys.

He brushes some unseen fleck of matter from the corner of the desk.

—She is, in all these dealings, loud and highly visible. We do not exist within a vacuum. The uninfected world is the medium in which we are forced to live. Vibrations cannot reach us without first traveling through that medium. Yes, those vibrations must be decoded, but that does not mean that others cannot learn the code. She is putting us all at risk. This is not solely a matter of Coalition doctrine being controverted, this is a case in which the concerns of all the Clans are being drawn under fire by the willful hand of a child who is not even of our ilk.

I stop fiddling with my toe and give him a look.

—*Of our ilk?* Christ, Predo, is that a little racism I hear?

His fist shatters the desktop, pen and papers flying, gun dropping to the floor.

—She is trying to find a cure!

His foot lashes and the desk skitters down the ballroom trailing splinters and kindling.

—A cure!

His fists ball, knuckles whiten.

I point.

—Your tie's a bit askew there, Mr. Predo.

He closes his eyes and his mouth twists slightly.

His eyes open.

—Word will spread.

I nod.

—Yeah, I know.

He lets a breath drop in, lets it out.

—Infecteds that know no better will flock to her. There will be desertions from the Clans. Refugees from off the Island.

—I know.

He opens his fists, flexing his fingers back, relaxing them.

—Our careful balance will be undone.

—I know.

He shrugs the collar of his jacket back into place.

—And when she fails, there will be chaos and discord.

He runs fingers through his hair, brushing his bangs back into place.

—And finally.

He touches the knot of his tie, pulls it straight.

—We will have war.

He tugs at the French cuffs of his shirt.

—And we will all die.

The throbbing where my eye was comes from the nerves regenerating. I'd be better off if the Vyrus left them dead. Not like they're gonna have anything to plug in to. Without that eye, they'll just be raw and disjoined. Something that can cause pain while serving no real purpose.

I look at him.

—You say that like it's a bad thing.

He waits.

I look at the floor, see the picture. Amanda Horde. Changeling child living somehow in the infected world. Genius. Mad. Not as in angry, but as a hatter. I look at the designer gun that's come to rest next to the photo. Wonder how many shots I could get off if I got to it before him. Wonder if I could get any of the bullets into his head with my one eye. Figure he did Mrs. Vandewater easy. Figure I've felt what it's like when his fist hits my jaw. Figure he can take me anytime and anyplace. But I look at the gun for a bit longer anyway.

Then I look at him.

—I won't kill her for you, Predo.

He smiles.

—I don't want you to kill her, Pitt.

He bends, picks up the photo, looks at it, looks at me.

—I want you to join up.

The Andrew Freedman Home was finished in 1924. Endowed by an eponymous millionaire with ties to Tammany Hall and subway financing. And if that doesn't suggest something about the nature of his fortune and how dirty his dollars likely were, nothing else will. But pretty much everything you need to know about this guy you can tell by the house. A massive limestone palazzo on the corner of One Sixty-six and the Concourse, he left pretty much all of his fortune in trust for the thing to be built as a home for the elderly.

Exclusively for the elderly who had at one time been rich, but who had lost their fortunes.

Luxurious in the manner of a Gilded Age private club for rail barons, the Home kept the busted rich in a manner to which they had become accustomed.

1

Good old Andrew Freedman, looking out for the little people.

Whatever, it was his money. Man should spend it how he wants. Especially after he's dead. Besides, whatever Andy's wishes may have been at one time, the place ended up a broken-down community center for run-of-the-mill poor old folks.

Proving again that time gives fuckall about who you are or what you want.

I manage to glean this knowledge from a plaque as Predo leads me from the subsiding ballroom on the third floor through several corridors artfully decorated with sagging plaster and rat droppings.

—Dregs.

He points ahead and one of the enforcers flanking us moves to a door and opens it.

—That's what she's collecting.

We pass through the door into an echoing stairwell, climbing.

—Rogues. Off-Islanders. The dross clinging to the fringes of the Clans. All those who lack the wherewithal and fortitude to understand that the Vyrus has made us different.

He pauses on a landing, waits as I negotiate around some broken glass with my bare, mangled foot.

—That there is no going back.

He starts up the next half flight.

—Traditionally, that kind of offal weeds itself from the community. Viewed as an engine of evolution, the Vyrus is a most powerful instrument for defining the fittest of the species. One can argue at length as to whether we are human any longer. Coalition precepts hold that we are. Regardless, the Vyrus insists on extreme levels of fitness, resilience, adaptability. Without those qualities, the runts die out quite rapidly. Our primary concern is not how best to steel them to this life, to aid in their adaptation, but how to make their deaths as rapid and as invisible as possible.

He stops at the top of the stairs, waiting while one of the enforcers opens the door and sweeps the area beyond with the barrel of his weapon.

I point at him.

—He making sure no sleeping pigeons are waiting to get the drop on us?

Predo waits for a nod from the enforcer and goes through the door ahead of me.

—Our intelligence on the Bronx is far from extensive. But we have heard about the Mungiki.

I step out onto the roof, a river breeze in the tops of the high trees that grow from the grounds below, a few hazy stars above.

—Mungiki are in Queens.

He stops next to one of the half-dozen TV aerials that sprout from the roof.

—We heard some were still left.

—I hear they're all out. Whole crazy pack of them in Queens.

—Is that what the drums tell you, Pitt?

—No, that's what being exiled up here for a year tells me.

He studies a spray-painted tag on the back of a cement urn decorating the edge of the roof.

—A year.

He looks at me.

—A year in the Bronx.

He looks me up and down.

—And, until the last few hours, very little worse for wear.

He resumes his walk, skirting a sag in the tar paper where rainwater has pooled in the shade of one of the trees, greened with scum.

—But you have always shown the resilience I was speaking of. I doubted it for some time, thought your sentimentality would get the best of you. Labeled you overly reckless. But I was wrong. Your natural ruthlessness serves you well. A particularly useful adaptation for this neighborhood, I imagine.

I think about what I learned growing up in the Bronx, who taught me the nature of ruthlessness. I wonder if Predo knows this is home turf for me. Wonder if it matters what he knows.

He looks back at me.

—No comment?

He's right, no comment.

He shrugs, stops at the southwest corner of the building where the tops of the trees part, the sky opens up and the view carries straight to the lights and towers across the river.

—Perhaps you have some comment regarding that.

I look at the City, but I still have nothing to say.

He lays a hand on the snapped base of another of those urns.

—We do not want her killed, Pitt.

He looks at me.

—The wreckage that now floats around her would become unmoored, drift into the open. She has established herself, in her hubris, in the midst of our turf. An entire apartment building in the near center of Coalition territory. She's housing them, providing for their needs. A welfare state. Were she to die, that flotsam would bob into our streets. We could not contain them all. A strike of any scale on the building would draw far too much attention. Our influence spreads to certain circles in the uninfected community, but not so broadly that we can conceal a paramilitary raid in the heart of the Upper East Side. No.

His hand wraps the jagged stump of cement.

—As appealing as assassination may be, it is out of the question. We must rather proceed with greatest discretion. We know her ultimate goal.

He looks upward.

—A cure.

Shaking his head.

—But we need to know by what organizing principles she will

proceed. If she is pledged to secrecy, working on her own under the auspices of her father's biotech labs and with no outside research partners, we have some amount of time and leeway in our plans. If she intends to make this a public effort, marshaling evidence that the Vyrus is some form of illness, and then launching a public-health campaign via a grandstanding news conference or similar stunt, we shall have to act posthaste.

I grunt.

He looks at me.

—Yes?

I'm still looking at the City, the Empire State Building's spire lit up in red, white and blue.

—Nothing. I just like to make a mental note when people use words I've only read in books before. *Posthaste.*

—Well, in an effort to broaden your vocabulary, allow me to use another word: *genocide.*

—Yeah, I heard that one before.

—Good. Then I do not need to define it for you. You can picture it on your own. How it will proceed if she tries to launch an effort to cure the Vyrus as if it were African famine relief or a similar faddish cause for dissipated fashion models and rock stars to champion.

I step closer to the balustrade, eyes on the lights.

—Maybe we'd get our own concert.

—The best we might hope for, Pitt, would be an orchestra of our own imprisoned kind to serenade us as we filed into the showers.

—Yeah, well I'm not arguing the point.

—No. Nor would I expect you to. Occasional lapses into romanticism aside, you have always been clear on what fate waits us if we are revealed.

I give him a look.

—Wonder.

—Yes?

—What's Bird think of all this? The Society? Rest of the Clans?

He folds his arms.

—Tensions, unsurprisingly, are high. Your former employer, Bird, still feels that our long-term best interests can only be served when we all unite and present ourselves en masse to the public eye. He does, however, allow that the moment is not yet ripe. That the girl's efforts are destabilizing. The Hood, while still maintaining a war stance on our northern border, have taken a similar position. D.J. Grave Digga will not pursue hostilities while this matter is unresolved.

I measure my heartbeat, let five slow beats count off before I go further, knowing Predo will fish out my interest if it is not guarded.

—I'd think the idea of a cure would send Enclave over the edge.

He pulls his arms tighter around himself.

—Daniel would have had some opinion on the matter. Insane as he was, he would have had a measured response. The idea of a cure for the Vyrus might well have been a heresy to him, but Daniel would never have considered that it was an actual possibility. I expect he would have bided, as he did in most all Clan matters. But.

I count more heartbeats.

—But?

He unfolds his arms.

—But Daniel is dead. And there is a new head of Enclave. And he has declared that Enclave no longer communicate with *heretics*.

He looks back at the city.

—Daniel was as fanatical as the rest of them in their childish superstitions, but he was, at least, vaguely grounded in the Clans. I could make some judgments regarding how close they might be to launching their eventual crusade. Now they have sealed themselves off, we have no idea of their intentions.

He shakes his head.

—I don't know whether to be relieved or terrified. But, they are, in any case, not at issue just now.

He turns to me.

—At issue is simply the need for information. And so, you will join her *Clan*. You will gather all the intelligence you can, and you will deliver it to me.

I consider.

—Fuck you.

He nods.

—Yes, of course, the prospect of doing the smartest thing, of taking the action that will best ensure your own security along with everyone else's, does not appeal without some promise of remuneration. I did not expect it to. I will forgo threatening your life. That, I trust, is implicit in any offer I may ever make to you. But something more.

He points at the City.

—Manhattan. Civilization.

He trails his arm, offering.

—You are unwelcome there. So vicious and unreliable in your nature that you even went so far as to bite the hand that fed you. So far that even Bird could no longer tolerate you.

—Technically speaking, I didn't bite him. I shoved a couple nails in him.

—So I heard.

He allows the corner of a smile.

—As much as I might like to do the same, it does not change your circumstance. He will not have you back. And you were never embraced by the Coalition. You lack the pigment for the Hood. Daniel's fondness for you is as dead as he. Perhaps you might find a home hiding at the foot of the Island, among the other cast-aways, but that would require that you traverse all of our territories. And sooner or later you would be sniffed out. And now, well, here am I, standing in front of you, in the Bronx. So tell me, Pitt.

He allows rather more of a smile.

—Where would you scurry to next? To what hinterland? Where to be certain that I could not find you again?

He holds up a hand.

—More simple for you to erase that question. Replace it with this one, *What would you do with open passage on the Island?*

I watch the black waters between the Bronx and Manhattan, as Predo spins words at me.

—Go to the Horde girl. Join her. Find her intentions. Strengths. Weaknesses. Report them. This will serve all the Clans. Once done, I will secure you a Coalition visa. And ensure rapprochement of some kind with Bird.

He's to my left, in my new blind spot, invisible. I turn so I can see him.

—How many of your people did you already put inside?

He lowers his arm.

—Five.

—How many has Sela sniffed out and killed?

He slips a hand inside his jacket and takes out the folded photo and looks at the young girl's Amazon minder.

—Four. She's somewhat more efficient than I suspected.

—And none got close enough to the girl to find shit.

—No.

He looks up from the photo.

—But you have a history with her. She is fond of you. And Sela trusts you.

—Let's not get carried away.

I look back at the City, letting him slide into darkness, outside my vision.

—Once I'm back, once I do this, I won't pledge Coalition.

—Don't be silly, we wouldn't have you. We will simply facilitate your return and offer securities against your life.

—You'll tell everyone to leave me the fuck alone or you'll have them killed.

—Yes, just so.

So many goddamn lights. A whole world on a chunk of rock in the middle of dark waters.

—I want the name of the one you still have inside.

—Why?

—So I can fucking pretend to find him on my own and hand him over to Sela for execution. That way she'll know I'm on the up and up.

I hear a pen uncapped, smooth roll of expensive ink on stiff paper.

He offers me the photo, a name written on the back.

I take the photo, stuff it in my pocket, and look at him.

—When do we go?

He smiles, shakes his head.

—*We* do not go, Pitt. *I* go. *You* find your own way. After all.

He shrugs.

—It wouldn't look at all right if someone were to see me dropping you off at Eightieth and Lexington, would it? In addition, as unified as Clan intentions may be on this matter, trust is more than usually at issue. Ms. Horde has sympathizers at all levels.

—Got spooks of her own?

—Not as such. But certainly there are individuals within the Coalition, Society and Hood who are quite willing to volunteer information to her in hopes it can help her to her ultimate goal. And more pragmatic others willing to offer similar information at a price. Thus, while Digga might be willing to allow you passage across Hood turf to the Coalition, I have chosen not to inform him of the operation. A truism of intelligence is that the more people who know about an operation, the more it is at risk. And we cannot risk Horde or Sela knowing that you and I are associated. Hood surveillance is not up to Coalition standards, naturally. I expect you'll have little or no trouble circumventing it. Much better for the sake of verisimilitude if you worm across the river yourself and pick your way with great caution to the girl.

—There had to be a hitch in the deal somewhere.

I look down at my bloody clothes, my one remaining boot.

—Do you think verisimilitude could suffer to the extent of a couple bucks so I can find some clothes that won't have people pointing at me and screaming for a cop?

He waves one of the enforcers over from the eastern corner of the roof.

—Petty cash.

The enforcer takes an envelope from his side jacket pocket and drops it in one of the scummy puddles.

I look at Predo.

—You rehearse that move in advance?

He shrugs.

—Actually, not. This one has initiative.

I bend and pick up the envelope.

—Charming quality, that.

He starts across the roof.

—Don't take too long with your tailor, Pitt. I'll want a report soonest.

I flick stinking water from the envelope.

—Yeah, get right on it. Chop, chop, and all that.

He pauses at the access door to the stairs.

—Do that. The line of those waiting to dismember you should you fail has grown rather long.

I take the money from the envelope.

—Well it was never short.

He considers.

—Yes, always a popular man.

I count the bills.

—Speaking of popularity.

He waits.

I look up from the envelope.

—That Dickens fan you have working up here, the one with the Fagin fetish. Lament?

—Yes.

I flip through the bills, making sure it's not Monopoly money.

—I'm gonna have to kill him.

He looks at his shoes, looks up.

—Complete the assignment, Pitt. After that, how you spend your political capital is your own concern. However, killing a Coalition resource could well nullify any other aspect of our deal.

I stuff the cash in my hip pocket.

—Well, seeing as I always assume you'll fuck me over in the end, that doesn't really change my approach.

He nods.

—Not unwise, I will admit.

He turns. Stops.

—One thing, as long as killing has come up, I think I must renege on my earlier statement.

—What was that?

—When I said I'd forgo threatening your life. At the risk of becoming redundant, let me assure you that this is by far the most pressing issue on which I have ever employed you. And let me further assure you that if you should betray me in any way, I will kill you when we next meet. With my own hands. For the sheer pleasure of it.

He raises an eyebrow.

—Need I add that failure in this case will be deemed a betrayal? No. I think not.

And the door swings shut behind him.

I turn to the City.

It's there. Right where I left it.

Is she? Is she where I left her? In the harbor of Enclave. Is she as I left her? With a new thirst she never asked for?

Is she alive?

Evie.

I look away from the city, the ghosts of the lights still in my eye.

I'm gonna die. I'm gonna die any minute now. Any second. I'm gonna up and die right here if I don't get a fucking cigarette in my mouth in about one second.

I hobble down the fire escape from the roof of the Freedman Home, along a weed-choked path to the street and look down McClellan at the glowing storefront of a twenty-four-hour bodega. I'm not overly concerned about going in there with one bare foot and a considerable amount of dry blood on my clothing, this is the Bronx after all, but best to minimize the visual impact I might make.

I cut over to Walton and head north. There's a little A.M. action on One Sixty-seven around the tight cluster of stores. They're all dark except for another bodega, but it's the same grouping of shops and signage you see on every merchant block up here.

Send Money, Cash Checks, Income Tax, Abogado, Peliculas, Cell Phone, Discount Fashions, Unisex Salon, Long Distance Pre-Paid, Travel.

At the corner some kids hang around the subway entrance passing a blunt and a couple bagged forties. Two gypsy cabdrivers stand outside the bodega drinking *café con leche*.

I cross the street far down from them, my eyes scanning the tops of streetlamp posts, tree branches and the telephone and cable TV wires that cross between the big apartment blocks that line Walton.

At Marcy I spot what I'm looking for and shimmy up a lamp-post and untangle the pair of sneakers that some kid has tossed up there to dangle in testament to some shit that I have never figured out as long as I have lived in this city.

I sit on the curb and stuff my feet inside, leaving the laces undone. They're too small, but the right one fits a little better than the left. Not having a big toe is already paying off.

Farther up the street I jump and grab the bottom rung of a fire-escape ladder, pull myself up and climb two stories to the landing where someone has left their laundry out to dry overnight. I take a green Le Tigre and a pair of khakis, drop them to the sidewalk and climb down. In an alley between buildings I strip out of my bloody shirt and pants and pull on the clothes.

No, not exactly what I'd buy for myself, but they were the first things I saw that looked big enough to fit.

I ball my old clothes and stuff them deep in a garbage can. All except my jacket. I roll that into a bundle inside a few sheets of discarded newspaper and put it under my arm.

At One Seventy there's another strip of shops. No one lingers outside the bodega here. I limp up the street and inside and the proprietor looks out from behind his Plexiglas kill-shield and his eyes just about bug.

Seems I could have spared the bother of getting rid of my other outfit. One-eyed white guys in full preppy mode make an impact all their own. But, bottom line, I'm too freakish just now to be anything other than a junkie. And this guy knows what to do with a junkie.

—The fuck out.

I don't get the fuck out.

He takes his hand from under the counter, shows me the can of pepper spray it's holding and points at the door.

—Don't make me come out there and spray you, *blanco*.

I point at my one eye.

—Better have some sharpshooter fucking aim you want that shit to do any good.

He thinks about that.

While he's thinking, I drop a twenty in the tray that cuts under the shield.

—Just give me a couple packs of Luckys and some matches.

Cash changes everything, even in the hands of a guy clearly wearing someone else's polo shirt.

He drops two packs in the tray.

I look at them.

—No, no, not that shit. Give me the real ones, the filterless.

He looks at the display of smokes behind him.

—I got the filters or I got the filter lights. Don't got filterless.

I toss another twenty on the tray and point.

—Give me that pair of scissors hanging there.

He rings up the scissors while I open both packs of smokes. I knock the bottom of one pack until just the filters stick out, open the scissors, and slice them off. I repeat with the second pack and leave the trash in the tray with the change from my purchases.

The guy points at the mess as I make for the door.

—Not your garbageman, motherfucker.

I hold up one of my modified smokes.

—Buddy, you're lucky I didn't burn this fucking place to the ground.

So much for keeping a low profile in the Bronx.

Then again, so much for the Bronx.

. . .

Rounding onto Rockwood I run my hand along the bars of the fence that separates the little playground on the corner from the rest of the world. My fingers snag one by one on the bars. Kids play here during the day. I know because I can hear them when I use my bolt-hole next door. This time of year they mostly run in and out of the spray from a little fountain, returning again and again to push the silver button on a red post, triggering the water when it times out.

Not a bad sound, those kids.

Sentimental. Romantic.

Predo knows shit. Just likes to throw words like that at me. Figures they'll get my goat. Figures I got some problem with being who I am. What I am. Figures he can worm under my skin and make me jumpy.

I ever bothered time on who I am, I might get worked up about it. But why fret on something you can't change.

I come even with tonight's cave, one of a half dozen or so that I like to rotate between. A crumbling garage surrounded by ruined cars at the back of a mechanic's asphalt lot. The business itself is a block over on One Seventy-two. This place here the guy uses as dead storage.

I scale the chain-link, drop inside and edge between a wall and an old red van. Back of the van are a couple steps down to a door held shut by rusty hinges. A stone ram's head worn smooth by rain is wedged into a notch over the door. The walls are crumbling stone and brick. A limestone foundation visible at the foot of the wall.

It's fucking old.

I push the door and it grinds open about eighteen inches before jamming on an engine block just inside. I work myself through the gap. Inside, I push the door closed. I could have gotten a lock for the door, but it was open when I found it. Figure the sudden appearance of a lock might attract someone's interest. Some places are so forlorn, figure they're safer if they look like anyone could come in and lie down to die anytime they please.

I reach inside one of the empty cylinder chambers on the big V-8 block and find my flashlight and flick it on. If the windows weren't all boarded, enough light would filter in for my eye to work with, but that's not the case. Pitch isn't so black.

The light shows me the piled heaps of twisted rust and grease. It looks like someone bought the scrapped wreckage of a hundred demolition derbies and dumped it all in here until it could be made use of.

How lucky for me to find such cozy lodgings.

I skirt the piles, working my way to my burrow at the base of the north wall under the buckled hood of a '49 Ford. Behind the mix-and-match seats I've wedged together for a cot, I find a filthy nylon laundry bag.

Worldly goods.

A couple plain black Ts mean I can scrap the pastel thing I'm wearing. Rarely felt better about getting rid of an article of clothing. Spare boots means I can get my feet unpinched and out of the sneakers. No backup pants just now so I'm stuck with the khakis, but they're getting nice and greasy now, so that's not so bad. Spare works. I open the kit and make sure it's all there: hose, needles, blood bags.

No spare gun or switchblade or Zippo.

But lots of paperbacks. Moving from place to place these days, a DVD player is a bit of an encumbrance. And an expense. I find the copy of *Shogun* that I couldn't get through, unsnap the rubber band that holds it closed, open it, and take the brass knuckles and straight razor from the hollowed pages inside.

A faucet scabbed with peeling lead paint juts from a wall at the back. I take my jacket, the Le Tigre shirt, and a small box of detergent from a Laundromat vending machine, and go squat by it. I get the shirt damp and sprinkle some soap powder on it and start to work at the blood on the jacket.

Not the first time I've done this.

Back outside, I pull the door closed and look at the City of Light Christian Center across the street. Is it ironic, me crashing across from a church? No, it is not fucking ironic. What it is is fucking business as usual in the Bronx. Churches are like hair salons up here. Can't go two blocks without passing at least one.

Pentecostal Church of Jerusalem II. Cherubim and Seraphim Church. Congregation of Hope Israel. Healing of the Heart Worship Center. Concillio de Iglesia Pentecostal Vision Para Hoy Inc.

Danger isn't that you'll burst into flames should you accidentally rub against one, danger is that all those fucking places are breeding grounds for superstition. Not just the usual shit about the virgin giving birth and her son growing up to get crucified and come back to life. These people, they believe in all kinds of crap.

Not least of all, some of them believe in vampires.

The fact they believe in the kind that can be chased off with garlic and by invoking the name of the Lord is beside the point. Simple fact is, they believe.

I hit the corner of Rockwood and the Concourse at the big apartment building that looks like Charles Addams was a big inspiration in its design, and cross the Boulevard.

Believers are a problem.

Believers keep me moving from shithole to shithole up here. Mean, you slap a reputation for nocturnal habits on top of the white skin, and some of these churchy types get even more nosy than usual.

But the Bronx isn't the only place where believers make trouble.

That scene cooking over the river. That isn't about believers facing off for a dustup, I don't know what it is. Everyone putting their back in a corner, going into a big stare-down, waiting for someone to twitch and turn their eyes away. That happens, someone blinks, and the rest will be on their throat. Whittle themselves down till there's two left, circle, sniff and hit the floor with their teeth buried deep in each other's flesh.

Smells like a lot of dying getting ready to happen.

I think about Predo's little presentation on the Horde girl and everyone's reaction to her plans. Trying to pry the truth from the cracks between all his lies isn't worth the time. I've tried, and never come away with more than bloody fingertips.

Only way to get to the heart of what Predo's up to is to pick up a knife and start digging under the skin till you hit a gusher.

One could ask, *Why bother?*

Why jump when the little prick comes calling with a setup that could be straight and narrow, but that just as clearly won't leave room to squeeze out at the end? Things so bad up here? So miserable just eking it out? Life lack some kind of meaning when it's lived this close to the bone? Willing to put your neck on the block just for a chance to live back in Manhattan? Mean to say, Joe, it's a great city and all, but the rents are out of fucking control!

And I could answer back, *Mind your own fucking business.*

Man have to have a reason to do something stupid?

Man got to be more than just bored and sick and tired of what he's got right now to decide to risk a pile of worthless crap on a crooked wheel?

So.

Figure I got a reason. Figure I got a couple reasons. Figure there's some people over there important to me. Figure there's two of them.

Figure one of them I got to kill.

The other. Well, figure that's a little more complicated. Figure the other is a girl. That's always more complicated.

Figure a chance to get across the river with a little time to work with is all I've been breathing for. Get picky about who comes offering everything you've been dreaming about for over a year, and it'll slip away, never to be seen.

So it's a crooked deal. So I'm angling to get myself real fucking dead. So what?

I play this right, I may get to see my girl again. Fact that if she's alive, it could mean she's just waiting for a chance to kill me doesn't enter into the situation.

I like her anyway.

Besides, you got something better to die for?

Past the Morris Hair Salon and Spa, the svelte figure of a yellow neon woman standing in for the *i* in Morris, Bonner dead-ends in a cul-de-sac of weeded gardens. One yellow-brick tenement, a three-story town house of rotted wood shingle, a gray aluminum-sided row house with a rooster weathervane bolted above the porch, and another fucking Pentecostal church.

Juan 3:16 on a green sign.

For God so loved the world that he gave his one and only Son, that whoever believes in him shall not perish but have eternal life.

Funny thing. Live in this life, do the things we do to stay alive. Know that if you do it enough you could go on living for a very long time, sometimes you think funny things.

Like that line about drinking His blood and eating His body.

Guy like me hears that and he could get ideas about what was really going on at the last supper. Not that I'm saying anything. Just that I like to give myself a good laugh every now and then.

Back of the church, behind chain-link, is a yard of high green weeds and low-hanging branches that screen the rear of a dingy white row house seated off the cul-de-sac. I go over the fence, through the brush and scratch at the red backdoor of the place.

Nothing happens. I scratch again. More nothing. So I knock. Same result. I pull my hand back to give the door a good banging and smell the gun oil on the barrel of the shotgun before it tickles my neck.

—You wake my neighbors and I'm gonna be mad as hell.

I raise my hands.

—You use that thing and they'll wake the hell up all right.

—They will. But they'll be too scared to look out their windows.

—Good point.

She takes the gun away.

—The hell you doing here, Joe?

I turn and show Esperanza my new scar.

—Hoped you'd have a pair of sunglasses I could borrow.

—Thought you had a quiet night planned.

I settle into the ladder-back chair in the corner of her basement room.

—So did I. Ran into a guy named Lament had other ideas.

She puts the .20 gauge on the floor next to her old army cot.

—Lament.

—Got in a tangle with some of his kids.

She pulls a drawer open on an old bureau.

—You hurt any of them?

I point at my face.

—I look like I hurt any of them? Want to see where that crazy fucker bit my toe off?

She digs in the drawer.

—No, I do not.

—Didn't think so. Between that, losing an eye, and my bad knee, I'm gonna be roadkill any night now.

She looks up from her search.

—Kind of doubt that.

I light a smoke and drop the spent match in one of those ash-trays with a plaid beanbag base.

—Doubt all you like, but I'd have to contract dire leprosy to start losing parts any faster.

She takes a green and gold sweatband from the drawer and stretches it between her fingers.

—How'd you get away?

—Cut a deal.

She drops the sweatband back in the drawer and looks over.

—Cutting deals isn't Lament's style.

—What can I tell you, I cut a deal.

She scratches her upper thigh just under the hem of the flan-nel boxer shorts she wore outside to threaten me. I'm assuming she was wearing them already and didn't put them on special for the occasion.

—Guess it's not unheard of.

She's washed her usually slicked hair and it hangs black and glossy to her jawline.

—I cut a deal with him once.

There's an old Ewing poster above the cot, corners ripped by thumbtacks.

I stretch my leg, feel the gravel in my knee grind.

—Don't say. Didn't know you know the guy. Truth is, before tonight, I didn't know he existed.

She twists a hank of hair.

—Like I said before, you don't look to get involved in the neigh-borhood, you can't expect to know what goes on.

—True. True. So you one of his kids?

She tucks the hair behind her ear.

—Yeah. I started over there.

She cocks a hip, rests a hand on it and leans against the bureau, flashes some attitude.

—But I didn't like the way he ran things.

—So you cut a deal.

She works a cigarette from her pack on the bureau top and puts it between her lips.

—I cut a deal.

I watch her look for a match, and take mine out of my pocket.

—Having seen his operation, that sounds like it was a wise move.

I flip her the matchbook.

—What kind of deal did you cut?

She lights a match and puts the flame to her smoke.

—I cut the kind of deal where I dragged him out of the sun when the Mungiki would have let him burn.

She crosses and drops the match in the ashtray.

—Deal was, he was too fucked up at that point to do anything but whine while I kicked him in the face before I left.

She drives her bare heel into the floor a couple times.

—I was smarter, I would have *left* him in the sun.

—What stopped you?

The tip of her tongue appears between her lips, slips back inside.

—I was afraid. Stupid. Afraid he'd be able to do something if I killed him.

She knocks some ash.

—He has a talent for that.

She takes a drag and smoke rides her words.

—A real gift for making kids afraid.

The tips of our cigarettes flare a few times.

I stub mine out.

—Never too late to make up for past mistakes.

She nods.

—Yeah, I've thought about it. Every time I hear another kid went missing up here, I think about going over and finishing that deal.

—Something holding you back?

She walks back to the bureau.

—Yeah.

She rests her smoke on the edge of the bureau and starts digging again.

—I'm still afraid of him. How funny is that?

I think about my parents, about urine running down my leg as they came at me.

I watch her, and try to read the dark tattoos on her dark skin in the dark room.

—Nothing funny about that at all.

She takes a pair of big geriatric sunglasses and a compact from the drawer, crosses to me and slides them on my face.

She tilts her head and gives me a once-over.

—Just like you just went to the eye doctor.

She palms the compact open and holds it in front of my face.

I take a look at myself in the huge black goggles.

—Oh yeah, very inconspicuous.

She clicks the compact closed.

—Better than walking around with that hamburger showing.

She takes the glasses.

—It gonna grow back?

—No. But it'll heal some. Part of the eyelid might grow back. Probably skin will just seal it up.

She sets the sunglasses and the compact on the top of her boom box next to the ashtray.

—Gonna be light in a few hours.

—Yeah.

—Just saying, you may as well stay here.

I shift in the chair.

—No, I gotta—

She holds up a hand.

—Don't tell me what you *gotta*, Pitt. I didn't ask. I don't need to hear your excuse. And, for the record, I didn't mean anything by the invitation.

She goes to the bureau for her smoke.

—You've made it plenty clear you're not interested. I've made it plenty clear I am, and that there's no strings attached. I don't need to be turned down twice in one night. When I say, *You may as well stay,* I'm picturing me in my cot and you on the floor. Not that I'd suddenly play hard to get if you climbed under my blanket, but you've let me know that's not the way it's gonna be.

She crosses her arms over her cutoff WNBA tank.

—So you staying or going? Cuz I'm ready to get some sleep.

I look around her little bunker room. Knicks posters, the scratched bureau, boom box and a stack of hip-hop and reggaeton CDs, small collection of basketball shoes, microwave, few groceries stacked on milk crates, chem-toilet in the corner, pile of books in both English and Spanish, that little cot.

The chambers of the Queen of the South Bronx.

The idea of climbing off that floor and into her cot, well, a man would have to be flat-out dumb as mud to pass on a chance like that.

But two people would break that cot.

—I can't stay.

She heads for the cot.

—No problems. Door is right there.

—I need to go.

She lies down.

—Don't tell me your plans, Pitt, just get going.

I lean forward and rest my elbows on my knees.

—I need to go across the river.

She looks at me.

I look back.

—And I need help.

I rub my chin.

—Tonight.

She laughs.

I nod.

—Yeah, funny, right?

She laughs some more, stops, looks at me.

—No. Not funny. Just I get it now.

She puts her hands behind her head.

—Man I was freaking *out* on it.

—What's that?

She laughs again.

—Why you kept saying no. I mean, I've been turned down, shit happens to any girl. And I don't usually offer twice. You, I've put it out there a bunch of times. I mean, a girl thinks, *What's wrong with me?* I didn't know if it was the whole jock thing, like you like your chicks more feminine, or maybe you don't like Latinas. I could not figure that shit out. I mean, Pitt, there ain't that much up here to choose from if we want to stay in our own kind. You don't look so bad, you can talk when you get the urge, and you're not some freak running 'round gnawing on anything with blood in it. And I know I got something that works. I could not figure this shit out. Why the fuck we never hooked up.

She rolls on her side and points at me.

—You got yourself a girl over there.

She laughs.

Women. You tell me they're not all witches, and I'll tell you you haven't been paying attention.

—It's not that easy.

—You do it all the time.

She raises a finger and wags it at me.

—OK, first, I do not do it all the time. I do it every chance I get, but that is far from all the time. Second, what I do on my own, and what you need, those are two very different things.

I look at the clock.

—It's the same damn river, Esperanza.

—It may be the same damn river, Pitt, but we are two very different people.

—Which means?

She points at her skin then points at mine.

—That need to be spelled out any clearer?

It doesn't.

—I still need to get over.

She taps a bare toe on the shotgun lying next to her cot.

—I hear that. But they don't want you over there. I mean.

She raises her hands over her head.

—You came up here, you had to know that was like a one-way ticket.

I walk to the bureau and look at the high school basketball trophies lined on the top.

—I need to get over.

She jabs a finger at me.

—They. Don't. Want. You. I cross over, it's one thing. Mean, I been hitting Rucker since I was a kid. Before Lament ever got his hands on me, I was a face over the river. Once I got infected and then got clear of Lament, I started going back. Didn't take long before one of Digga's rhinos saw me play. He sniffed there was something extra in my game. But they're cool with me. Digga called a sit-down, spelled out the rules: As long as I tithe over a percentage of what I take from the boys I school playing one-on-one at Rucker, I can come and go.

She gets up and comes over and takes one of the trophies from my hands.

—Don't fuck with those.

She puts it back in place.

—You can't just go back, man. That ain't the way this works. You got sense, you know this. Shit, you're from over there. You know damn well they don't want any of us outer-borough trash coming over. I wanted to pledge Hood, Digga might have me, but that's as much because I'm an earner as it is I'm brown. They don't want no more mouths to feed over there.

She rubs her thumbs on the chipped leg of a gilded ball player.

—Why I stay here. We want anything, we got to make it better over *here*. Fuck their Island. Shit can't be sustained. How you going to keep the population down? Think on that. It's a goddamn virus, no way to keep it from spreading. Mean, I barely stayed in school enough to play ball, but even I can read enough to get that straight. Island can't last. Future is over here. Where there's room to spread.

She lifts her chin.

—Wait and see. Years go by, it's gonna be the other way around. Gonna be their asses trying to cross over. Get to this side.

I take one of my custom-cut smokes from the pack.

—No argument. But it don't change things.

I light up.

—I need to get over.

She throws her hands up and walks away.

—Like you're not even listening.

I study the scratches on the cement floor.

—I'm listening. I'm just not hearing anything that helps me.

She turns.

—If that's what you're waiting for, you should get moving.

I look up from the floor and study her young face.

—I'm not asking you to hold my hand. I'm not asking you to carry me across. Way I figure, chances are no one will even see me. How many subway platforms can they cover? How many trains can they ride looking for refugees? Coalition can't keep everybody from crossing their turf, someone always slips through the cracks. Coalition has cracks, the Hood has to have holes you can walk through. All I'm asking is, *Where are the holes?* I get snatched, I get taken to Digga, I got a history with the man. Maybe he cuts me loose. Doesn't matter. Time is an issue. 'Sides, I don't want anyone to know I'm over there. I don't want anyone to know I'm back.

She touches her earlobe.

—What's that about?

I smile.

—I'm hoping to surprise a couple people.

I hold out my pack and she comes over and takes a smoke.

She leans in to the lit match and looks at me.

—That's a nasty smile you got, Pitt.

The smile stays where it is.

She blows out the match.

—I like it.

She takes a deep drag and exhales.

—That girl you got over there. Turns out she don't know what she has in you, you bring that smile back over to this side of the river. We could get some things done here.

I put the smile away.

She lifts her shoulders.

—And there it goes.

She reaches past me and pulls open a drawer and takes out a pair of knee-length cutoff jeans.

—They move around.

She puts the smoke between her lips and pulls the cutoffs on.

—Only got so many people to watch their border, so they move them around. Got apartments they move in and out of with views of the bridges. Shift others from station to station and line to line, sniffing for refugees. Buses and trains. Got some guys work the graveyard in the toll booths. How's that for security? Others got MTA jobs, down in the tunnels. Conductors. Motormen. Maintenance. Only the Hood can do that. What's the last time you saw someone white working the subways? First of never, that's when. Coalition tried to put one of theirs in a job underground, everyone'd be like, *What the fuck?*

She points at a Starks jersey on the back of the chair.

—Toss me that.

I toss it to her and she peels off her WNBA top.

—Don't be staring at my tits. You had your chance.

I take a drag and look away as she pulls on the jersey.

She's right, I had my chance.

And I passed on the best the Bronx has to offer.

So.

Back to the fire.

I stand at the foot of the Macombs Dam Bridge, leaning against one of the Tudor abutments, smoking, looking down the length of the swing bridge at the Island, a little over two thousand feet away.

Esperanza watches the approach.

—Should be a gypsy around anytime.

—They don't like to stop for me.

—Why not?

—Why do you think? I'm white. They think I'm a transit cop or something. Looking to bust them for hacking without a medallion.

—I can flag one for you.

I flick my butt over the rail of the bridge. The wind off the Harlem grabs it and spins it away.

—I'll walk.

I take the cash Predo gave me out of my pocket.

—How much?

She shrugs.

—Guy I called, he'll need a couple bills.

I peel off two hundred.

—And you?

She points over the river at the FDR.

—That stretch of road, just that couple blocks, know what it's called?

I look at it.

—Nope.

—Three Hundred Sixty-ninth Harlem Hellfighter's Drive. Black regiment. First fought in World War I. Spent one hundred and ninety-one days under fire. Suffered over fifteen hundred casualties. Guy named Private Henry Lincoln Johnson, and his buddy Private Needham Roberts, they fought off twenty-four Germans. Just the two of them. When Roberts was shot, Johnson used his bolo knife and rifle butt to hold off the krauts.

She turns, looks over the Bronx.

—Johnson won the Croix de Guerre. First American ever.

She looks at me.

—Good to have someone to put your back against when the close work starts.

She spits over the rail.

—So how about you owe me on this one. Sometime I need someone to have my back, maybe I give you a call.

I fold the bills over.

—Can't say it's a safe bet I'll be around long enough to pay off.

—I'll take that chance.

I put the money in my pocket.

—If that's how you want it.

—That's how I want it.

She starts to walk backward, away down the bridge approach.

—Guy said the bridge was clear. No watchers. Grab yourself a ride on the other side. Said steer clear of Marcus Garvey Park. Said Malcom X is clear all the way to One Ten. Once you cross to Coalition turf, who knows what the hell you find. But in a car, I don't know how they go about spotting you.

I raise a hand.

—Stay alive.

She raises a hand.

—That's the plan.

She turns away, takes a couple steps, turns back.

—Joe.

—Yeah.

—Little advice.

—What's that?

She points at my trousers.

—Lose the khakis. They do nothing for you.

She turns again and breaks into a trot, jogging smooth and easy till she boosts herself over the rail, dropping into Macombs Park, lost from view.

I find a cigarette to put in my mouth and start over the bridge.

Summer wind is blowing, taking the smoke downriver. A couple cars roll past, vibrating the bridge plates. I slap one of the beige-painted trusses and it tolls like a low bell. I cross the midpoint, feel my feet start to hurry, make them pace slow.

Is my breath short?

It is.

Past the little stone hutch where the operator sits when the bridge swings open, I hit the western approach. Look down, see the river disappear behind me, land under the bridge.

Crossing Hellfighter's, coming onto the Island, fingering the straight blade in my pocket.

At Adam Clayton Powell Junior and One Fifty-three I raise my hand in the air then step in front of the gypsy that tries to drive past me. The driver looks at the color of my skin and his door locks snap down. I show him the color of my money and the locks pop up.

He watches me in the rearview as I slide into the back.

I point.

—South.

He starts rolling.

—How far?

I lean into the leather, light a smoke.

—Not too far. But take Malcolm, will you.

He takes the left onto One Forty-five.

—Right. The scenic route.

I roll the window down and smell the summer stink of Manhattan.

—Sure. The scenic route. Why not.

How you know you're being watched is, you have clandestine arrangements with someone you don't trust under any circumstances that don't involve that individual being tied up and held at gunpoint. It also helps if the individual involved shares a similar attitude toward you.

The rest is easy.

See, once you've established a level of trust like that, the only question you have to ask yourself is, *Assuming I don't want to be followed, where do I go?*

The obvious answer being, *I go where they expect me to go.*

And then I go somewhere else.

The gypsy drops me at the corner of Second Avenue and Seventy-third. For a moment I sit there with one foot out on the sidewalk, thinking about pulling my leg back in, closing the door and telling him to roll farther south.

It passes, and I get out and close the door and he drives off.

No. That's a lie.

I get out and he drives away, alright, but it doesn't pass. The gravity pulling from below Fourteenth doesn't go away. Back on the Island, it just pulls harder than ever.

How you ignore a thing like that is, you move. Create momentum. Build velocity to carry your mass outside the influence of the body pulling at yours.

I walk east on Seventy-third, aligning myself with a new trajectory, knowing that what happens beyond the event horizon cannot be described until you are caught in its tide.

The building is mid-block between First and Second, only four stories, but stretching the width of three tenements. Big ground-floor windows covered in sheets of dark paper in a manner to suggest some kind of renovation within. A half-full construction Dumpster at the curb. Upper-story windows heavily draped.

A double stoop leads up to a portico entrance.

The sky's holding the day back yet.

Time enough to make a courtesy call and be on my way.

I go up the steps and push the buzzer.

It's a mess.

Like there was ever any doubt, right?

Something like this, the only way you think it's going to be anything but a mess is if you're one of those people they call an idealist. Those people, I generally prefer the word *asshole* when I describe them. Not that I fault a person for doing their own thing, but *assholes* of the *idealist* strain have a habit of fucking things up for everyone else.

Nothing like a person with a dream and a vision for getting a load of people all fucked up.

But Jesus it's a mess.

It reeks. Rank with overcrowding.

Fear. Desperation. Misery.

All these most pleasant human emotions have a smell. None of them enjoyable. The air in here is heavy with all of them. A man could gag.

—Um, mind your step there. Just. Yes. Just kind of, um, step over them and. Obviously these are less than ideal conditions. You're certainly not seeing us at our best. But I, um, assure you that this state is only temporary. Once the renovation is complete we'll have these people housed, um, properly.

I follow his advice and just kind of step over the people sleeping in the hallway. Not that they're actually sleeping. What they're actually doing is watching us pass, tracking us through slitted lids. I hear one or two sniff at me as I weave through their jumbled limbs and bodies.

—Hey, hey, man.

I look down at the hairy face looking up at me from his spot, reclined along the wainscoting.

He scratches his fat belly through his Superman T-shirt, pointing a rolled-up copy of *Green Lantern* at me.

—You got anything?

I step past him.

—No. I ain't got anything.

He sits up, waves his comic book at me as I follow my guide.

—Bullshit, man! That's bullshit! I can smell it on ya! I can smell it, man! We can all smell it!

Bodies rouse, the more lively ones tilt their faces up and inhale.

My guide tugs at the shirttails that hang ever so stylishly from the bottom of his argyle sweater.

—Um, just a little, um, more briskly here. Just up here.

He picks up the pace, doesn't pay enough attention, steps on someone's fingers.

—Hey, fuck!

—Sorry, um, so sorry.

—Watch where the fuck, Gladstone.

—Yes, um, sorry.

The comicbook geek is on his feet.

—Can't get away with this shit, Gladstone. Come through here, stomp on people, bring some asshole that's holding and won't share out.

More sniffing from the bodies.

Voices.

—Who's holding?

—Fuckin' Gladstone.

—Holdin'?

—I smell it. I smell it.

Gladstone stops at the door at the end of the hall, sorts keys.

—Yes, um, so sorry, yes, my mistake, didn't mean to. Yes, um, just in here if you will.

He slips a key in the lock.

—Just, um, in here and. Um. Yes, if you'll all please just be patient, I'm sure we'll have something for you all just as soon as, um. Yes. Um.

I pass through, glancing back, seeing the comicbook geek flipping us off.

—Fuck you, Gladstone!

The others in the hallway settling back into torpor and misery. These being easier and more comfortable than action and rage.

The door closes and Gladstone locks it tight.

—Um, Sorry, um. Normally we'd have taken the elevator to the office level. Not walked through the, um, residences, but, um, the elevator is out and, well, there are some difficulties involved with getting it serviced. So, um. Up here and, yes.

He pulls at his lower lip.

—By the, um, way, are you holding any?

I walk past him, up the fire stairs.

—No. Just I couldn't get all the blood out of my jacket when I cleaned it last.

He comes after me.

—Oh, yes, that would, um, explain it.

—It's a fucking mess.

—I know.

—And it's getting worse.

—I know.

—And it's going to happen again.

—I *know*, Sela.

—Um, yes, excuse me.

I watch Gladstone's back as he sticks his head a little farther into the room beyond the door he cracked open only after knocking politely about ten times and finally deciding the people fighting beyond it had not heard him.

The folks inside take note of his presence.

—What? What?

—Um, I. So sorry, Miss, but I, I did, um, knock, and.

—What, Gladstone?

—Nothing. I mean, um, someone, a, um, new, um.

His arm is waving at me, indicating my presence, despite the fact that it is invisible to the people he's speaking with.

—A new, um, applicant. And I, um, know you like to greet each one, um, personally, so I.

—An *intercom*, Gladstone. We have a perfectly good one. Or has that broken now too?

—No, I, um, I. I buzzed and. Would you like to, um?

—Wait. Gladstone.

The other voice has taken over, the one that shares my opinion about things around here being a mess.

—Um, yes?

—Is there someone out there?

—Um, I.

He pulls his head back, looks at me to make sure I'm still there, then sticks his head back into the room.

—Yes, um. There. Yes.

—Motherfucker! See! See! A mess! These people. No regard for security. No understanding of protocol. Is it any wonder things like this shit come up?

—They're not *these people*. They're *our people*. You, of all people, should get that.

—Don't, not now. This is no joke. And it's no time for remedial lessons in compassion and understanding. You!

Gladstone's back stiffens.

—Um, yes?

—You bring someone up here again without clearing it through me, you'll be back in the dorms.

—I, um, yes, I. It's just, I did buzz and, um.

—Shut the fuck up.

—Um.

I grab the edge of the door and pull it open, move Gladstone out of the way and step into the room.

Sela goes for the piece strapped into the shoulder holster she's wearing over her tank top.

Her hand freezes on the butt.

—Oh Jesus.

I raise a hand.

—Yeah, good to see you too.

Her hand stays on the gun.

—Did I say it was good to see you, Joe?

—No, but I always try to read between the lines. Figured you going for your gun was how you express affection these days.

—That not how she expresses affection at *all*, Joe.

The girl comes out from behind her desk, puts a hand on Sela's arm, rubs her thumb across a vein that swells down the muscle.

—Chill *out*, Sela.

Sela takes her hand from the gun, but I'd be hard-pressed to describe her as chilled out.

—Don't get too close to him.

The girl comes toward me.

—Don't be *silly*, it's Joe. What's he gonna do, *kill* me?

She comes closer.

—He'd *never* do that. He'd never hurt me at all.

She smiles.

—Well, except for *maybe* that time he slapped me.

She squishes her face.

—But I *was* being pretty bratty. Giving him a bad time about things.

She stops in front of me.

—Well, come *on*, Joe. What do you *think*?

She gives a little spin, displaying her slacks, French-cuffed shirt, suit vest and expensively shorn hair.

—Have I grown up right?

I take off my huge sunglasses and show her the fresh scar tissue.

—I don't know, maybe I need a better look.

She claps, wraps her arms around me, turns her face into my chest and inhales.

—Oh, Joe, you *always* know just what to say to make me feel safe.

I stand there with her arms around me, my own arms at my sides, looking at Sela.

She shakes her head.

—She her own thing, our girl, isn't she, Joe?

—The *logistics* of it are just devastating. I mean, it was one thing to *say* we were going to establish a Clan, take in anyone who wanted to join, supply them with *blood,* and then make the cure available to them once I *find* it.

She points at the twin flat-screen computer monitors on her desk, the piles of paper.

—But it is *so* another thing to actually be doing it.

She flops back in her leather office chair and kicks her heel against the floor, spinning slow and lazy.

—Don't misunderstand, I do *not* have any regrets. I'm *young,* I have the energy, God *knows* I'm smart enough to handle it all, but I'll *totally* fess that it's *way* harder than I expected it to be.

She stops spinning, launches herself from the chair and begins circling the desk, plucking papers at random.

—I *completely* miscalculated demand. I mean, the numbers are way out of whack. There's only a few *thousand* infected on Manhattan, right? The ones aligned with Clans, why would they take a risk, move over to us? We assumed mostly we'd get Rogues. How *many* could that be? With a food source strictly limited by the land available, it's just common *sense* that predators not operating with a pack are going to get squeezed out. So we assumed a couple dozen Rogues, at most, a like amount of crossovers from the Clans, people willing to take that *chance* because they were committed to the idea of a *cure,* and some refugees who got the word and managed to make it over to the Island.

She shakes one of the papers.

—At this point, in our first year, we were assuming a *max* membership of eighty. We prepped for *one hundred*. Just to be safe.

She crumples the paper and throws it on the Persian rug underfoot.

—Two-hundred and sixty-one.

She shakes her head.

—I mean. Holy shit. The *renovations*. The initial renovations were hard enough. But you buy a building, grease the right palms, bribe the *tight asses* on the neighborhood committee and get to work. Once the materials start moving in and out, the people on the street have no idea what you're *actually* doing inside. The rooms were *so* nice. We really went the extra mile. No Pottery Barn or IKEA crap, really nice beds, furnishings. Tried to give each room a *character.* Like a boutique hotel. That's what the builders thought we were doing.

She goes to the door, opens it and points at her outer office.

—Now? Did you see it? In the *halls.* On the *stairs.* How do we bring a crew in here to tear out the walls and turn the second and third floors into the barracks we need? How do I take delivery on a *hundred* bunk beds? Like no one is going to *notice* and ask what the hell is going on. Little things. The elevator. I can't get a repair service in because I don't have room to *hide* all these people. A building this size, things are *constantly* breaking, wearing out. We're taxing the plumbing like you *wouldn't* believe. The longer these things go without maintenance, the worse everything gets.

She throws the papers in the air, stands there as they snow around her.

—And food, just regular food, we're sneaking it in. So the neighbors don't know how many are here. I *mean*, the FreshDirect truck can't be rolling up every day and unloading enough groceries for a cafeteria, can it? I *mean*. My God. Jesus. *Shit.*

She sighs, looks at me, smiles.

—*Listen* to me. I mean, could I sound a little *more* like my dad? He'd come home from work, it'd be just like this. The lab or the office or both, something was always blowing up. All he wanted to do was be up to his eyes in research, but it was always patent *this* or government oversight *that* or board of directors are *cocksuckers*.

She rubs her forehead.

—And that's what really *kills*. Not being in the lab. I mean, I *know* I have responsibilities here, and I took all this on and I *have* to deal, but it's not *even* what I want to be doing. I mean.

She drops her head back and opens her mouth wide.

—Gaaahhh.

She rolls her eyes.

—This stuff is *so* boring. And I mean, the whole point is a cure, right? I mean, that's why these people are packing in here, right? I mean, why name the Clan *Clan Cure* if I never get to work on it?

She leans against the desk, opens a cigarette box and takes out a clove.

—And *that* place. It's a whole different headache. 'Cause the *Vyrus,* it's testy as hell. It's really, what's so sad, it's really a *pussy.* I mean, there are other viruses that are *way* more robust. Think about it.

She comes over and puts her cigarette in her mouth and leans in.

—Light?

I snap a match and she touches her cigarette to it.

—Thanks.

She moves away, blows a cloud.

—Think about it. The Vyrus, it can only live *inside* the human body. It can only survive in a human body. It can only *spread* itself blood to blood. And it's so *hyper,* it colonizes host cells so quickly and burns them out, that it needs to have its environment *constantly* refreshed. And it *kills* its host and rarely gets a chance to reproduce. I mean, is that inefficient or *what*? *Seriously,* it is one crap piece of engineering. One of those evolutionary steps that's *so* random and poorly designed that it actually proves evolution. I mean, why would God bother with a thing like *that*? Intelligent design? *Not*.

She crosses to the window. Lifts the hook that holds the shutters closed behind the curtains.

—Something fussy like that, just getting a look at it is a *pain*. Creating a stable environment for it outside a host? Talk about *tedious*. And then, a thing like this, finding a cure for a virus, you don't do that alone. Not even when you're smarter than *everyone* else.

She opens the shutter a crack, puts her hand through and parts the curtain.

—There's just *way* too much busy work. I mean. Cultures, batches of *this* and *that,* computer modeling, archiving. It's like working on a code. Like how when they try to break a *code* they sometimes give just a *piece* of it to each team. So they don't really *know* what they're working on. Keep them isolated from one another. I have to do that. I *mean,* the lab I assembled for this at Horde Bio Tech, it's not staffed with *assholes*. Well, some of them are assholes, but they're really fucking *smart* assholes. Show these people the whole Vyrus, let them get a good look at it and see its behavior? You will see some *serious* freaking out. But.

She turns, light from a streetlamp drops through the curtain and crosses her face, makes her perfect skin glow.

—It is *amazing*.

She lifts her hand to the light, stares at it reflected there.

—That's one of the things that's *amazing*. Light. Like we've been doing things with *light*. These guys at ASU, they've been *blasting* viruses in blood samples with a laser. Like fifty megawatts per square centimeter. Which isn't *half* as nasty as it sounds. And so, like, we've known for a *long* time you can kill viruses with UV radiation, but that causes *mutation*. And mutation leads to *adaptation* over time. So, these guys, they've been using visible light pulses. And it works. It.

She holds up her cigarette, wiggles it, creating a jagged stream of smoke.

—It vibrates a virus, physically disrupts the virus shell, this thing called the *capsid*. It cripples the virus it affects. Virus can't function, and *dies*. So.

Her eyes are big, staring a million miles.

—The Vyrus, your Vyrus, goes *haywire* when exposed to solar UVA, it mutates. But not adaptive mutations. Or not that we can see because it happens *way* too fast. But, but, maybe we can find a wave of radiation, a *visible* wavelength to shatter the Vyrus' capsid? It's so, it's *way* outside the box, but the Vyrus isn't in the box, so this is the kind of stuff we have to. I *mean*.

She stares farther, going away from the room, deep inside some other place.

—It is so fucking *cool*.

She takes a big drag.

—It's *like*, like being a *pioneer*. Like none of the rules *apply* and you can try anything. *Anything*. Nothing is out of bounds. And. Oh, and I said about *computer* models. The good thing about having too many people here, it gives us a *really* good pool to draw samples from. And, because the Vyrus, it *does* mutate. *Radically.* From person to person. I *mean*, we've got a couple people here who infected other people here. And even then, the *same* strain passing from host to host, it mutates. But within a range. I *think*. So we can draw samples. And like I said, the Vyrus is a *total* puss, and if you mishandle a specimen it croaks like *that*, but if you do it right we have time to log the mutation. So we're creating a database of mutations. *Like*, we can look and see its favorite tricks. How it *hides*. How it *defends* itself. Maybe get an idea why some infecteds get a lot stronger, and some *not* so much. Or *healing*. Like some strains seem to mutate in a fashion that really enhances new cell growth. But not all of them. And.

Her eyes slide sideways, unfocus, and someone cuts her strings and she's hitting the floor.

Sela gets to her before I do, feels her pulse, takes the burning cigarette from between her fingers and stubs it in an ashtray on the edge of the desk.

I look at her as she brushes loose strands of perfect hair from Amanda's forehead.

—She OK?

Sela doesn't look at me, just lifts the girl's head into her lap.

—She's exhausted.

—Yeah, well I guess being crazy will do that to you.

She looks at me now.

—She's not crazy. She's a visionary.

She looks back at her lover's face.

—She's special, Joe.

I fish a smoke from my pack.

—Specially fucked up, Sela.

I drop a match in the ashtray, see Amanda's clove still smoldering and crush it.

—She had mind-fuck parents and they mind-fucked her. She's got too much money and she's too smart for her own good and she's seen too much and she knows things that are too weird. And that's all fucked her up. She's not normal. She's bent as hell. She's crazy.

Sela rests her hand on the girl's forehead.

—You calling yourself normal these days, Joe?

I smoke some more.

Sela looks at me.

—Yeah, I didn't think so.

She slides out from under the girl.

—She works harder than any of us. She never stops. She's here in this office or she's at the lab. I can barely get her to sleep two hours out of every thirty. She never stops. She never gives up. Everyone who shows up on that doorstep, she says yes to. She takes them all in.

—Like I said, crazy.

She steps to me, every flawlessly cut muscle on her is rigid.

—She never stops working, Joe. For us. She's not infected, but she never stops trying to help us. She works harder to help us than we work to help ourselves.

She raises a finger and shows me the short, sharp, red nail at its end.

—So be careful how you talk about her.

She angles the finger at my face.

—You only got one eye left to poke out if I lose my temper.

It's true Sela wouldn't even know the girl if I hadn't been around. It's true I've known Sela since she was a punk-attitude pre-op tranny down with the Society, as opposed to a fashion-plate, lipstick pre-op up here with Amanda. It's even true she saved my life once.

But none of that will save my eye if she decides she's got a hankering to see it on the end of her finger.

Diplomacy is required.

—Sure thing, Sela. I get it. Mean, the fact she's investing her energies in trying to save a bunch of people who look at her like food, fact that she's filled a building with them, all of 'em close enough to smell her all the time, that doesn't indicate anything about her sanity. Stable as a rock, your girl there.

She pulls the finger in, joins it up with four or five others, and I get a second to wonder how far my head will fly if she decides to knock it off my neck, then she lowers her fist.

—Yeah, you're right about that part. That part's a problem.

She steps back.

—Those people downstairs, that's a problem.

She folds her arms.

—Think it's tough getting enough burgers in here to feed all them, imagine what it's like getting enough blood. We've got the money. We just got no place to buy from. They're starting to starve. Couple already have. Burned out. Went berserk. Want to know how good it was for morale when I had to bring those ones down? Not good at all. And last night. That thing we were getting into when you showed up. One of our members went hunting last night. Just a block away. On our doorstep.

—Sloppy.

—Desperate.

—Witnesses?

She rubs the back of her neck.

—*Witnesses.* No. Not to the act. But he left one majorly fucked-up corpse. I expect to see coverage on that the second I take a look at New York One.

—Where's the guy?

—He's here. He's locked in the basement for now. We're trying to sort out what to do about him.

I take the last drag off my smoke and stub it.

—Kill him.

She shakes her head.

—No. That's not what we're doing here. We're making something different.

—Fine. Make something different. But the smart play is you kill him. You know that. He went off the reservation. So now you kill him. And make sure everyone in the place knows you killed him.

—That's what I've been telling her.

We look down at Amanda, her eyes open, fiddling her hair back into place.

—I mean, I want there to be room for compassion around here, but we're on the brink. Order has to be maintained at some point.

She holds out a hand and Sela pulls her to her feet.

—Easy, baby.

—I'm *fine*. It's just a little sugar crash.

—It's severe exhaustion and borderline malnutrition is what it is.

Amanda twists her hand free.

—I *said* I'm fine. I just need a *smoothie* or something.

—You need a proper meal and sleep.

—Sela, back *off*. I love you, honey, but give me just a little space here before I positively *freak* out.

She turns to me.

—I *mean*, you don't see Joe going all *fluttery* on me just because I got a little dizzy.

She brushes the back of her hand across her forehead, fusses her hair some more.

—That's like one of Joe's great assets. He doesn't get *fluttery*, do you, Joe? He just sees what needs to be done and deals with it. After that, it's all just like a question of whether you do it and accept the *consequences*, or don't do it and accept some *different consequences*. Like with this problem today. Joe *gets* it. I mean, you get it *too*, Sela, but Joe gets it in a *different* way. Joe sees the consequences of *not* handing out some kind of punishment here. Don't you, Joe?

I shrug.

—If you say so.

She bunches both fists, tucks them beneath her chin and smiles wide.

—Oh, Joe! I'm *so* happy you're here. I mean, I always *knew* you'd come sooner or later, but it's just perfect that you came when we really *really* need you. Having you join us, that's going to make all the difference for *so* many reasons.

—Yeah, well, thing is.

I take a drag.

—I'm not here to join you.

I take another drag.

—I'm just here to spy on you for Dexter Predo. Now that I've done that.

I point at the liquor cabinet.

—I'll be looking for a drink. After.

I point at the door.

—I'll be looking for the rear entrance.

—No.

—Can I *finish*?

—No.

—I *mean,* so, what, just out of hand, you won't even *listen*?

—No.

—Joe, really, all I'm asking is for you to listen for a *minute*. Just a *couple* minutes while I explain just what it would mean to us. I mean, this is really *really* important.

I toss down my drink.

—And all I'm telling you is *no*.

She sips on the smoothie Gladstone brought her.

—What is that about? I *mean,* I know you don't like to be *in-debted* to anyone, but I'm not even talking about a favor. I'm talk-ing about a *business* transaction. And you just want to sit there and be *all*.

She makes a stone-face, drops her voice an octave.

—*No. No. No. My name is Joe Pitt and I don't do nuthin' I don't want to do and I won't even listen because I don't know a good thing when I have it and I'd rather be all fucked up and tragic and sad and go hurt people.*

She points at me.

—And you're doing it right now, you're thinking about hurting me.

She shakes her head.

—You are *so* thin-skinned.

She leans forward and puts her elbows on the desk.

—But *OK*, you don't want to *join* us. You don't want to do *business* with us. But you're *here*. I mean, there *has* to be a reason why you're here. Besides *spying* for Predo, I mean. I *mean*, I'm not saying that's not what you're doing, but there's a *reason*. Because.

She folds her hands on the desk and lowers her face and rests her chin on them.

—I know you, Joe. I know you like people to *think* you just run around from job to job looking to stay ahead. But I know you have things that get you worked up.

She winces.

—Like when you slapped me? When I was *talking* about your girlfriend that time.

She looks at Sela.

—Sela *heard* what happened.

I run a finger around the rim of my glass. Crystal, it sings a pure note.

Amanda bites her lower lip.

—You tried to infect her. That's what she heard. And it didn't work.

It's quiet, just the glass repeating its song.

—I *know* I never met her. But she *must* have been something, Joe. I know that. I mean, she must have been *something else*.

She lifts her chin from her hands.

—So now, I *mean*, I guess that means you're alone. Like, not just alone like you like people to think you are, but really, *seriously*, alone. Sooo. So, I'm guessing that's why you're here. Because I don't know where you've been, or what kind of deal you made with *Predo*, but, and please don't get all *pissy* with me about this, but I think that the reason you took his job is because you were tired of being alone.

She stands.

1

—But being, like, *you*, you couldn't just come here and say, *Hey, guys, mind if I hang out?*

She comes around the desk.

—So here you are, too stubborn to just jump in and join the family. OK. But, I *mean*, you came up the stairs, you saw those people. Those people, Joe, they're starving. I mean, it's getting bad. The guy we're talking about that went hunting, that's, like, that's the tip of the iceberg. Pretty soon, there's gonna be more of that. And more. And we're not going to be able to contain it.

She sits on the edge of the desk.

—It is going to get so ugly. So fast. And so soon.

She rubs her face.

—We've just.

She looks me in the eye.

—We've got to have more blood. Now, we think we know where we can get it. But it's going to be a serious pain in the ass.

She reaches out and rests her fingers on my knee.

—And we need your help.

—You shouldn't be asking him.

She looks at Sela.

—Why not?

Sela points at me.

—He's spying for Predo.

Amanda looks around the room like she's missed something.

—*So?* I mean, he told us that. He's obviously not all *Coalition* all of a sudden.

Sela watches me as I pick up the bottle from the desk.

—It doesn't mean anything. Predo may have told him to tell you. This could be their game.

Amanda grabs the sides of her head.

—Well if you're going to get all *twisty-turny* about it we'll never get *anywhere*.

She holds out her arms.

—I *mean,* what's he going to tell Predo? What are we *hiding*? We're like all of twelve blocks from his office. *He* can come take a look if he wants. Shit, far as I'm concerned, he can come *join* if he wants. We're *here,* we're taking *all* comers, and we're finding a *cure.* What's the big *secret*?

Sela puts her hands on her hips.

—I don't know! But he wants something. And he sent Pitt here to find it. And letting him stay is fucking dangerous no matter what your feelings about him are. It's stupid. And you're not stupid.

Amanda rolls her eye.

—Baby, you know what, fuck *you.*

Sela cocks her head.

—Excuse me?

Amanda cocks her head to the same angle.

—Oh don't whip out that *sistah* attitude and throw it around in my office.

Sela raises an eyebrow.

—Uh-huh. Alright, I won't bring the *sistah attitude* in here. I'll leave it at the door. I'll leave all that shit outside as soon as you stop acting all Mata Hari. Like you know how this is played. Because, little lady, you do not. You may be the smartest one in the room, but there is shit you do not know. This guy, your precious Joe, sure he comes across sometimes. Sure he's turned up in the right place at the right time once or twice, but mostly what he does is he gets people killed. And a lot of them, they get killed because he has a history of playing off both sides. You want to get all sentimental about him because he saved your life, I get it, but he has been in Predo's pocket for years. Fuck, he's been in everyone's pocket one time or another. He comes out and tells us he's here for Predo, that means shit. All that means is whatever he's after, whatever Predo's after, it has nothing to do with him being here spying.

She looks at me.

Amanda looks at me.

I set my empty glass on the desk.

—Well, I had my drink.

I stand.

—Now can you show me that back way out?

Amanda watches as Sela enters the code and unlocks the door that leads to the alley.

—You're wasting *so* much time, Joe.

I lean against the wall.

—I don't know about that. I had a nice drink, got caught up with old acquaintances. Worse ways to spend an hour.

She gives the eyeroll she's been perfecting since she was nine.

—*Not* what I mean. And you know it.

She reaches over and grabs the sleeve of my jacket.

—This is the *place* for you. This is the last place for you. What we're doing here, it's *real*. You can huff and makes *faces* and act like you think I'm *crazy*, but you know I'm doing the right thing. And you know I can get this done. Anything you do between when you walk out that door and when you come back and tell us you're with us, all that will be *such* a waste of time.

I look at her.

—Sweetheart.

I come away from the wall.

—I don't think you're crazy.

I gently twist my arm free.

—I know it like I know life ain't fair.

I make for the door, stopping to give Sela a look.

—Try to keep her alive.

She opens the door.

—It's what I'm here for.

—Yeah.

I point down toward the basement.

—It'll make your job easier if you do like she says and kill that guy who made the mess.

I start down the rusted steel steps that lead into the alley.

Sela stands there watching.

—We're not all like you, Joe. Some of us don't take to killing so easy.

I walk toward the gate that leads out onto Second.

—Not my fault.

On the street I find a yellow. The driver asks me where I want to go.

I can't go there yet.

So I tell him to take me to the Bowery.

The nice thing about a place like the Whitehouse is they don't feel compelled to announce you if you drop by at an unusual hour to visit a guest. The bad things about a place like the Whitehouse, listed alphabetically, start somewhere around *armed robbery,* run past *cockroaches* and *dirty needles,* hit their stride with *mass murder,* start to tail off at *rape,* and end with a classic: *zoophilia.*

Add in the smattering of semi-functional resident bums, midwestern teenage runaways, and gagging-drunk European tourists on a budget, and you've got a holocaust of vomit and shit smells that draw up the stairwell like smoke pouring up a chimney.

I can almost see the reek as I climb through it.

Coming onto the top-floor landing, I have to turn sideways to fit down the narrow yellow hallway punctuated with close-set white doors. I hear snoring, early morning fornication, someone listening to Kraftwerk so loud on their iPod that they might as well hook it up to some speakers, a toilet flushing and clogging in the communal bathroom, and the distinct sound of someone moaning through a gag while a belt is applied to bare skin.

I long for matches and gasoline.

End of the hall, front of the building, I stop at the final door.

There's silence behind the door. Not even the grinding of teeth I would have expected. The lock is the worst piece of shit I've ever seen in my life. I flip my straight razor open, slip it in the half-inch gap between the door and frame, and start to edge the bolt out of its socket, pulling hard on the doorknob to create friction so the bolt doesn't snap back into place.

The door to the bathroom opens and a girl with the hem of her short skirt tucked into her panties, a ring of hickeys around her neck, and a shiny pink wig askew on her head, staggers down the hall to the room where I heard the fucking sounds.

She tries the knob and it doesn't open.

She bangs the door.

—You fuckers! Stop fucking and let me in!

The panting and groaning behind the door gets louder, faster.

She bangs again.

—Fucking open up! I'm not waiting out here till you guys cum.

The fucking goes on.

She puts her forehead against the door and slouches and turns and looks at me, my razor working the lock.

—Hey.

I watch the pulse that makes one of the hickeys on her neck flutter.

—Hey.

She licks dry lips.

—Thought that guy lives there.

I look at the door I'm working.

—This guy?

She closes one eye, trying to think over the rising volume of her friends' fucking.

—Yeah. Said he lives there.

—When'd he say that?

She looks down, sees her skirt, tries to pull it free of her waist-band.

—Shit. Uh, when'd he? Other day.

She pulls her panties down, gets her skirt straight, leaves her panties at her knees for the moment.

—He, um.

She covers her mouth.

—When I was blowing him. Said he lives there when I was blow-ing him. Said anytime I wanted to score I could come over for the same deal.

She drops her hand, points at the door.

—He wasn't lying to me, was he? I was fucking counting on get-ting some X off him for a party tonight.

I shake my head.

—He wasn't lying.

She smiles, reaches down and pulls her panties back up, catching her skirt in them again.

—Cool, that's cool.

There's a definite crescendo from behind the door, a shriek, a yelp, glass shattering.

She blinks a few times.

—Hey, if you, like, got something on you, I could really use it. Not for free, but like the same deal I made with your friend.

I shake my head.

—No, I'm not holding.

She sighs.

—Shit.

The door bumps her ass and she lurches upright as it swings open into the hall.

—Fucking about time.

She walks into the room.

—You're such a whore, I told you not to fuck him without me.

The door closes.

I pop the lock, go inside, shut the door.

The room is shin-deep in empty take-out containers, plastic baggies, dirty clothes and toenail clippings, the walls covered in photos of barely clad starlets and models torn from men's lifestyle magazines. Through the grimy barred window I can see an edge of sunlight is touching the roof of a building across the street. I pull it open to get some air in, then grab a dingy blanket from the bed to drape over the curtain rod. It's summer in New York City and the air coming in the window doesn't smell any better than the air already in the room. I light a cigarette and sit on the board-narrow bed and smoke and wait for the scum bucket that lives in the shithole.

Finally.

Back where I belong.

The cockroaches in the room, they move to avoid the blade of sunlight that cuts through the crack at the window's edge and slices across the floor. Roaches not liking daylight, it's no great shock that I don't have to wait long for my particular roach to come home.

I know him by the sharp report of nails worn through the heels of his ankle boots striking the hallway floor. Even over the stuttering pipes, creaking joints and bitter howls of the waking building and its occupants, I recognize his nervous step.

Outside the door he jitters the keys in his hand, simultaneously keeping rapid time with clacking teeth. The key jams into the lock and the door jerks open and I smell his greasy pomade.

He steps in, closes the door, freezes with his hand on the knob and looks at the blanket blocking out the day.

—Oh.

It's a small room, a very small room, a room with more in common with a closet than with other rooms. It takes his eyes less than a heartbeat to look it over and see the dark silhouette on his bed.

He holds his key to his face, looking at the fob that dangles off it.

—My bad. Wrong room. I'll just. Don't get up. I'll just.

Not the brightest bulb, but not the dimmest, he knows that people who wait in your room with the window blacked out are bad news.

He just doesn't know how bad the news is yet.

He starts to open the door.

—I'll just. Go to my own room, yeah? Right. Sorry about this. My bad. Totally my bad. This place, so cheap, right? Have like ten different locks in the whole joint. Open someone else's room by accident. Happens all the time. My bad. Really, don't get up.

I don't get up.

—No, you got the right room.

He stops vibrating.

—Oh shit.

I watch a roach skitter across the shaft of daylight.

—Close the door, Phil.

He closes the door.

I stomp on the roach.

—Got some things I want to talk to you about.

If it wasn't daylight I could take him by the ankle and dangle him out the window and cut to the chase.

Instead I have to be subtle.

—I'm going to cut your nose off, Phil.

He holds his hands up.

—Whoa! Whooooaaaahhh! Who said? *Cut* me? How did we get to? Hey, man, I'm sayin', *How did we just skip all the way across you're gonna beat the shit out of me, kick my teeth in, put a cigarette out on my forehead, and get all the way to cutting my fucking nose off?*

He drops his jaw.

—Like, what happened to conversation? What happened to getting all caught up?

He crosses his arms over the front of his dirty silk Hawaiian print shirt and moves his head to one side.

—Hey, great to see you, Joe. Long time. How ya been? Fine? You been fine?

He puts his hands on his hips, moves his head to the other side.

—*Sure, Phil, I been fine. How you been? What you been up to?*

Back to position one.

—Me, oh, I been OK, the usual. This and that. And, you know. Mostly what I been up to is.

He throws his hands in the air.

—Mostly I been spending my days and nights making sure no one cuts my nose off.

He covers his nose.

—I'm saying, *Seriously fuck, Joe!* Cut my nose off? My nose?

He walks in little circles, kicking the trash out of his way.

—Why not an ear? My lips? Fingers? Jeezus!

He stops, holds a hand up.

—Not, mind you, that I'm making suggestions, expressing a preference, mind, just that, you know, fuck. You know?

He stands and pants.

I show him the razor again.

—You want to let me finish?

He pulls his head back.

—Oh, there's more? There's more after you're gonna cut my nose off? You got more that comes after that? Here, let me pull up a chair, let me get comfortable for this, I can't fucking wait to see how it ends.

There's no chair in the room, so he takes a seat at the end of the bed, crosses one leg over the other, rests his hands on his knees and cocks an ear my way.

—By all means, man, proceed.

I balance the razor on my finger, watch it jump slightly with every beat of my heart.

—What I was gonna say, Phil, was, *I'm gonna cut your nose off.*

He nods.

—Yep, yep, got that part, got it. *Gooo ooon.*

I flip the razor, catch it so it rests easy in my palm.

—*I'm gonna cut your nose off,* I was saying. *I'm gonna cut your nose off if you waste a single fucking second of my time,* is what I was saying.

I look from the blade to his face.

—If that makes any difference in your reaction, Philip, that is what I was saying.

His jaw tightens, clicks twice, he nods.

—Yeah, yeah. Sure. That makes a difference. Um.

He points at his nose.

—Too late.

I fold the razor.

—No, man.

I slip the razor into my pocket.

—It's not too late.

He queases a smile.

—Great, Joe, that's great. You know I want nothin' but to help an old buddy like you. Never want to waste a second of your time. Time being, you know.

He rubs fingers against thumb, hopefully.

—Time being money. You know what I mean.

—Yeah, I know, Phil.

I take my hand out of my pocket.

—I just thought we'd do this one the old-fashioned way.

He sees the brass knuckles on my fist.

—Aw, Joe, we coulda worked it out like gentlemen.

I give him a closer look at the knuckles.

Much closer.

He slams into the wall and drops in a jumble on the floor.

I stand over him, using one of his old dirty wife beaters to wipe the blood from brass.

—Shut up, Phil.

I point at the crushed mass that used to be his nose.

—Just feel lucky you still got that fucking thing.

—I need to know how it stands.

—Right, right.

—There a bounty?

—A? A what? A bounty? Jeezus, man, what do you? A bounty?

I knock the brass knuckles on the side of the sink where he's washing the blood from his face.

—Stay focused, Phil.

He flinches.

—Yeah, focused.

He looks in the mirror, sees the bib of blood spread over his shirt.

—Oh for fuck! Maaan. That sucks.

I clink the knuckles again.

He snaps to.

—Yeah, focused. Yeah, bounty. Yeah. Like I was sayin'? Fuck do you think, Joe? Stab Terry and all. You think there's a bounty? Fuck yeah, there is.

—How much?

He pulls a baggie from his pocket, starts sorting through the pills inside.

—Man, this'll teach me to focus exclusively on the ups. I mean, fuck, I don't got a single painkiller in here.

He fingers a couple chalky white pills from the bag and pops them in his mouth.

—Still, any port in a storm.

I slap the back of his head and he coughs and the pills fly out of his mouth, bounce off the mirror and drop to the floor.

He stares at the pills, one resting at the edge of the pube-clogged scum-grate in the middle of the room, the other rolled to the base of a toilet inside one of the doorless stalls.

—Oh, that, that was utterly unnecessary. That was totally fucking flagrant.

I put a finger beneath his chin, raise his eyes to mine.

—Phil, perhaps I'm not communicating my urgency here.

I fit my hand around his jaw.

—It's early in the morning and you're burned out, distracted. I know. It's hard for you to focus. But.

I exert pressure, squeezing the hinges of his jaw.

—If you pay attention, you'll notice that I'm talking more than I usually do, giving you more chances than I usually have in the past to tell me what the fuck I want to know before I give you some new scars.

His jaw creaks. Phil whimpers.

—That might give you some idea of just how thin your ice is.

I stiff-arm him into the wall, careful not to shatter his jaw. I don't want to shatter it yet, not until he's talked.

—And just how bad things are going to get if you don't focus immediately.

I relax my hand and take it from his jaw.

—How much, Phil, how much has Terry put on my head?

He works his jaw up and down, listens to it click, rubs it.

—Twelve pints.

I look at him.

—Again?

—Twelve pints.

—A blood bounty?

He wipes some of his own blood from his face.

—What I said.

The door swings open and Phil's next-door neighbor comes in wearing a stained bed sheet like a poorly wrapped toga. She walks past us, eyes all but closed, goes into a stall, hikes her sheet, sits and places her elbows on her knees with a yawn.

I grab Phil's shoulder and aim him at the door.

—Come on.

He looks back at his lost pills, straining against me.

—Just a sec, man, just a sec, really, man, I can't afford to let that shit go.

I shove him at the door.

—Yes, you can.

He bangs out into the hallway and I follow him.

—Twelve pints.

He walks backward, trying to get a peek through the swinging bathroom door.

—Man, that fucking chick is gonna snag my shit.

—Anyone scooping that stuff off the floor is hard up enough to deserve it.

He raises a hand.

—Well there you go, man, you just described *me*.

I give him another shove and he bounces off the door to his room.

—Twelve pints is an interesting number, Phil.

He gets the key from his blood-stippled high-waisted trousers.

—Fascinating, I'm sure. But, like, you don't understand what I got going here.

He points at the bathroom.

—That chick there gives it up for anything. Mean, I could probably lay off some NoDoz on her and come away with a hand job. Thing is, I'm not saying *I* wouldn't eat the shit on the floor back in there *myself,* but with this deal I don't have to. I can just give them to her and still get a hummer out of it.

He sticks up both thumbs.

—It's win-win, man.

He lowers his thumbs.

—But if she sees them on the floor she'll eat them just out of fucking curiosity. Man, I'll be out the pills and the hummer.

He points both thumbs down.

—Lose-lose.

—Hey, asshole.

The girl stands in the open bathroom doorway.

Phil points at himself.

She nods.

—Yeah, you. That stuff you gave me, that was like total bullshit, wasn't it?

He shakes his head.

—What, huh? No, no, that was good stuff, I wouldn't, you know.

She puts her hands on her hips and the sheet falls off one shoulder, exposing a tit topped by a scabbing Betty Boop tattoo.

—Yeah, like you said you wouldn't cum in my mouth either.

He shakes his head.

—That was like I told you, like an accident, like I lost focus for a second at the point of impact and next thing I knew, BANG.

She narrows her eyes.

—Yeah, bang, my ass.

Phil puts a leer on.

—Hey, if that's what you're into.

She makes a fist and starts down the hall.

—Don't even, you dick. Cumming in my mouth is one thing, but that shit you gave me was almost all baby laxative.

Phil backs into his door.

—Hey, no way.

—Bullshit. I've had the runs all morning.

—Look, this is the big city, you got to expect shit to be cut a little.

The girl's door opens and a guy with too many gym muscles sticks his head out.

—What the fuck, that the guy ripped you off?

Phil raises a righteous finger.

—*Ripped off?* I. Man, I never in my life. This shit is like a calling for me. I. Out of the kindness of my, I, I, like I barely have any shit for myself and I cut a deal with this girl, throw her a little help when she's in need and now. I.

He folds his arms.

—I'm fucking insulted.

Too Many Muscles comes fully out of the room, bare-assed, showing the rest of his muscles.

—Fucking rip-off artist.

Phil opens his mouth and I dig a thumb under his arm and turn him to his own door.

—Open it.

He looks at me.

—Sure, sure, just no one likes being called a rip-off artist.

—Open it.

He opens the door.

Too Many Muscles is trying to catch my eye so he can flex and make it clear that I shouldn't fuck with him. The girl is shaking her fist in Phil's face, her voice rising, telling him she better get some good X off him if he expects another blow job. The corridor is filled with smells of shit and smoke and sweat and fungus and incense and fast food and spilled cheap wine and puke and the residue of the last corpse that rotted unnoticed in its room for a week before it was found.

It's distracting.

So distracting I don't register for a beat that Phil never put his key in the knob I locked before we went to the bathroom to clean his nose. So distracting I don't hear what I should hear, don't smell what I should smell. So distracting that after I shove Phil into the room I stand frozen for a moment when the side of beef disguised as an arm comes out of the dark room and fists a gloved collection of bratwurst into the collar of my jacket.

And then I am pulled inside by a force not unlike being roped to the back of an MTA bus as it pulls from Penn Station, and the door is slammed shut behind me on the suddenly retreating couple in the hall.

— He's still giving me that look, tell him again it wasn't me.

—I know it might be a little hard to believe, the situation being what it is, but he's actually telling the truth, Joe.

—See, it wasn't me, man. I mean, just basic logic at work, man, I mean, do the math. Like, two and two does not make five, and for it to have been me, well, you'd like have to go back and make that apple not hit Galileo's head and make two plus two equal like eleven. If you get me.

—Newton.

—No thanks. I'm not hungry. Like, the way he's looking at me, I'm never likely to eat again the way it makes my stomach jump.

Terry shakes his head.

—No, the name you were, you know, searching for, it's Newton.

Phil scratches his head, careful not to disrupt his pompadour.

—Name? What name? I don't know any names, man, I don't

know a thing. I'm like barely involved in this shit. Innocent by-stander.

Terry taps my razor against my brass knuckles.

—The man who got hit in the head with the apple, who invented, although *discovered* is a more accurate word, gravity, his name was Newton. Sir Isaac Newton.

Phil holds up both hands in denial.

—I'm telling you, Bird, I never heard of the guy. Like with Joe here, he just showed up. I'd known he was coming I woulda called you. I was gonna call you.

He looks at me.

—No offense, Joe, and not like there's anything in it for me, but if I want to stick around these parts I got to do what's smart.

He raises a finger.

—But I did not, in fact, make that call. Cuz why would I? For what? And when?

He shows the raised finger to Terry.

—And this Newton character? Never heard of him. He's around, I'd never know it.

Terry looks at the mass of shadow behind Phil. It comes away from the wall and taps him on the chest and Phil goes down hard into the corner of the room.

The mass looms over him.

—Siddown an' shutit, Philip.

Phil cowers.

—Yeah, sure thing, Hurley. It's shut.

He covers his mouth with his hands.

Hurley turns to Terry, rolls his neck.

—Dat good enow, Terry?

Terry sets my weapons on Phil's narrow dresser.

—Yeah, that's fine, that's fine. Just we all need to relax a little. Get a little less chatter in here, clear the air of static and confusion.

He adjusts the set of his Lennon glasses on the bridge of his nose.

—Like, for instance, Joe, while yeah, Phil is a nasty cockroach of a Renfield and would sell his, I don't know, his soul, mother, anything like that, for a few bucks or a handful of black beauties, he didn't have anything to do with this.

He combs his soul patch with the nail of his index finger.

—Truth is, you weren't the victim of any kind of, I don't know, betrayal or setup, you were really, when you get into it, the victim of your own nature.

He places a hand on the inner thigh of his often-mended hemp jeans.

—What I'm getting at here is that you, over the many years of our association and, if I'm opening up, which I am, over the many years of our *friendship,* you were given a lot of slack. Yards and yards. Part of that was in tribute to the bond between us.

He points at the window where the gap of daylight has grown brighter.

—You know they closed it? CBGB, they closed it. Outbreak of sudden hostilities between the guy who owned the place and his landlords. A homeless charity, of all things. Couldn't be negotiated. They, there's some some irony in this, the homeless charity people, they gave him the boot.

He looks lost for a moment.

—The Bowery without CBGB. What's that? Like, and it's not an overstatement at all, you know, like the end of an era.

He looks at me.

—Big landmark in our relationship, yeah? The Ramones. That gig. Man that was a great gig. One of their best. I was having an amazing night. Right till I went in the can and found you all opened up and bleeding on the floor. Tell you, till very recently, I don't know, I always hoped I'd find the guy who did that and, don't get me wrong, but thank him.

He spreads the fingers of both hands across his chest and bows his head.

—I know how that sounds. Believe me.

He raises his head.

—But the point isn't to thank the guy for causing you pain, for infecting you, for sending you into this life and all the, you know, complications that come with it.

He lowers his hands from the front of his East Village Organic Foods Co-op shirt.

—The point would have been to thank him for dropping you in my way. For facilitating whatever, I don't know, whatever energy it was that knew I needed someone like you at that time. I mean, man, over the years, we got some things done. Not always seamless, I'll be first to cop to that, but we got some things done. So.

He points at the window again.

—For a long time I always had this vague kind of feeling that guy deserved some thanks from me.

He touches that spot on his thigh again.

—You know, until you got Hurley there shot to pieces and did your best to kill me.

I light the smoke I've been paying attention to while he's been talking.

—Terry, let's face it, when all that went down, I wasn't at my best.

I wave my hand, leaving a rising trail of smoke.

—I'd been at my best, you'd be dead right now.

A sharp light comes to the corner of his eye.

—Well, that's a point that could be debated. Isn't it?

I nod.

—Sure. Feel like you maybe want to have Hurley step into the hall and we can debate it now?

He runs a hand over his head and down the length of his ponytail.

—No, Joe, that's not going to be the way this happens.

He comes and sits next to me on Phil's sagging bed.

—What I was getting at before, about how, I don't know, Phil there didn't have anything to do with us being here, about how that was your own fault, that wasn't a minor point. See, the fact that you were, for all intents and purposes, sitting on death row when you made your break, that's not exactly an extenuating circumstance. More like that's further grounds speaking against you.

I find a blue and white cardboard coffee cup on the floor and knock some ash into it. Not that I'm too worried about making a mess, just that I'd like to avoid burning the place down. Till I'm certain that's my best option, anyway.

—Yeah, I follow, Terry. Thing is, you were planning to put me in the sun. So I'm hard-pressed to see what you can do at this point that's any worse.

He takes his glasses off.

—Worse, yeah, worse. Well, that's part of the whole picture thing here. Like how the reason we know you're here, that's *because* you're here. Which, I know sounds deliberately circular, but it's really not.

He taps my knee with one of the arms of his glasses.

—The way you left us, that big bang you went out with, that required a great deal of effort on my part to, well, not so much to *cover up,* but to keep in perspective. That story had circulated too widely, it would have destabilized things. Not a situation we can afford in already unstable times. Yeah. So. When we took it to the street, the picture that was painted was very much of our making. But based on your own work.

He folds and unfolds the arms of the glasses.

—So, your failed attempt to infect your girlfriend, that was retouched a bit. That became a, I don't know, a situation where you fed on her to save your own skin. The thing is.

He puts the glasses on.

—You have down here, or, you know, *had,* kind of a folk status. You may have been the security arm of the Society, but people felt like they could depend on you for a fair shake. Plus everyone likes a badass. Everyone likes telling stories about a badass. And everyone likes the idea that their badass is badder than everyone else's badass. And people, turns out, had this idea that you were their local badass.

He shrugs.

—We needed to change that, *whatever,* that perception.

He scratches his shoulder.

—So we let it be known you'd iced and drank up your own girl. That we'd put you in custody. And that before your trial, you backstabbed a couple partisans and slipped out on your belly like a snake and ran north to the Coalition.

He shakes his head.

—Turns out, people hate nothing like they hate a fallen folk hero. So when someone caught sight of you down here on the Bowery, they didn't think twice before making the call. And granted.

He holds a hand flat, wiggles it side to side.

—That's a chancy call to receive. People are so, I don't know, eager to lay you to rest, they see a big guy with dark hair and a leather car coat and they're placing the call. We've followed up on more than our share of bad numbers.

He steadies the hand.

—But someone seeing a guy fitting your description coming here, to Philip Sax's flophouse? That needed immediate executive attention.

He gestures at the window.

—As it was, we just made it over before things got dicey with the dawn.

He sits, looking at the garbage between his feet, lips pursed.

I flick some more ash, look down myself. I can't see the half of the room on my left. The other half of the room is pretty much filled with Hurley, leaving a scrap of space on the floor for Phil to occupy. Hurley'd barely need to move to grab me if I started something. Grab me and hoist me up so my head either flattens against the ceiling or pokes through it into the room above. Or he could just pull one of the two .45s he's always got on him and blow a few chunks out of my brain. My other option, jumping out the window, seems similarly unwise.

The whole *burn the place to the ground with everyone in it* idea is picking up serious traction. I scan the floor for any tinder that looks especially flammable.

Terry unpurses his lips and looks up from the garbage.

—Anyway, the tone of things being what they are, your unpopularity with the masses being what it is, this isn't so much a matter of trying to find the most miserable way to send you to your death. I wanted to do that I could just call a general assembly of the Society and toss you in the middle of the room and watch the madness of crowds take over. No, Joe.

He stands.

—This is simply a case of expediency.

I watch as he moves to the farthest corner possible in the tiny room.

—Phil, you may want to cover your eyes.

Phil covers up.

Terry looks at me.

—He can be smart when he needs to be.

He gives a slight, sad wave.

—Hurley.

Hurley grunts.

Terry nods.

—Kill Joe.

The bratwurst hands come out of the gunny-sack pockets of

Hurley's overcoat and go around my throat. I am levitated from the floor, trying not to thrash, knowing the torque might snap my neck.

I wheeze through the pinhole Hurley's grasp has reduced my larynx to.

—Huuuneee.

Terry squints at me.

Phil peeks from between his fingers.

—Jeez, oh jeez, oh shit.

He covers his eyes back up.

I force the last bit of air in my lungs up past the crushing fingers.

—Uuhhhnneee.

Phil peeks again.

—Man, that's so fucked up. Is he calling you honey? Is that normal for this kind of shit?

Terry raises a finger.

Hurley relaxes his thumbs just enough to let some more air slip down and out of my throat.

—Muhhnneey. Muhhney, Thhheery. Muhhneee.

Terry nods, Hurley squeezes, Phil re-covers his eyes.

My legs thrash, I can't stop them, my body twists, I have my hands on Hurley's fingers, trying to pry them loose, but I may as well be trying to bend the barrel of one of his guns. I try aiming a kick at him, and graze his thigh and he holds me at arm's length, putting me out of range.

Terry watches me dying, tucks his toe under a mashed pizza box, flips it, watches roaches scurry for cover.

He looks up.

—Take Phil out, will you, Hurley. You can let him go.

Hurley's hands open and I drop.

—Sure ting, Terry, whativer ya say.

He collars Phil and hauls him up.

—C'mon, ya wretched piece oh shite, it's some fresh air yer wantin'.

Phil writhes.

—Aw, man, it's my fucking room, man. How come I'm the one that's gotta take a stroll? I mean, so OK, obviously you guys can't take a walk right now, but how come I gotta? Not like I'm any friend of the daytime either.

Hurley shakes him once.

—Yer takin' a walk cuz the alternative is ya take a dive offa da roof.

Phil pumps his legs.

—Hey, a nice refreshing stroll, a perambulation, yeah? Sounds good. Do me good.

They go out.

Terry comes and stands over me.

—Tell me exactly why I should care about the money you mentioned.

I inhale, smoke rasping over the raw inside of my throat and down into my still-parched lungs. I exhale, cough long and hard, and draw a trembling one and a two in the air with my cigarette.

—Twelve pints.

I look at Terry.

Terry watches the numbers drift.

—Yes?

I exhale again, blowing the numbers to scraps.

—Twelve pints. Contents of a human body. As close to exact as possible. What you were offering for my head.

I rub the bright red finger marks on my neck.

—Out of character for you, Terry, offering a blood reward. Out of character for the Society. Especially a number like that. Suggests someone's gonna die for you to pay off on that bounty. Kind of contrary to your whole thing about coexisting with the uninfected community. Places a certain kind of value on me. Also sends a different kind of message to the troops than you like to. Me.

I put a finger in my own chest.

—I figured you'd offer money. Don't want the members thinking about blood as a commodity, after all. Then I remembered.

I snap my fingers.

—Money's a little tight for you these days, isn't it?

Terry nods, combs his soul patch again.

—Yes, losing the Count's income has been a blow to our liquidity.

I turn my head side to side, listen to hear if anything grinds that shouldn't.

—Sure, hard to keep fighting the good fight without some greenbacks in your pocket.

He stuffs his hands in his pockets, shrugs.

—So, OK, Joe, you have my attention. Hurley is at bay for the moment. Here's your big reprieve. Yes, we, sad as it is to say, we in the Society need money as much as anyone else. Would it was not so. Yes, the resources we had on hand before we lost the Count had allowed us to expand the kind of support we offer to our members, better housing, improved medical care. We were, if you can believe it, we were able to put one of our members who had been a grief counselor before she was infected, we were able to pay her a salary, keep her from having to take a night job, make her available full-time to counsel the newly infected and help them to make the adjustment. It was a real boon, putting the Count's family's petrodollars to good, healing work. So, OK, so we've gotten by on far less than we have now, but it's a hard time to be cash strapped. So, yes, there's something to talk about here, but it's going to be a very brief dialogue if you don't have something substantial to offer in the next, I don't know, the next half a minute. And I'm sorry if that sounds unreasonable.

I nod, use some of my thirty seconds taking a drag, use a few more blowing out the smoke, and offer something substantial.

—The Horde girl.

Terry takes his hands from his pockets, looks at them.

—Yes, that's substantial.

—It's not so much that I don't trust you, it's more that I'm not sure that money, even a great deal of it, will be of more value to the Society in the long run than your death.

I shift on Phil's mattress, moving myself from one collection of broken springs poking me in the ass to a different collection of broken springs poking me in the ass.

—No argument out of me, Terry, it's a conundrum.

Terry, on the floor, his back against the dresser, shifts his legs away from the line of daylight that continues to track across the room.

—Yeah, that's it, Joe, a conundrum. Well put. Certainly, I don't doubt Miss Horde's affection for you. I think the chance she took abetting your escape last year speaks volumes about her, I don't know, feelings. And her resources are well known. I am as certain as a person has a right to be certain of anything in this life that I could send her word that you're in our custody again, and that she'd be more than happy to open several large offshore accounts accessible by the Society's not-for-profit corporation.

—But then you can't kill me.

He juggles his hands.

—Well, yeah, sure we could still kill you. It might cause some problems, but let's not split hairs. Let's just say it's the, forgive me this, it's the money or your life.

I grimace.

—Jesus, Terry.

He holds up a hand.

—Pun unintended. I swear. Cheap humor when talking about a person's life has never been my style. You know that.

I look at the collection of water stains on the ceiling. No, joking about killing has never been Terry's style. His style has always been more about making declarations regarding the greater good, and then telling me who needed to die for it this time.

Interesting, the shoe being on the other foot, my death being the one supposed to promote the greater good. Who knew I had it in me?

I open my flip-top and look at the butt ends of my last couple smokes.

—Doesn't matter anyway, you can't make a deal with her nohow.

He raises his eyebrows.

—I can't? That's an odd point to make. Doesn't really seem to speak in your favor.

I put a smoke in my mouth, light it.

—Bargaining a ransom. Kind of a serious business proposition. So tell me.

I light up.

—You start cutting deals with Cure, how's that gonna sit with the rest of the Clans? I mean.

I pick a flake of tobacco from my tongue.

—The minute you enter into that kind of negotiation, it gives them legitimacy, yeah? Can't imagine that'd go over with anyone. Least of all the Coalition. Seems unwise. Things being as unstable as you say they are.

He smiles.

—I'm anything but close-minded, Joe. Tell me what you're suggesting.

—Let me go, I'll make the arrangements. You'll get your money.

He pushes out his lower lip.

—Like I say, I'm not what you'd call close-minded. Always looking to see the bigger picture in life, my whole forest-and-trees thing, but this is a tough one for me to wrap my head around, man. So, just for fun, because I like a good theoretical discussion, tell me how it is I can trust you in this scenario you're spinning.

I grin.

—Fuck, Terry, who said shit about trust?

He extends an index finger like a saber.

—Touché.

I drop my grin.

—But you're missing a big piece of things, man. For a guy who likes the big picture, you're missing a big fucking piece of things.

—Please, I love nothing more than to be educated.

I point at the door.

—Terry, what the fuck am I doing here?

He cocks his head.

I point at him.

—Strange, yeah? Why, of all places, come down here? Am I that stupid? I want to die that bad?

He temples his fingers, put the tips at his lips.

—OK, yeah, I follow. Go on.

—Terry, there is one reason, and one reason only for me to be here.

I point north.

—The Bronx sucks. There's no infrastructure for us. Hell, there's no structure at all. It's a bunch of free agents, with life spans preset to a couple months, running around trying to get all they can lay their hands on before they burn out. It's a place for dying fast. And so maybe I've always looked to have as much leeway as I could get away with, but turns out I maybe didn't know what that meant. Turns out maybe I didn't know just how much the Clans do to make life possible for a guy like me. Maybe I didn't know how good I had it.

I rise.

—I want back. I want back in the world. I want civilifuckingzation, man. And you want to know why I'd get the girl to shovel some serious cash your way and come back down here and be at your fucking mercy? Well that's why, man. I am tired of living with the savages. OK, so maybe it's gonna be hard to rehabilitate my reputation, but it's got to be better than what I was doing up there.

I plant myself in the middle of the room.

—I want to come home, man. I'm not saying it will be like it was, I know that can't work, but I want to be back downtown. Find me a corner, somewhere out of sight, just get me back down here, man. That's all. That's all.

I let all my air out, deflate.

—That's all. I just want to come home.

Terry considers me from the floor, touches the tip of his nose.

—Well, I won't deny it, Joe, I'm a sucker for a good redemption story.

He pulls his legs in, rises easy, stands in front of me.

—But I'm not a sucker.

I look him in the eye.

—I know that.

—Sure you do. Well. Cards, then.

He fans an imaginary poker hand.

—We need the money. Negotiating with the girl would be bad for business. You can get the money. And.

He drops the cards.

—I believe you need to be down here.

He tucks a strand of hair behind his ear.

—I don't believe your sob story about wanting to come *home,* but I do believe that you want to be down here.

He inspects my face.

—Why is that, Joe, huh? What's down here, besides familiar ground, that you have to be so close to it? You leave a score unsettled? It *that* old story?

I hold his gaze.

—Just what I told you, Ter, just that I need to get out of the jungle.

—OK, OK, that's cool. I can play it like that. Just, if it is a revenge thing, be careful about who you take a bead on. Your slack is played down here. You go up, get the money, come back, and yeah, I can figure something. We can find a corner for you. But it'll be a quiet corner, man, and you'll have to keep it that way.

—All I'm asking for is a second chance.

He gets tired all of a sudden.

—Yeah, you find one of those, you tell me how I can get one for myself.

I smile.

—Yeah. I find where they keep them second chances, I'll share them around.

I get rid of my smile.

—Speaking of second chances, or second bananas I guess, can't help but notice you're making policy decisions without Lydia around.

The tiredness that came over him a moment before stakes a claim on more of his face.

—Well, man, I'll tell you, that's true, she's not here for this. Which, if you put a little, I don't know, a little thought into it, it might become clear why that is. I put some thought into it, Joe. I'm not claiming to be cerebral by nature, instinctive moves are more my style. I like to think that energy, personal energies, are a medium I have a small talent for reading. But that's maybe not the point. The point is, once you think about it, her feelings of animosity toward you aside, you can't help but notice that when you've had your back against the wall with the Society and managed to find your way to, forgive the pun, to daylight, that Lydia always seems to be in the know in a certain kind of way that suggests, I don't know what, involvement of some kind. So maybe it's an intuitive leap on my part, or maybe it's just obvious as hell, but I thought, seeing as I was coming over here to have Hurley kill you, that it would be best to leave her out of the loop this time.

He tugs his soul patch.

—Lydia has always operated her Lesbian, Gay and Other Gendered Alliance with a fair amount of independence within the Society. Always swung that bloc of votes to wherever she felt, I don't know, justice was best served. These days, she's, and this is her right, she's started going it alone more than in the past. She's, this is, this is a real strength of hers, the narrowness of vision thing, so she's really pushing for more direct action. For the Society to move more aggressively toward making the Vyrus and the infecteds public. She's talking timetables and benchmarks and action agendas for taking the final step and putting ourselves out there and seeing if people are ready to accept us. Me, I'm still trying to keep mouths fed, trying to keep us all together and on message so we can have unity before we make that push. Needless to say, there's some distance between us right now. And I admire her moral and ethical solidity, the strength of that structure of values she's built her life on, but that woman, she can be a real pain in the ass when it's time to get our hands dirty.

—She's a ball breaker.

—Not how I would put it myself.

He blows out his cheeks.

—But I wouldn't argue too much over it.

I wave a hand.

—Yeah, Lydia, always a stickler for procedure and due course and all that crap. Woman like that, she just has a way of screwing up a good old-fashioned political assassination.

The tiredness leaves his face, replaced by something a bit sharper and less inclined to take my shit.

—True is true, Joe, and we've made a deal here and all that, but this is a bit of a sensitive subject. So you might want to put a sock in it.

—Sure, man. Just sorry to hear the two of you aren't getting along.

He touches his thigh, where I drove the nail into his flesh.

—I'm not a fool. You know that. And I know Lydia was involved. And it hurt, Joe. In more ways than one.

—I know you're not a fool, Ter. And it wasn't supposed to tickle.

He taps the edge of the left lens of his glasses.

—What happened to the eye?

I shake my head.

—Peeped one too many keyholes.

—Well, bound to happen the way you get around. Speaking of which.

He goes to the door to let Hurley back in.

—While you're working on getting some money out of the girl, you might, I don't know, take a look around her operation. I hear they're having some tough times over there. Dealing with some crisis management issues.

—Where you hear that?

He shrugs.

—Just something I hear. But I'd be curious to know how she's going about things. How she's handling keeping things, I don't know, keeping things afloat. Idealistic causes always take a hit when there's not enough loaves and fishes to go around. After all, not like I'm against what she has to say. The idea of a Clan that supports all its members equally, that's not far from our charter, I'm just concerned about her larger goals. The whole idea of a cure is outstanding in theory, but it's a real disruption. That kind of thing has to be planned, coordinated, not just dropped like a bomb. What I'd really like.

He puts his hand on the knob.

—Is for her to know she has more of a friend down here than she maybe thinks she does. Certainly, you know, more of a friend here than she has in the Coalition. That kind of thing, Joe, she should hear that.

He looks at me over the tops of his glasses.

—She should hear it from someone she trusts. Someone not in any kind of official Clan hierarchy.

I take the penultimate smoke from my pack, regretting that Terry already cut Phil loose and that I can't send him out for more.

I light up, shake out my match, nod at Terry.

—Sure, Terry, I follow. From someone she can trust.

He looks at the slash of light that's crept to the wall.

—Guess there's nothing for it but to wait.

—Guess so.

I flick the extinguished match into the piled mess on the floor.

Now all I got to do to survive the day is listen to a few more hours of Terry's bullshit. I touch my neck.

Maybe I should have let Hurley break it.

I get an escort.

—Ya ought ta do sumptin' 'bout dat eye, Joe.

—What do you recommend, Hurley, a contact lens?

I point at the smoke shop on Second and St. Mark's.

—Mind?

He looks at the scratched face of his ancient wristwatch.

—Naw, don' mind. Just ya be quick 'bout it. Terry said nae fookin' 'bout.

He waits by the door, casting his eyes about for sudden moves on my part while I buy a couple packs of Luckys. Down here in civilization, they actually have the ones without filters.

The guy slides them to me and I knock the plastic case next to the register.

—And I need a lighter.

He sticks his hand inside the case

—Want one with the titties?

His hand hovers over a Zippo with a bare-chested pinup girl enameled on the side.

—No. And I don't want one with a Jack Daniel's label either. Just give me the plain one.

He takes one of the plain ones out, sets it next to the smokes.

—Anything else?

—Flints and some fuel.

He takes a yellow plastic tab, laddered with tiny red flints, from a hanging rack of them behind the counter, reaches below the counter and sets a yellow and blue Ronsonol squirt bottle with the rest of the stuff.

I give him some cash and fill my pockets.

On the street Hurley steers us north.

—Naw, ain't contact lenses I'm talkin' 'bout, Joe.

I look up from the delicate work I'm doing in my hands, unscrewing the little shaft in the bottom of the lighter to slip in a flint.

—Huh?

He points at his own eye.

—Yer eye. It's a bit what dey call *conspicuous*. Doesn't do fer us, ta be standin' out ina crowd.

I drop the flint in the shaft and use my thumbnail to screw the cap back into place, reflecting on the idea of this semi-retarded Irish behemoth in the double-breasted overcoat and fedora lecturing me on the topic of standing out in a crowd.

I flip open the nozzle on the Ronsonol bottle and send a stream of fluid into the exposed wick folded into the body of the lighter.

—Well, I tell ya, Hurley, I had a pair of sunglasses that hid it pretty well, but they got crushed when you grabbed me and yanked me into Phil's room.

—Ach.

He shakes his head.

—I'm sorry 'bout dat, Joe, truly I am.

I close the bottle, drop it back in my coat pocket and slip the lighter into its brushed-chrome sleeve.

—Not a problem, Hurl, you've done worse by me and it's never interfered with our relationship.

He touches the brim of his hat.

—Sure an dat's true. Dat's true.

I thumb the lighter's wheel, a spark jumps and a large flame trails greasy black smoke from the new wick. I touch the flame to a cigarette and inhale the mixed flavors of smoke and burning cotton and lighter fuel. I snap the lighter shut, bounce it on my palm once, feeling the warmth of the just-extinguished flame, and drop it in my pocket to clink against my arsenal of brass and sharp steel.

He stops as we reach the south side of Fourteenth.

—Well, dis is it fer me. On yer own from here.

I linger, looking south down Second. The marquee at Twelfth Street advertises a midnight double bill of *The Killer Elite* and *Soylent Green*.

Date night at the old Jewish vaudeville theater.

Hurley taps my shoulder.

—C'mon, Joe, no time ta reminisce, yu'v got miles ta go till ya sleep 'n all dat.

—Yeah, miles to go.

I look at him.

—By the way, Hurl, you're looking a lot better than the last time I saw you.

He rubs his stomach.

—Sure, an why wouldn't I be? Tell ya, only ting hurts worse den all dem bullets goin' in is pickin' out da ones din't come out da udder side.

—Yeah, well, sorry about that.

He waves a hand, shakes his head.

—Come now, wasn't yer doin'. Ya didn't pull da trigger. An' like ya say, me an you, we always bin professional wit one 'nother.

—Yeah. Sure.

I look north.

—Know something?

—What's dat?

I look over my shoulder at him.

—People down here who thought I was the badass, they must never have met you.

He smiles, showing me horse teeth.

—Well an' its nice o' you ta say so.

—Ta, Hurl.

—Ta yerself, Joseph.

I start across the street.

—An, Joe.

I look back.

Hurley covers his left eye.

—Tink 'bout a patch. It'd suit ya, it would.

How you know if you've successfully ditched a tail by going where you were supposed to and then where you were not supposed to, is you show up someplace where you *really* don't fucking belong. If they're there, your ruse has failed. The best way to avoid having your ruse busted in this fashion is to never reappear where your tail *can* follow you.

Figure Hurley marching me right to the Coalition border at

Fourteenth, and standing there watching until I cross over, effectively blows that part of my plan.

I need a cab.

I need to get my distinctively one-eyed face into a fucking cab right away before the Coalition spotters that roost about Fourteenth make me. Naturally, my need being desperate, there's not a fucking cab in sight.

I start trotting, making for Union Square. I should be able to score a cab. Worst case, I can jump the L train to Eighth Avenue.

Border of no-man's-land.

All I need is a little shard of luck and I can cross back over the border and onto turf where no one goes, before Predo's tails pick me back up.

Unfortunately, God has no luck to spare tonight.

So when the limo pulls to the curb in the middle of the block and the back door swings open, I don't wait for anyone to point a gun at me before I climb in.

—Was I unclear about both the urgency of this assignment and the need for utter discretion? Did I in some way fail to communicate to you that your only option was to go directly to the Horde girl? Did I leave any room for confusion as to what the consequences would be if you failed to execute precisely as I told you?

—No, you were actually very fucking clear about all of that. Did I do something that suggests otherwise?

Predo makes a gesture taking in the downtown streets we're leaving behind.

—Does this detour not suggest otherwise?

I lean forward from the rear-facing seat.

—No. What it suggests to me is that I'm doing my fucking job.

And, for the record, almost getting throttled in the fucking process.

My shaking hand spills more cigarettes into my lap than even I can smoke at once.

—Fuck.

I shove them back in the pack, breaking several.

—Fuck.

Predo observes.

—Nerves, Pitt?

I get an intact cigarette in my mouth and light it.

—Nerves? Hell yes. You ever had Hurley's paws around your neck?

—I cannot say that I have.

I spew smoke.

—Well count yourself well fucking blessed.

He leans forward, touches a slightly depressed square of leather on the bar to my right, it eases open, revealing a gleaming and perfectly unblemished ashtray.

—Perhaps you should explain.

I blemish the ashtray.

—I'll explain. I'll explain that Horde is as nutty as her father. I'll explain that as nutty as she is, she knows to listen to Sela. I'll explain that only a fucking moron would see me on their doorstep and not have some questions about my loyalties.

He looks out the window, watches as we glide past snarled taxis and buses, the limo apparently obeying some other set of traffic and physical laws.

—Did you tell them about my mole?

—How do I do that? How do I walk in the door and expose a mole in the first hour? How do I know something like that unless I'm around for a while to poke? No. What I did was tell them to put me to the test.

—And?

—*And.*

I lean back.

—And Amanda Horde told me to go downtown and talk to Terry Bird.

Night outside.

His face is doubled by the dark glass.

Does he know the nervous beat of my heart is telling a story different from the one my mouth is?

—And?

I rub my forehead.

—She's looking for an alliance. She's looking for one of the Clans to acknowledge her. She's looking for legitimacy. So where's the first place she's gonna look?

It's possible that we turn a corner, but it's impossible to say for sure from within the infinite smoothness of the car.

Predo's hands are folded in his lap, he unfolds them, looks at his manicure.

—And you saw him?

—Yes.

—And he let you go?

I wave a hand at all the expensive leather and wood.

—Well here I am, right?

—Yes.

His eyes flick to my face and away.

—Here you are.

He touches the glass, leaving a fingerprint on his reflection, where a good Catholic would receive a smear of ash before Easter.

—Tell me what you told Bird.

—I told him the truth.

His mouth opens as if to laugh, and closes without making a sound.

I shrug.

—Yeah, funny. But it's what I did. I told him Horde wants a sit-down.

—What else?

—That's it.

He studies the reflected set of his own blue eyes.

—He wasn't curious as to how you effected your escape from the Bronx?

—He didn't ask. And why should he? Far as he knows, I'm with Horde now. She's got the cash to get anyone out of anywhere.

A slight nod allows this point.

—And so.

He blinks slowly.

—What is it he wants?

He looks away from his own reflection.

—Hurley had his hands on your throat.

He indicates the fading marks on my neck.

—I can see that much is true. But what was it that compelled Bird to release you? I know him well enough to know he would not seriously consider formally acknowledging the girl's *organization*. So what offer did you make to secure your freedom? Why are you not dead, Pitt? You did not, by any chance, sell me out?

He tilts his head.

—Did you?

I stub out my smoke.

—He wants money.

I light a new one.

—Your enemy is in the red, Predo.

He makes a sound, could be amusement.

—And you are to get it from Horde.

—Yeah, funny how everybody's needs always seem to dovetail.

—Funny.

He watches me smoke.

—Very well. Things shall proceed. Only.

I let him watch me smoke, not trying to hide the sweat or the slight tremble in my hand, knowing I have ample reasons to fear. Not knowing which reasons he may be able to read, but incapable of hiding any of them.

—I am curious.

He leans forward.

—What are you after, Pitt?

We both watch smoke tremble from the end of my cigarette.

He squints.

—Something. A return to the Island, certainly.

He leans back into his seat.

—But why so desperate?

Returns his gaze to the brightly lit night outside the dark glass.

—I should like to know that. But, of course.

He smiles at his face in the glass.

—Of course I will know.

He closes his eyes.

—Before this is over.

Dropped into the masses in Times Square, where my appearance is least likely to be noticed, I feel gravity's pull, again from downtown.

Turning north, I strain away from it.

Too many forces in play now. Too many tiny uncharted objects flying on random trajectories. An obscure path is best. Travel by the course others have plotted.

Look for the chance to veer back to your own.

My return is hardly unexpected.

—Back so soon?

I go to the liquor cabinet and get a glass and the bottle I'd started emptying during our last chat.

—Looks like I'm a little more persona non grata than I thought I was.

Amanda joins me at the bar.

—That come as some kind of *surprise*?

I raise my chin, display the almost faded bruises on my neck.

—Didn't expect the fatted calf to be slaughtered. But I also wasn't figuring on having to face down Hurley my first hour back on the turf.

Sela juts her jaw.

—How's he look?

I pour myself a drink.

—Hurley? You know, looks like a guy you should have shot in the head when you had the chance.

I raise my glass in her direction.

—Seeing how happy he was to see me, I'd say you're best staying off his beat.

She puts her hands on her hips.

—Hurley never scared me.

—Then, lady, you're a better man than me.

I take a drink.

Amanda scoops some ice into a glass of her own and pours vodka over it.

Sela frowns.

—You shouldn't be drinking. You're worn to the bone.

Amanda clinks her glass against mine.

—Joe's come home. I *have* to drink to that.

She drinks to that.

I drink, but not to anything at all.

She crosses to Sela and gives her hand a squeeze.

—Just chill a *little* bit, baby.

Sela keeps a grip on the girl's hand.

—I'm trying to look out for you.

Amada touches her cheek.

—And you're doing a *great* job. But right now I need a *drink*. And I need you to be my *girlfriend* for a few minutes and not my fucking *nanny*.

Sela takes a step back, removing her face from the girl's touch.

—It doesn't switch on and off. I do not work like that. I don't go from one to the other. Being your lover, that's not separate from being your bodyguard. And I can only keep you safe and healthy if you listen to me.

Amanda sighs.

—*OK*, I'm listening.

She pulls on an attentive face.

—*What* am I doing wrong now?

Sela bares her teeth, covers them.

—Aside from running your body down with stress and lack of sleep and too much booze and not enough exercise, aside from putting everything we're working for at risk, putting all these people here who believe in you at risk by not taking care of yourself, aside from all that, you are inviting a major *security* risk into your confidence.

She points at me.

—He. Cannot. Be. Trusted.

She points at Amanda.

—And that is more true now than ever.

She looks at me, shakes her head.

—He just skipped down to see Terry Bird? Just went down there, had a little run-in with Hurley, and skipped back up here? How's that compute? I'll tell you how. It does not. First he's spying for Predo. Drops that gem on us and then, *ta-ta*, and he's gone.

I raise my hand.

—I never said ta-ta.

She shakes her head.

—Uh-uh, hold that shit in, Pitt. Don't get cute with my ass. You say I should do the smart thing and kill one of our own, kill that poor, starving, desperate son of a bitch in the basement? OK. Tell you what sounds like a smart move to me.

Her long muscled arm extends and she points her fist at me.

—Killing you sounds like a smart move to me.

Amanda looks into her glass.

—Don't say that, Sela.

Sela slowly uncurls her index finger from her fist, taking a bead on my face.

—He is dangerous. I said it before, *He gets people dead.* He's working both fucking sides. We don't know what they *really* want. We don't know what he really wants. And there's no way to be sure anything he tells us is the truth.

I clear my throat and pick up the bottle.

—Predo, he *says* he wants to know what your research plan is.

I start pouring bourbon, decide I got no reason to stop, so I pour till my glass is full.

—Wants to know, are you going to go public with the Vyrus, ask for help finding a cure? Or are you going to do like you said to me, keep it in-house? Says he wants numbers of members, security, layouts. Stuff he'd need if he decides he needs to send a crew in here. That's what he *says.*

I drink.

—What he doesn't say is that all he's really interested in knowing is if you can *do it.* What he really wants to know is if you're making any progress. He wants to know if a cure is possible. He wants to know if you can actually find it in this century.

I get a smoke up and running.

—Terry Bird, he let me go, said he'd let me back on Society turf if I came up here and poked around. Said he wanted me to arrange some back-channel communications. Said he wants to start a *dialogue*. See if there's *common ground*.

I take my bottle and my glass and my cigarette and go to a chair and take a seat.

—What *he* really wants is the same damn thing that Predo wants. And he wants it for the same reason.

I point my cigarette at her.

—Because, bottom line, if there's a cure, if the Vyrus is destroyed, it all goes away. The Coalition. The Society. All the alliances and backdoor deals and spycraft and manipulations go away. All the *power,* it goes away. They don't want that. And if there's a scrap of a chance you can come up with a cure.

I drink whiskey.

—They'll both want to know the best way to kill you yesterday.

I take the picture Predo gave me from my jacket and drop it on the desk.

—Name on the back of that is the last mole Predo has in here. I don't know for sure who Bird has on the inside, but he definitely has someone reporting to him on conditions in here. I was gonna take a guess.

I point at the floor.

—I'd pick that fat comicbook geek you got living in the hall. He come over from the Society?

Sela blinks.

I nod.

—That's what I thought. He's got it written all over his lazy fucking ass. Yeah, he's your man. So.

I drink some more.

—I guess that's two more people I'm gonna get dead. What *I* want, little miss junior psycho. Is for you to tell me what you meant before when you said *business arrangement.* As in, I want to know how much of your money you're going to give me if I help you feed the starving people in this building before they realize you're more valuable to them as a meal than as a savior.

Amanda folds her arms, sets her jaw.

—*I'm Joe Pitt, and I'm here to chew bubble gum and kick ass. And I'm all out of bubble gum.*

I wait.

She unfolds her arms.

—OK, Joe, well, I'm going to give you a *whole* lot of money. Enough to make you *super* wealthy. And really, you don't *even* have to do that much for it.

She points east.

—All we need you to do is take a quick trip to Queens and find out where the Coalition gets their blood.

They have it, everyone knows they have it, she says.

I don't argue with her.

Why argue when someone's right? They do have it. And everyone knows they have it.

Biggest Clan on the Island, and then some. And the only one that has enough blood to supply all their members. Only one can keep them fed well enough that they don't have to worry about someone going berserk and hitting the street to make a spectacle like the one Amanda and Sela are trying to keep under wraps. No secret that they got it. Hell, get down to it, it's pretty much advertised.

Best advertising you could ever have to attract Vampyres is a well-known reputation for keeping your members in the red.

Why keep it a secret.

But there *is* a secret. There is a big secret. There is the biggest secret.

Where the hell does it all come from?

Enough blood to keep hundreds, maybe over a thousand, members alive and kicking.

You figure that some Vampyres are more equal than others, figure that guys like Predo are getting quite a bit more in their fridges than the average infected slob on the street, and then figure a minimum of a pint a week to keep the rank and file happy.

I didn't pass math. Shit, I didn't pass anything. But I can figure that number in my head.

Know what that number equals?

Equals: *Where the fuck do they get it all?*

A question most folks dwell on from time to time. But most definitely not a question folks like to ask out loud. Ask that kind of question out loud and someone might hear you asking it. And whether you're Coalition, Society, Hood or Rogue, you don't want to be heard asking that question.

See, figure everyone comes up short from time to time. Everyone has their off quarters when they don't make quota. Which means everyone goes to the bank for a little extra now and again. Society, the Hood, they get pinched hard, can't keep their people healthy, they might be known to make a call, cut a deal.

Only in emergencies, mind you, but shit happens.

Don't it?

So who wants to rock that boat?

Answer: *no one*.

Coalition doesn't want anyone to know where it comes from. You had the lockdown on what everyone wanted, what everyone needed, would you want to share where it came from?

Don't lie. You're not that altruistic. No one is.

Society and Hood need a little help now and again, they can't afford to look nosy. Can't afford to have their people look nosy.

And Rogues? They can't afford to do anything makes anyone notice their unallied asses are hanging out in the wind waiting for someone to take a shot at them just because it will take one more mouth off the market.

It's there. We all know it's there. It's the thing that just about the whole fucking Clan structure spins around.

And we all pretend it doesn't exist.

Shhh.

Only someone crazy would poke into this shit. Lucky me, I know someone really fucking crazy.

I sit there.

I sit there some more.

I look at Sela.

—Shouldn't part of keeping her safe involve telling her when she's talking about doing something that will kill everyone?

I hold up my hand.

—No, never mind, I totally fucking forgot that your whole fucked-up *Clan* is based on trying to do something that's going to get everyone killed.

—They *have* it, Joe.

I look at Amanda.

—You already said that.

She turns in place, holding her drink over her head, rattling the ice cubes.

—OK, OK, I know it's this *total* secret hush-hush thing. I know we're not supposed to talk about the hundred-pound pink *poodle* in the room.

She stops turning and spreads her arms.

—But the whole point is that we're *seriously* trying to change things.

She takes a sip.

—And you don't change things by doing what everyone has always done before.

She comes over and perches on the edge of her desk.

—So here's the *deal:* We need more blood. Plain and simple. I can get a lot through the lab, from medical supply houses, but not as much as you'd *think*. They mostly deal in *plasma* and other *blood components*. And the Vyrus only feeds on *whole blood*. Did you *know* that? *Tried* it. Tried using plasma. Tried using platelet serum. Not what it wants. So we need more blood.

She blows out her cheeks.

—But the Coalition won't *deal* with us. We could pay like *way* over market price, but they won't even open a fucking *dialogue*. Which is *super* funny considering how they kissed my parents' and my asses for so many years before I started Cure.

She empties her glass.

—So the thing is, we have to do something.

Sela steps forward.

—If you tell anyone about any of this, Pitt.

I look at her.

—Sela, if I decide to commit suicide, I'll do it with a gun like normal people. I won't do it by telling people about little chats I'm having to plot a raid on the Coalition's fucking reservoir.

Amanda shakes her head.

—It's *not* a raid. We're not even *talking* about that kind of thing. I'm talking about just some *surveillance*. *Intelligence*. That's *all*.

She taps her own forehead.

—I mean, *think* about it. They have to get it from *somewhere*. They can't just *make* it. They have to have a supplier. Maybe they have a *bunch* of them. I know that's, like, the most *reasonable* possibility. They've been around forever. So they've, like, built up these weird relationships. Totally *backdoor* stuff that no one can get in on at this point. They must get it from *dozens* of places. Hospitals. EMT workers. Blood banks. They bring it into a central warehouse or *something*. All we know is that when it comes in, it comes in from *Queens*.

She leans.

—What we need to know is, who some of those suppliers *are.* If we know, like, who to talk to, we can *totally* outbid the Coalition. Or we can *force* a deal. Tell the Coalition that they can either sell to us or they can face some competition in the market. See what they do when I throw some *real* cash into the supply and demand equation and their suppliers start driving their trucks to *our* door. That's all.

That's all.

Just go to Queens. Just leave the Island right after I got back. Just go poke around the Coalition's biggest secret. *The* biggest secret.

Just leave again.

Just leave.

Gravity pulls. Pulls at the center of me. Pulls at a part that I didn't know was there till I took it off the Island.

If I pull too hard in the opposite direction, will it snap?

Jesus. Who am I?

I move the girl's hand from my knee, I look at her.

—It's going to cost.

She does the eyeroll, letting me know again that I shouldn't bother talking about things that she doesn't give a shit about.

I nod, stand up.

—OK. Maybe we should start by asking some people some questions.

I look at Sela.

—And then making them dead.

Amanda slips off the edge of the desk.

—See, baby, I told you he was the man for the job.

Sela turns away.

When the math is done, it's not two people I get dead, it's three people I get dead. Amanda suggesting, not unreasonably, that maybe I could deal with the slob in the basement who caused all the problems for them the other night.

One more. Sure. Why not? Who's counting at this point?

Terry's mole, he cops to it. I don't have to touch him or even threaten to tear up his back issues of *Amazing Spider-Man* to get him to cop to it. I just let him watch while I deal with the others. Then I tell him I'll do him different, more easy, if he tells me if he's the one been making calls to Terry.

He says he is.

Could he be lying?

Sure. Why not? I watched someone do what I do to Predo's mole, and *I* got given a chance to say something might let me avoid the same discomfort, I might lie myself.

But I don't think he was lying.

And if he was?

If he was, then I guess it makes what I did to him that much worse. And if there's someone watching the things I do, watching and judging, that's one that will go against me. Assuming there's any more room in the AGAINST column.

Doesn't matter, I couldn't let him live no matter what. Not after he watched. Not after he heard the questions I asked Predo's pawn.

Far as that guy goes, mostly it's too bad he didn't know anything. Makes life that much harder for me. Certainly made death that much harder for him.

But I'm not worried about it. Because no one is watching me. No one is judging me. No one is weighing my actions and making book on where my soul is gonna finish when the race is over.

I'm the only one watching these things I do. I'm the only one counting. I know the number.

And I've known for a long time what I've got coming someday.

I'm not trying to get out of anything.

I kill the guys. And I don't make it easy for them on the way out. Because I got no doubts they deserve it.

Only maybe not as much as I do.

Tough luck how that works out sometimes.

—Hey.

—Who?

—It's Joe Pitt.

I hear salsa music doppler in and out of the background.

—What?

—Joe Pitt.

—Yeah?

—Yeah.

—And?

I clear my throat.

—Remember how you said you'd rather I owe you one for when you need someone to have your back?

—Yeah.

—How'd you like to make it two?

I hear catcalls in Puerto Rican–accented Spanish, and her own retort: something about someone's dick and a knife and their throat. But my Spanish isn't good enough to get the subtler nuances.

The catcalls fall silent.

—You still there?

I nod, even though she can't see it.

—I'm here.

The phone carries the sound of a train crashing and screeching on overhead tracks.

—You ask a lot, Pitt.

—Yeah.

—I got ex-boyfriends, kind of guys never have a fucking job, you know?

—Sure.

—Kind of guys, they let a girl pick up every check, pay for their new Nikes, give them walking-around cash they're gonna use to take their shorty out later. Know what I mean?

—Sure.

—But you. You I never even broke off a piece, and you got them all beat.

I shift the phone to my other hand so I can get at my smokes easier.

—Yeah, I like to go that extra mile.

—Yes, you do.

—Yeah. So, not to waste anyone's time, I don't have anything to add to the pot. You want to help out or not?

Esperanza grunts.

—Girl likes maybe just a little sweet talk sometimes.

—How 'bout that.

—Yeah. OK. What is it?

I get a cigarette in my mouth.

—What it is, is it's funny you brought up ex-boyfriends.

—How's that funny?

—Funny like maybe I'd want to meet one of them.

Silence. I look at the screen of the phone Amanda gave me to make my call, making sure the connection hasn't been broken. It hasn't.

I put it back to my ear.

—Hear me?

—I heard you, Pitt. I'm just trying to figure out how to say *ha-ha* without it sounding too sarcastic.

Getting me out is also on the tricky side.

Seeing as the Cure house is smack in the middle of Coalition turf, getting anyone out is a trick.

Figure that under normal circumstances the Coalition would

weed out anyone tried to put roots in their turf. But there's noth-ing normal about Amanda Horde. Nothing normal about her or her big brain or her money or the Horde family name. She was right about the way Predo used to kiss her and her parents' asses.

Before he plotted to have them all assassinated.

Plot didn't work out.

Someone got in the way.

Chalk that up as yet another reason on the long list that Predo has for looking forward to the day he gets to watch me boil in the sun.

But back before that little misunderstanding took place, the Coalition was neck-deep in dealings with the Horde family. And Horde Bio Tech, Inc. Far as I know, they still have holdings in the company. But the little girl holds all the important strings.

Still, it's too late in the day for them to make a sudden move on her. She's too well connected for something like that. Too bright a star on the map of the sky. Not the Page Six fixture her mom was, but definitely someone the Manhattan gossip mill has an ear and an eye for.

Poor little orphaned rich girls who run their family's biotech-nology holdings and are always accompanied by their sexy but suspiciously muscular black female bodyguards tend to be a hot item from time to time.

Figure the Coalition couldn't do much when she decided to open housekeeping on their doorstep. But figure they keep as many eyes on that house as they possibly can.

Predo knew when I went in the first time.

And he found out that I left.

So I have to use an alternate route this time.

—Don't be particular, Pitt.

—I don't think I'm being particular. I think I'm being perfectly fucking reasonable.

—There's no time for this shit. Just bag it and get in.

—Oh, that's funny.

—I wasn't trying to be funny. Shut up and climb in.

—Fuck.

But I shut up and climb in.

Because Sela was right when she spelled out how it'd work. This is the best bet on short notice. But knowing something is the best bet, that's doesn't make it a sure thing.

I lie down on the greasy, shit-stained, olive-drab sleeping bag on the floor. Sela kneels at the foot and pulls the zipper up.

—Bunch up a little, Pitt.

—Fuck.

I pull my knees up, hunch my shoulder and duck my head.

Amanda steps closer.

—Hang on.

Sela stops with the zipper at my chin.

Amanda puts a hand on Sela's shoulder and bends to look down at me.

—Hurry back, Joe. We need you.

I wriggle deeper into the sleeping bag.

—Yeah, and it's so nice to be needed like this.

Sela yanks the zipper, catches some of my hair, and gives it another yank, tearing the hair out and sealing me inside the reeking mummy bag.

Then she grabs the top of the bag and drags me down the steps behind the building and out to the alley.

—Hey. Hey, you could carry me, couldn't you?

Her heel clips the back of my neck.

—Shut up.

I hear a gate squeal open, sounds of the street, an idling diesel.

Then she hoists me high, and shoves, and I feel air beneath me, for a second, then a bunch of hard stuff.

The tone of the diesel changes, gears grind, there's a jerk and the load in the back of the truck shifts and some more hard stuff tumbles on top of me.

And we roll, the driver of the Waste Management truck hauling the construction Dumpster that had been parked in front of the Cure house, doing his best to hit every fucking pothole and divot from the Upper East Side, across the Queensboro, and down along Dutch Kill and Review Avenue to Maspeth.

By which time I have found the zipper tabs are stuck on the outside and cut my way out with my straight razor, so I'm ready to vault out when we wrap around the back side of New Calvary Cemetery.

Twenty-four hours?

Not even that. Not one full day on the Island. And somehow, somehow I find myself someplace worse than the Bronx.

You don't have to work hard to land in this kind of shit. You just have to let go of whatever you're hanging on to. The shit is right down there under our feet, waiting for anyone who can't keep their grip.

The next bit, the next bit is the tricky part.

Keeping your mouth closed when you go under.

Maspeth.

One of those names comes from an Indian word that got all fucked up. Someone told me once it means something like *At the bottom of the bad water place*.

Swamp.

Swamp and landfill.

And the choicest landfill groomed, sodded, planted with nice trees, and filled with dead people.

I lived in Maspeth, I'd look at those massive cemeteries lining the L.I.E., Calvary, New Calvary, Mount Zion, Mount Olivet where they buried the unclaimed dead from the Triangle Shirtwaist Fire, I'd look at them, and I'd look at the dust and the muck where the row houses and the tenements took root, and I'd start digging up dead people and dropping them in Newtown Creek.

But I don't live in Maspeth.

Finally, something going right.

Standing at Fifty-fifth Ave. and Fiftieth, where my meet is supposed to take place, I get to celebrate that little fact for about a second before a dozen gibbering cannibal warriors with filed teeth and machetes come boiling over the fence from the truck-filled lot behind one of the warehouses that choke the dry land on either side of the Creek.

Know what's funny?

Nothing.

No. Really what's funny is what I forgot.

See, what with all the hubbub and urgency, all the need for me to speed on my way because shit is coming unhinged at the Cure house and this needs to be done last fucking year, what with all that, I forget to ask for a gun.

How funny is that?

Not funny at all.

Not if you're the clown who just took a job to cross the water again. Not if you're that sad fucker who just made a call to make a date with some savages.

Still, I almost laugh when I remember I forgot.

Almost.

Instead of laughing, I run. I make it across the street before the bare slapping feet catch me, and fingers capped with chrome claws drag me down.

. . .

—She's a special lady.

—I'm not arguing.

—That's wise.

I don't tell him that wisdom isn't a virtue I've often been credited with.

As for him, he keeps his own counsel, clinking the honed tips of the claws on his right index finger and thumb against one another, in time to a drum no one else hears.

—If I were a better man. If I had been a better man, she might be here.

I let my eye take in the stifling abandoned shipping container we're all crowded inside of. Only Menace has a chair. The rest stand or sit on the piles of old books and newspapers that fill the whole container.

—Think what she's missing.

His claws stop clinking.

—I do not care for sarcasm.

I think for a moment, come up with nothing better, shrug.

—I could try not talking at all.

—That sounded like more sarcasm.

I scratch my head.

—Like I said, I could try not talking at all.

He holds his hand high over his head, light from the candles illuminating the container reflected in points on the bias-cut sections of sharpened silver pipe fitted at the end of each of his fingers.

—I could flay you and wear your skin as a cloak, and caper in the streets in the moonlight.

He lowers his hand.

—But some might consider that crass treatment of a guest.

I nod.

—Well, some people got no sense of humor, do they?

He brings his hand to his chest, dimples the tight, brown skin over his sternum with the point of a claw.

—I am one of those people.

I take a good long look at Skag Baron Menace. The claws, the filed teeth, the bare feet with soles calloused to leather, the bracelets of finger bones, the broad blade of the machete leaned against the leg of the camp stool he's sitting on.

I get a cigarette from my pocket.

—Kid.

I light up.

—Why would I think you have a sense of humor?

He nods.

—Yes.

He looks at his crew, all kitted out pretty much like himself.

—Yes.

He looks at me.

—I see your point.

He rises, picks up his machete.

—We'll take a walk.

He gestures and the candles are snuffed, dropping us into a black pit. Only light coming from the tip of my smoke.

Breathing. Shuffle of bare feet. Claw scratching steel. Steel grating on steel as the lock-bar is unlatched and the door swung open by the sentry outside.

In the starlight that filters in, Menace sweeps his machete in an arc, waving me ahead of him.

I get off the floor and walk toward the door, waiting for the bite of the machete blade in my back, the rake of claws on my neck.

But they don't come.

Yet.

Put your money on something happening down by the water.

That's where I'd do it. So much easier to get rid of a body when there's some water at hand.

Wedged into an angle created by the Kosciuszko Bridge, Fifty-sixth Road, and the Newtown and Maspeth Creeks is a fish-shaped bit of land. The tail occupied by yet another warehouse. The body of the fish an open plain of concrete and asphalt, broken by empty foundations, corpses of abandoned refrigerators with the doors still on, swamp grasses pushing through the pavement, and a glittering sheen of broken glass that seems to pebble the whole surface in nearly even perfection.

Menace walks on the glass, leading us toward the water.

—I cannot say for certain, but I think this was once the home of Cord Meyer's Animal Carbon Plant.

I kick at some of the glass, rearranging the huge, senseless mosaic.

—What the hell was that?

He shakes his head.

—I am not certain. But I believe this is where it was. Whatever it was. I simply like the name. It sounds ominous. Like much of the industry that found a home here after the American Revolution.

He points with his machete at a truck yard over Fifty-sixth.

—Cating Rope Works.

Indicates a warehouse up the water.

—Fisk Metal Casket Company.

Another industrial mass.

—Alden Sampson Oil Factory.

Another.

—And Peter Cooper's Glue Factory.

He lowers the machete.

—No need to wonder where the sinister quality in that name comes from.

A damp, stinking breeze blows off the water.

—Yeah, sure. Boiling horses. Dreadful.

He stands at least a head shorter than me, looks up, shakes his free hand, rattling bones.

—Esperanza said you had trouble with Lament.

—I did.

—She said you cut a deal with him to get away.

—I cut a deal.

The machete flickers through the air, cutting the tops from a thick tuft of grass shoved up through a crack in the concrete.

—Not something to recommend a person, having cut a deal with Lament.

I look at the distant lights of Manhattan, wonder if Maspeth is where I'll finally die.

—Yeah, he seems to have a great fondness for you too.

He balances the machete.

—He mentioned me?

—Yeah. Seemed a favorite topic. I was to judge, I'd say he goes to bed mumbling your name, and then dreams about nailing your head above his door.

He smiles, moves the tip of his tongue from pointed tooth to pointed tooth, realizes what he's doing and closes his mouth.

—Yes. I am certain he does.

He looks north toward the Bronx.

—And considering the roll he played in educating me, I do not imagine it is any coincidence that I have similar visions regarding his own head.

I spit in the oily water we walk along.

—He has one of those heads people think about cutting off.

—Yes. He does.

He rests the flat of the machete blade on his shoulder.

—When he took me off the street, I thought it was the greatest piece of luck. I was finally going to be part of a crew. Make some money. Other kids, they would join crews. Soon after they would be showing up at school in fresh K-Swiss, And1. Hilfiger jeans. Burberry caps. Soon, the ones who lasted would have cars. Leased Escalades and Mercedes. Tricked-out Nissans.

He frowns.

—I wanted to be in a crew. Everyone I knew wanted to be in a crew. That was how you got things. Kicks. Clothes. Wheels. Respect.

His frown deepens.

—All the things a boy desires. That is a skill of Lament's.

He catches his lower lip between the points of two teeth.

—To know what young people desire.

His teeth draw a bead of blood from his own flesh.

—After I was infected by one of the older boys, I felt less as if I had been lied to, and more as if I were being invited deeper inside something special. Of course.

He wipes the drop of blood away with the back of his wrist.

—By then Lament had taken my name, christened me Menace. A process of physical starvation had begun, soon followed by a more intense deprivation when he withheld blood. And physical abuse. And emotional abuse. The easiest thing, the thing most of us did, was to surrender. After all.

He drops the blade of the machete from his shoulder and angles it to catch a bit of the sliver-moon.

—Once you have been told that you are worthless, and treated as if you are worthless, put in a place where you are all set against one another in a contest for one person's approval, approval that is never consistent in how it is rewarded, it is the easiest thing in the world to succumb to that conditioning and believe yourself to *be* worthless.

He brings the blade up, touches it to his own forehead, like a warrior knighting himself.

—But I am not worthless.

He lowers the blade.

—He had me cleaning. Digging out the piles of papers and magazines he had accumulated.

He shakes his head.

—I have no idea why the word caught my eye. I do not believe in destiny. For whatever reason, I saw it, and I needed to read about it. And so I did. I do not even remember the magazine. *National Geographic*? *Time*? It does not matter.

He inhales, exhales a word.

—Mungiki.

He nods.

—Kikuyu farmers. They banded together in defense squads against Nairobi government forces during a land dispute. The government was dominated by the Kalenjin tribe. Enemies of the Kikuyu. The Mungiki prevailed. And thrived. They moved into the cities, the slums. Provided protection, brought down crime rates. They did this through violence.

He nods again.

—Beheadings. Amputations. Vicious beatings. Torture. And they became a source of terror. Blood drinkers. Madmen. Savages so brutal, neither the police nor the military would go into their slums.

I look at the long flat span of empty cement around us, the other Mungiki scattered about. I look at the water. Water's the way out. Whether I have to jump in it, or that's where they dump my body, it looks like that's where I'm going.

He stops nodding.

—They inspired me.

He shakes his head.

—Not that I knew anything about the Kikuyu. Not that I did, or do, have any care about the Kalenjin. I was simply inspired that these put-upon people, outnumbered, the lowest, rose. Made of themselves something to be reckoned with. Regardless of their methods. They made me realize that I could fight back. I could leave. So I did.

He shrugs.

—Physical security is not a concern of Lament's. He relies on his personality to keep his captives with him. Until he is ready to send them on their way. Escaping was relatively easy. But freedom. That was most difficult. I had already seen the uses of fear in my own conditioning.

He tinks a claw against a bone that dangles from his wrist.

—So. I set out to make myself fearful.

He indicated the black leather vest worn open over his bare chest, the combat fatigues cut off at the knees. The outfit his crew sports as well.

—I designed a uniform for myself and the friends I convinced to join me. And we did things. Engaged in acts modeled on the Mungiki. Are they still afraid of us in the Bronx?

I flick ash.

—They are.

He points north.

—And we are not even there.

He lowers his arm.

—It is strange. That causing fear in others can help produce freedom. But it is also true. It clears a path before one. Creates space, a perimeter within which one can operate with abandon. I am not saying that it is true freedom. But it is a start. And it has given us the space and time to become more dangerous.

He brings a claw to his temple.

—I am not the boy I was. I do not crave the material things of MTV culture. I am not the slave I was. I do not crave the attention and occasional kindnesses of Lament. I am not even the savage I made myself after my initial escape. I do not crave blood for blood's own sake. I am a rational man. I have made myself into this. I have read and studied and applied myself. I am clear in my thoughts. And in how I express them. While I cultivate mystery about my person in order to project the fear that frees me, I want none of that mystery in my speech. I am capable now of great subtlety. A word I could not have defined just a few years ago. I am capable of that subtlety, but I prefer bluntness. I am all these things, all my past selves, and my new self, because of one reason.

He aims the claw at me.

—Because I have a purpose. And succeed or fail, I have aimed myself solely at that purpose. With no time for anything else. And yet.

He turns his hand over, shows me his pale palm.

—Even a man with a purpose can have regrets. My own regret is that I could not convince Esperanza Lucretia to join me. Though I still have hopes that she might. So, seeing that you know her, and that she recommends you to me, I agreed to deviate my attention from my purpose to meet with you. In return, I will need you to do something.

I wait.

He looks away.

—Tell her I miss her.

I flick my butt into the water, pull out a fresh one.

—Yeah, I know how that goes.

I light up.

—I can do that for you.

He nods.

—Well, then.

He squats, puts the tip of the blade on the ground, folds his hands over the leather-wrapped grip.

—What do you want?

I inhale smoke, killing the smell of the rank water.

—Like I told Esperanza. I don't know Queens. She told me you two had history. I asked if she could reach out.

—You asked Esperanza Lucretia to reach out to the Mungiki.

—Not saying I was happy to be looking to talk to you. Just saying I don't know anyone in Queens.

He looks up at me.

—Then what you have to do in Queens must be very important.

I think about the Cure house, and the blood they need. I think about Terry, and the money he needs. I think about Predo, and the information he needs.

I think about me, and what I need. Where I need to be. Who I need to see.

Feel the pull.

—Yeah, it's important.

I look at my burning cigarette.

Say it out loud and you don't go back.

Say it in the open air and there's no telling where the words drift.

Say it.

—I'm looking for blood.

He raises an eyebrow.

—Are not we all?

I look up from my cigarette.

—No, man, I'm looking for a whole lot of blood.

He looks into my eye, nods, stops nodding.

—Did I mention, Joe Pitt, that I do not believe in destiny?

—Yeah, I remember something like that.

He rises, looks me up and down.

—Serendipity though, that is another matter.

He glances at the water.

—What's the worst thing you've ever seen, Joe Pitt?

I look at him.

I could tell him the worst thing I've ever seen. But he wouldn't see it the same as me. Tell someone the worst thing you ever saw was a dying girl being healed, they won't really get it. But I saw it. And it was bad. So I know better.

He watches me, nods.

—So you have seen many awful things.

I still got nothing to say.

Menace weighs his machete in both hands.

—Have they changed you, do you think? The things you have seen?

I find my lighter.

—How the hell should I know.

I flick the lighter to life, realize I don't have a cigarette in my mouth for it to light, and snap it closed.

—You are who you are. See things. Don't see them. You are who you are.

He studies the machete in his hands.

—I was who I was. I saw terrible things as a child. And I was who I was. Taken by Lament, tortured, I saw more terrible things. And I was who I was. Changing, yes, but always who I was. I agree with that. But as I told you.

He holds the machete tight in one hand, as he runs the palm of his other hand down the blade, cutting deep.

—I am different now. Remade. By a purpose.

He looks at the hand, watches the blood clot over the deep incision.

—Remade by what I have seen.

He shakes his hand, flecks of blood spattering the pavement.

—You should go home, Joe Pitt.

He looks at me.

—Or risk being a different person when you leave later.

He shrugs.

—*If* you can leave later.

I put my Zippo back in my pocket, take hold of my razor.

—You saying something?

His mouth twists down, tries to straighten, stays twisted.

—Rope works. Steel caskets. Animal carbon. Glue factory.

He swallows.

—Do you think the swamp draws such industry?

I slip my other hand in my other pocket, thread my fingers into the hoops of the brass knuckles.

—Not following you, kid.

He breathes deep a couple times, like a man trying to keep down his last ten drinks.

—There are things. Things you have to see.

Tears start in his eyes.

—Go home, Joe Pitt.

He raises the hand he cut, and the rest of the Mungiki encircle us.

—We are Mungiki. Savages. We are born for this.

He lowers his hand.

—It will kill you.

He bares his teeth.

—It will kill us all.

I lick my lips.

—OK.

I take my hands from my pockets, lighter in one hand, cigarette in the other.

—I'm suitably freaked out.

I light the cigarette.

—Now tell me where I go to see this thing.

He wipes tears from his face, leaving a small smear of his hand's blood.

—Not far.

He points south.

—English Kill.

He nods at the Creek.

—Do you know how to swim?

The Mungiki don't have guns.

Not that they have anything against them, just that they don't have much cash to procure them with. Under normal circumstances I'd consider it a bonus for the whole world that these guys are limited to machetes and handmade claws, but it does mean I can't borrow a gun for myself.

—Not even a zip gun?

—No. No firearms at all.

I look at the rank water below my feet.

—Shit.

I look back up at Menace.

—And you're sure I can't go on land?

—No. This is the only way.

—Shit.

There's a splash as one of the Mungiki tosses an inflated inner tube, scavenged from one of the truck yards, into the water.

I look at it bobbing on the scummy low tide.

—What's that for?

Menace squats next to me, angles his machete at the sandbar peeking from the middle of the Creek.

—Mussel Island. Even at low tide the currents around it are strong. Hidden rocks. You can get pulled down into them and ripped apart.

—Shit.

He picks up a shard of glass between the points of two claws.

—I will not see you again, Joe Pitt.

I unlace my boots.

—That's always a chance.

—No.

He drops the shard in the water.

—I will not see you again. You will not come back. If someone comes back, it will not be you.

I peel off my socks and stuff them inside the boots, shrug out of my jacket and pull off my shirt.

—Do me a favor anyway.

—Yes?

I point at my clothes.

—Hang on to that stuff. I got a feeling they'll fit the son of a bitch who does come back.

He was right about the currents.

The inner tube gets pulled from my arm and I get dragged under, sucking a lungful of contaminated creek water as I go down. I get spun, my shoulder bangs on the rocks, and then the current shifts direction and shoves me away from the tiny island and I break the surface gasping.

I knew the water was how I was going out.

I stroke hard, past the branch where fresh currents try to drag me down English Kill so they can crush me against the rocks below the silos rising above some kind of refinery. Farther down the waterway, I pass under the Grand Avenue Bridge, heavy trucks rattling the steel plates overhead. Ahead, the Creek splits. Disappearing beyond a huge warehouse and around a hard angle to my right, where Menace told me it dead-ends at Metropolitan. Crossing an invisible border into Brooklyn.

Going that way is one of my options. But I don't want to go to Brooklyn. I've been to Brooklyn. And I'm not welcome there.

On my left the water runs between an abandoned lot and a

school bus depot, washing up against wood pilings at the foot of a nameless street.

I grab hold of the long steel-and-concrete pier that anchors the middle of the bridge, the pivot on which it once swung open, when these waters were used as anything but a garbage disposal.

Rising between the depot and the warehouse, tons of gravel are drawn up long conveyors, dust floats, hazing bright halogens, a nonstop roar of crushed stone and diesel engines. And a high, white-painted cinder-block wall.

That's the place Menace told me about.

The place where he got changed.

I let go of the pier and swim down the channel to the bus depot, where there is no wall.

Where I can see what scares the savages.

Merit Transportation hasn't bothered with a wall or even a fence on the water side of their depot.

Why bother?

Who's gonna swim up in heavily polluted water to mess around in a bus depot? And what are they gonna mess with? Some tagger is industrious enough to frog-man his way in by this route and spray bomb the side of one of the buses, you may as well give the little fucker a medal.

No, there's no wall here. Nothing to keep out anyone mad enough to come in this way to do God knows what.

Dripping, my skin coated in chemically mutated algae, I haul myself onto the slick rocks and crawl up until I can huddle between two buses, the halogens above the grinding yard next door casting deep black shadows for me to hide in.

All I can see is the tops of those conveyors, raising the gravel high before it's dropped, churned, milled ever more fine.

I get down on my belly and worm under a bus, keeping my eyes on the dirt, hoping to find an especially long butt that someone may have tossed aside. A butt and a match.

No dice.

Ahead, there's a row of buses parked perpendicular to a bare cement verge; beyond that, the wall that hides the gravel yard, topped with a long twisted spring of razor wire. Brightly lit.

A tunnel would be nice.

Or a shaped but silent charge, to blow a secret hole in the wall.

Why am I doing this?

I look at the dirt. I crook a finger and trace a name.

Evie.

I'd be lying if I said it gave me courage. I'd be lying if I said it heartened me. I'd be lying if I said it made me stronger, resolved in my intent. Hell, I'd be lying if I said that name did anything but open wounds and grind salt deep into the meat.

But I get up and run.

I vault onto the hood of a bus, hop to the roof, sprinting, sheet-metal footfalls on the roof of the bus lost in the din.

The cement verge is at least six feet broad. The wall eight feet tall, the wire adding nearly two more feet.

Jumping from the rear of the bus, my bare foot pushing off from the end of the roof above the emergency exit, I have a vision of myself, feet snagged in a tangle of razor wire, hanging upside down inside the perimeter of the wall, spotlights pinned on my body, guards closing in from every quarter.

I look down, see my feet clearing the wall and the wire with inches to spare, then gravity catches me and sucks me down and smashes me into a gravel pile, crushing the air from my lungs and snapping three fingers on my left hand when I stupidly try to brace against the impact instead of going limp.

It's even louder on this side of the wall. And brighter.

Mounds of gravel and sand, the tower the conveyor belts climb and descend, a steel blockhouse of grinding machinery underneath, unpaved roads cut by eighteen-wheelers hauling open-topped trailers bringing in yet more gravel, smaller diesels with spinning mixers, painted in spirals, driving away with loads of cement. Everything gray, shot with patches and stripes of pitch-black shadow painted by the light towers above.

I roll out of the light to the bottom of a gravel pile, into a shadow, waiting to hear a klaxon, the machinery grinding to a halt, commands shouted back and forth between heavily armed guards.

Nothing happens.

Machinery roars, lights blaze, trucks roll in low gear.

I crawl to the edge of the pile and look for the enforcers who must be creeping up on me.

And see no one but the drivers in the trucks, a couple silhouettes in a small shack near the conveyors, and a uniformed man sprawled in a folding chair at the distant gate, waving the trucks in and out with barely a glance.

I duck back behind the pile. Wondering if I'm in the right place.

Maybe Menace meant the warehouse on the far side of the yard. Maybe he meant one of the warehouses I passed along the Creek. Maybe he's a fucking nutjob and I'm chasing my own asshole around Maspeth because he thinks he saw something.

Maybe he's a nutjob.

He's fucking named Menace. He's given himself fangs and little handcrafted claws.

No *maybe* about it, he's a fucking nutjob and a half.

This place is nothing but a gravel yard.

What am I thinking? What can that insane kid possibly know about the biggest secret the Coalition has? What could he possibly have seen and survived seeing?

I think about his twisted mouth. His gasping breath as he tried to tell me. The way he swallowed his own bile at the thought of the place.

Tears and blood on his cheek.

OK, so maybe there's something here to see.

I use the razor to cut a strip from the hem of my pants. I straighten the three broken fingers on my left hand, gritting my teeth, then I slip the brass knuckles over them, curl my fingers around the cold metal and use the scrap of dirty khaki cloth to tie my fingers into place. Then I roll around in the gravel and dust, coating my wet skin and pants, making myself muddy gray.

And I crawl into the light, brass tied to one hand, cold, sharp steel held tight in the other, waiting with my face pressed in the dust at the side of the road that's been graded by the tonnage of trucks and crushed stone. Coming to my feet as one passes, snagging a dangling chain and pulling myself aboard, huddling atop one of the gas tanks as it wheels around the base of the conveyors, circles, and pulls into the notch that runs between them.

Dust clogs my nose. I can't smell anything except diesel fumes and scorched rubber. The truck moves into the shadows beneath the conveyors. The tower of rust-streaked gray steel that the conveyors pour their gravel into shakes and shudders and sends thunder vibrating through the air. I'm deaf.

The truck jerks, turns, angles toward a road that leads to the gate.

Here under the towers, protected from the halogen day, the light is cast by yellow globes in wire cages. Someone coalesces out of the dust and sickly light. I jump from the truck, leading with brass, my broken fist sending a hot blast of pain down my arm as it hits the side of the man's face. I land on top of him, knocking his helmet and earphones off, smashing an elbow into his gut. No worry that his screams will be heard here.

I drag him beneath one of the jittering scaffolds that hold the conveyors and put my face close to his and inhale.

No Vyrus.

I scream into his ear, and he coughs, spits up, shakes his head.

I show him the razor, and he shakes his head again.

I cut his left ear off and almost hear his scream.

I yell into his remaining ear and he sobs and points at the steel tower.

I cut his throat. I drink his blood. Dust is in the first mouthfuls. Muddy and viscous, I swallow hard to make it go down. After that, it goes easy.

I don't linger to drink it all. It's not safe here for indulgence.

I leave his body in the shadows, his dusty jacket on my torso, his goggles, earphones and helmet on my head. I hadn't planned to kill him, but it was the smart thing to do, taking his blood to make me strong for whatever may be inside.

Things could get ugly in there.

It's louder. The machinery directly overhead amplifying the racket of pulverizing rock, blasting it down to this small, empty chamber. In the middle of the floor a staircase spirals down an ancient shaft, screwing itself into a deep darkness punctuated by the occasional scarlet glow of a safety lamp.

I start down.

Twenty feet below, the noise starting to fade, I come to the first light, a bulb in a cage above an unmarked steel door. I try the handle, it doesn't move.

I feel watched, look up, expecting to find the mouth of the shaft ringed by Coalition enforcers armed with machine guns, and find nothing.

Down.

Another light and another door. Locked.

Down.

The light just below me flashes twice, the door opens, pulled inward.

I tuck my knuckled fist behind my back, collapse my razor and palm it, raise my chin to the goggled and earphoned man coming out the door and dropping something into his jacket pocket.

He nods, waits, holding the door open.

And I slip inside, patting his side in thanks, taking the weight of the door from him, watching his back as he starts up the stairs, letting go of the door, then catching it before it latches.

I look at the key in my hand, the key that dropped there when I sliced out the bottom of his pocket as we passed in the doorway. Broad and thick, notched along both edges, I slip it into the lock and check to be sure it will get me out. It turns the bolt.

I close the door, steel and the sixty-odd feet of stone above finally giving relief from the noise, reducing it to an insistent grinding in the walls. Walls of moisture-seeping limestone, braced by rusting I-beams. Fluorescent corkscrews stick from old ceramic sockets mounted high.

Doors.

The first stands open on a room lined with cots. Floor covered in linoleum dimpled by nails driven through it and into the stone. Walls decorated by ragged pinups. A small fridge, a coffeemaker, microwave.

I plug each nostril in turn and blow hard to dislodge the dust and grit. I inhale. Room smells of men living in close quarters. Smell like a barracks or firehouse.

But there's more.

Close my eyes, concentrate, I can smell Vyrus.

And blood. Lots of blood.

I open my eyes. Menace may be crazy, but something is here.

I leave the room and start down the hall. Find a bathroom with showerheads sticking from the ceiling, a couple dirty urinals, empty stalls. It reminds me of the bathroom at the Whitehouse.

At the end of the hallway, a storeroom, canned foods, cases of beer, economy-size cartons of snack cakes and candy bars, pallets of toilet paper.

I leave the room, go back to the shaftway door.

Down.

Deeper.

The key opens the next door. I go inside. A similar hallway. More doors.

And more sounds. And smells.

Vyrus here. Recently.

First door. No dormitory this time. A single bed with a mattress. Blood on the mattress. Dried spots and streaks. I kneel. At the four corners of the steel bed-frame, manacles. My own blood beats hard in my temples, each pulse blurs my vision. I open my razor and cut my thumb deep and the pain sharpens me.

Next room, the door is shut, my key opens it.

Another bed.

Manacles.

The naked girl held to the bed by the manacles looks at me. She opens and closes her mouth, makes opening and closing gestures with her cuffed hands, spreads her legs.

—Hey, man, this room is occupied.

I turn and look at the man behind me, stripped to shorts and T-shirt and boots, gravel dust deep in the creases of his face and hands. I look at the clothes piled in the corner.

He reaches out and pulls the earphones from my head.

—You hear, man? I'm off shift, I had her brought up for me. Get one of your own.

The girl flinches when the man's blood sprays her.

I find a key on a hook on the wall and unlock the manacles. She lies there, pointing at her mouth, opening and closing it, spreading her legs wider. I sit her up and she tries to grind against me. I pull the man's work jacket from the floor and a plastic-wrapped snack cake drops from a pocket. The girl looks at it and whines. I hand it to her and she unwraps it and stuffs it in her mouth. There are more in the jacket. I give them to her, covering her with the jacket as she eats, feeling the jutting bones that poke from her skin.

Trying to slip her arm into one of the sleeves, I touch something hard, find a plastic IV catheter attached to her forearm, hoops of surgical steel, body-piercing rings, riveting it in place.

I look at the floor, the dying man has dragged himself into the hall, the blood pouring from his open stomach smeared in a single broad swipe like a giant's brushstroke.

He's lucky, dies before I can cross to him and make him hurt.

The girl eats her cakes, a pleased hum coming from deep in her throat. A sound comes from my own throat. I choke it. The room blurs, shivers, I can't catch my breath.

I cut myself again.

Again.

Again.

Vision clears.

I had her brought up for me.

I leave the girl, go back to the stairwell.

Down.

There's a guard when I open the next door under a red light. He turns to look at me, sees my face, freezes, his mouth slightly open under his thin moustache.

Then he's dead.

Low.

If the kid had never seen me before, he might not have been so surprised, he might have been able to do something to stop me from punching him in the temple five times, shattering his skull and crushing his brain. Instead he sits dead on the floor.

The brass knuckles came dislodged with the fourth blow. The bones in my fingers, that had started to reknit when I drank the man's blood on the surface, are broken again. I tie them back into place.

Low has a ring of keys and a truncheon.

I take the keys.

The noise from above is all but mute here, just a dull thud in the stone. But there are other sounds. Rustling, grunts, coughing, the occasional angry shriek.

First door opens on a white-painted room. Layers of paint, thick on the stone, the floor marked by boot scuffs, dry maroon stains. Steel tables with blood gutters down their sides, running to drains at their feet. Steel trays filled with used needles, some bent, some broken. Meters of looped plastic hose.

Down the hall.

Another storeroom.

Cardboard boxes filled with empty, paper-wrapped blood bags. Unused needles. Clean tubing. Gallons of bleach. Buckets of white paint. A dusty and broken autoclave, decades out of date.

An incubator.

The noise starts in my throat again. It's harder to stop this time.

The last door. Sounds are louder. Smells of feces and disinfectant and decay.

My key doesn't fit the lock. As I'm trying the keys from Low's ring, the door is opened from within.

—What the fuck, Low, it's the key with the piece of tape on it.

A scrappy kid with a Bronx accent.

He looks at my jacket and helmet and the earphones and goggles now hanging from my neck.

—What the fuck. You know your ass ain't allowed down here. You want a piece, call down and we'll send something up.

I don't see him anymore. I see the room behind him. I see the ranks of bunk beds. I see the skinny bodies filling the beds. I see skin waxed to albino paleness. I see a chemical pit at the back of the room that they squat over. I see bedsores and muscle atrophy. I hear their hisses and grunts and caws, their imitations of speech.

The Bronx kid pokes me with his truncheon.

—Motherfucker, time to go. You don't get to window-shop, asshole. You fuck what we send up.

I look at him.

Something crosses his eyes. He looks down. Sees my bare feet.

My hands are on the back of his head and my knee is pushing the bones of his nose back through his brain and I twist his neck and it breaks and I think I start crying.

But it's not why you think.

It's not why you think.

It's not why you think.

I'm simply angry at myself for killing him so fast, so easy. I'd have liked to take my time.

But in the whole universe there is not enough time. There are not enough minutes and seconds for what I'd like to do. For the things I could dream up if I had more time.

The things I could do to this world to make it pay for being the way it is.

I stare at the things that might have been people had they not been raised to slaughter. I look at the dead body I'm still holding. I drop it. There's a sound when I drop it, metal on stone. I kneel and find the gun under the kid's arm. I take it.

This gun. I love this gun. There are so many wonderful things I can do with this gun. So many people I can kill.

I turn and leave, eager to begin.

I kill two more workers on the stairs, at a total cost of two bullets. Two bullets for two human lives. I laugh to think that something as tawdry as a human life should come at the cost of something so precious as a bullet.

Climbing, I come to the second door I passed on my way down.

I don't need to go inside and look. I know what I'll find.

A key lets me in.

And I find it.

Another of Lament's creations is guarding this room. She's whippet fast and far more alert than the two I've already killed. Maybe it's what she's been charged to watch that makes her so present.

I don't care.

She takes three of my bullets. And snaps off the long scalpel blade she sticks in my right armpit before she dies. If I were left-handed, the blade would be in my heart.

Standing at the door of the room she guarded, I ask myself if I've seen enough.

Tiny things.

In my life I never think about them. Helpless, squirming, bundles of nothing but pure need. They have no place in my world.

Why are they suddenly here?

I turn as the steel door at the end of the hall opens, and I walk toward it, shooting, using the last of my bullets to kill the man in the black suit who is coming through the door.

I have to finish him with the razor, the body armor beneath his jacket having stopped the first two bullets I hit him with.

Groomed, manicured, fit.

Enforcer.

His gun is better than the one I took from the kid. I take it. I take the extra clips in the nylon pouches snapped to the back of his belt.

A fold of papers sticks from his inner breast pocket. I look at them.

Vouchers. Signed.

Nearby, a cooler rests on the floor, waiting, a number written on its top in black Sharpie matches a number on a voucher. I open the cooler.

Purple coils, thumb-thick, nestled in ice packs.

I go up the stairs with my new favorite gun. Ignoring the last door, the one closest to the surface, having no need to see the commercial refrigerators I know are behind it, or what is inside them.

Having no desire to be tempted.

There's a car outside the surface door, a low, black SUV. I open the passenger door and shoot the black-suited man behind the wheel. I take his gun, twin to the one I already have.

On my way across the yard, my feet cut again and again by the sharp rocks under them, I shoot the drivers of three trucks. I shoot the men in the shed.

I stand in the light and shoot the sky and the earth.

Then I run, I tear myself going over the wall and the wire, and I fall into the water and I let myself sink to the bottom, bullets thrumming around me, leaving white trails of bubbles.

On the bottom, clinging to the rusted-out shell of an oil drum, I open my mouth and let it fill and let the water run down my throat.

Only when it hits my lungs and I start to choke and my hands let go of the drum and I thrash toward the surface do I know.

It's not time yet.

Someone's still waiting for me.

—It is what he made us for.

Menace drops a dusty packing blanket over my shoulders.

—The final lie of Lament.

He pokes the coals with his machete and drops another dry, broken plank from an abandoned pallet onto the fire.

—We were baited with the promise of being a part of a crew.

The plank catches fire and crackles and spits sparks and Menace shoves it deeper into the blaze.

—Then, when he had prepared us, the secret was revealed. We were infected. Told we would be more than simple gangsters. We would be soldiers in a cause. Enforcers. Specially recruited and trained. Better than the others. Special. If we were worthy.

He thrusts the blade through the handle of an old enameled coffeepot and lifts it from the fire.

—And, of course, none of us was worthy.

One of his boys hands him a chipped mug with *World's Greatest Dad* painted on the side, framed by the stenciled outline of a football.

—And one by one we were all sent away.

He fills the cup and passes it to me.

—So when I found myself, and escaped Lament, I followed a trail. Rumors and scents. And it led here.

He puts the pot back in the fire and squats next to me.

—Getting in was not difficult. I was, after all, exactly what they were expecting. Another of Lament's products. A street child, strong and vicious. And with a regard for himself so low that he could never be expected to have regard for anyone else.

The firelight reflects off his claws, burnishing them red and orange.

—Once inside, I saw.

He looks into the fire.

—Lament's creatures, we are meant as herdsmen. To fodder and tend the beasts. Milk them. See that they are bred outside the herd. To keep the line hearty. See the whelps nursed. In exchange, feed at our will.

He closes his eyes.

—Though I saw signs that even our appetite can be fed to surfeit.

The fire has yet to warm me, the cold creek water deep in my bones. I drink some of the coffee and it scalds my throat.

—Where?

Menace opens his eyes.

—You know where, Joe Pitt. You know where they come from.

He points at my eye.

—You saw.

He opens his hand.

—And now.

He rises.

—Will you join us?

His boys come closer, into the firelight, ringing him.

—Will you stay with us, Joe Pitt? Will you file your teeth to bite out the throat of the world? Will you have claws to rake its hide?

I set the cup next to the fire and shrug the blanket from my shoulders.

—Where are my things?

Menace comes close.

—You are not the same. You cannot go back now.

—Are you planning to keep me here?

He shakes his head.

—No.

—Then where are my things?

He looks to one of the boys, and my jacket and shirt and boots are dropped at my feet.

Menace watches as I dress.

—Wear the same clothes, they will not hide your new skin.

I lace the boots.

—There's nothing new about me, kid. Nothing under the sun.

One of the boys dumps a bucket of water over the fire and it hisses out.

Menace stands in the rising steam and smoke.

—You cannot go back.

I pull on my jacket.

—Yeah, you keep saying that, and watch me walk out of here, back to where I came from.

He raises a hand, claws against the night.

—You died in there, Joe Pitt. We all die in there. Go where you came from, go to your friends, but it will not be the man who left that they see. It will not be a man at all.

I pull a smoke from my pocket.

—Who ever said I got friends to know whether it's me or not?

I start across the glass-covered concrete plain where the Mungiki haunt, smoke trailing from my mouth.

And it's me who goes west.

I am not changed.

I am not.

I have Predo's money in my jacket. I use it when I get to Vernon, waving down a cab that cuts past the parking lot above the mouth of the Midtown Tunnel. The hack boxes the compass from Vernon to Jackson to Fiftieth to Eleventh, and we're lined up, paying the toll, and underwater, traveling the exhaust-filled hole that will take me back.

I lost one of the enforcers' guns in English Kill, but the other rests in my pocket. I touch it.

It's good to have a gun again.

—What the hell are you thinking?

I make for the bar.

—I'm thinking I need a drink.

Sela follows me.

—We go to all that trouble to get you out with no one seeing you, and you just come to the goddamn front door and start banging on it? You think Predo suddenly got tired of keeping an eye on us over the last few hours? You think he won't want to know how you got out and where you went?

I pour a drink in a glass then pour it down my throat.

—It doesn't matter.

Amanda is still behind her desk, still holding the sheets of paper that were in her hand when I came through the door.

—You haven't been gone very long, Joe.

I pick up the bottle again, start to pour it in the glass, realize what a waste of time that is, and pour it in me instead.

—Thought you'd be happy. Thought you said there was a big hurry.

She sets the paper down.

—Well *yeah,* we're in a hurry. But I *mean.*

She gives a big shrug.

—That was really *fast.*

I look at the bourbon still in the bottle. Even if I drink it all at once, it's not enough to get me drunk, not with the Vyrus cleaning my blood.

—Fuck.

—Something the matter?

I take a drink.

—More than the usual? Not that I know of.

She flicks the edge of a paper.

—I don't want to rush you or anything, Joe, but I am kind of *totally* busy. I *mean,* if you have anything?

I look at the rug. Swirling mandalas. Rust background. Gold and white. Curls of thumb-thick purple.

I take another drink.

—You're right, Sela.

She clears her throat.

—Excuse me?

I wave the bottle.

—I fucked up coming in the front way. But.

I take another drink.

—Maybe Predo did pull off. That's what I was thinking. Maybe he wants to give me room in here. He told me he would.

—And?

—Be good to know for sure if I'm wrong about that. Someone should take a look. See if his peepers are out there. Not seeing them won't prove anything, but if they're visible, be good to know for certain that they spotted me coming in.

She doesn't move.

—What are you playing?

—Go take a look, Sela.

Sela looks at Amanda.

—What?

Amanda stands.

—Joe's right, go take a look, see *whatever*.

—Bull*shit*.

—Sela.

—This is bullshit. What the hell are you playing at?

Amanda comes around the desk and crosses to her lover.

—Baby, I'm not *playing* at all.

She points at the door.

—I'm *saying* go downstairs and take a look outside.

Sela's mouth tightens.

—Little girl, if you want to be finished with me, this is the fast track to getting there.

Amanda raises herself on her toes and kisses Sela's lower lip.

—Big girl, I'm never gonna be finished with you.

She lowers herself.

—I just think you should go take a look.

Sela looks at me, looks daggers. Looks sabers and spears.

—She trusts you, Pitt. I know better.

I wave the bottle.

—So you're a well-educated lady, go take a look like you're told.

She makes for me.

Amanda gets in her way.

—Baby, he's working your *nerves*. He's *totally* trying to get under your skin.

Sela grits her teeth.

—I know. He's doing a good job of it.

Amanda's fingers tangle with Sela's.

—Except you're *way* better than that.

Sela pulls her fingers free.

—No. No, I'm not.

She goes to the door.

I raise the bottle.

—Sela.

She doesn't stop.

—What?

—Make it a long look around.

She doesn't bother to reply. She also doesn't bother to come back across the room and kill me. Watching her slam out the door, I can't help but think I got off easy on that one.

I lift the bottle high, empty it in my mouth, and steel scrapes a nerve under my arm and I drop it, spilling the last of the bourbon.

Amanda comes over and picks up the bottle.

—Something bothering you, Joe?

I stick my left hand inside my jacket and poke around in my right armpit.

—I got a scalpel blade stuck in here that needs digging out.

Amanda nods, goes through a door on the other side of the bar, snagging a bottle of scotch as she goes.

—Come *on* then. I know this isn't your usual flavor, but it should get you through, *toughguy.*

She pushes the door open on a bathroom.

—And while I'm cutting, you can tell me what you saw that you don't think Sela can handle.

Sitting on the edge of the tub in the bathroom behind the bar, my hand held behind my head so the girl can dig into my armpit with a long pair of tweezers, after cutting the wound back open with my straight razor, I take slugs from the bottle of scotch. Not that it does anything for the pain, but it helps to wash out the taste of creek water still in my mouth.

—OK, OK, don't move.

I grit my teeth.

—I'm not moving.

—So don't *breathe,* OK? I can't get a grip on it 'cause it's slippery as hell.

I stop breathing.

She bites the tip of her tongue and yanks and pulls the scalpel blade free, along with a nice bit of my flesh.

—*Wow.* That is nasty, Joe.

I crane my neck to get a look under my arm.

—Could have cut a little cleaner.

She drops the blade and the tweezers in the sink, passes me a washcloth.

—Put that under your arm.

I put it under my arm, take another drink.

Amanda stands at the basin, looking at the blood on the thin rubber gloves she took from a first-aid kit and rolled onto her hands before slicing me open.

—Cord blood.

I drink some more.

She peels the gloves off.

I point at her bare hands.

—Be careful.

She frowns.

—It's dead, Joe. I *mean,* how many times do you have to be told? The Vyrus *dies* outside its host. It's a *pussy* bug.

She runs water over the bloody steel in the sink.

—The umbilicals you saw in that cooler. The Coalition must want the cord blood.

I watch the blood swirl, turn pink in the water, and run down the drain.

She stares at her reflection in the mirror over the sink.

—*Amazing* stuff, cord blood. Very rich in stem cells. Not like *bone marrow rich,* but *really* useful stuff. I mean, as soon as you start thinking about the Vyrus, really *thinking* about it and what it does, right away you have to start thinking about white blood cells. I *mean,* blood cells in general, because you know it can't have too much to do with *plasma.* And you don't think too much about platelets, either. I *mean,* sure, you can get caught up in them if you want to study *clotting factors* and stuff.

She turns and takes the cloth from under my arm.

The bleeding has stopped, the wound sealed.

—But that's *not* the essence of the Vyrus.

She squeezes the cloth, and my blood drips into the sink.

—The essence is that it *consumes.* It attacks. So it makes sense, I *mean,* this is *so* obvious, but it makes sense that it goes after *white blood cells.* Not just to attack them before they attack it, but to *invade* them. Make them do what it *wants* them to do. I *mean,* the T cell counts in infected blood is off the *chart,* especially *cytotoxic* Ts. Memory T cells, also out of *whack.* But suppressor Ts, like, *barely* there. Which means the cytotoxic Ts, the ones that fight invaders, should be going *berserk* and fighting the whole body. Killing everything. But they don't.

She drops the towel.

—'Cause the memory T count is so *high*. They keep the cytotoxics from getting out of hand. They, *right,* they remind them what to attack and what not to attack.

She looks at me in the mirror.

—Until you haven't *fed*. Then the memory Ts start to die. Poor little cytotoxic Ts don't know *what* to do. They go *totally* crazy.

She runs water over her hands, washing away the blood from the towel.

—But they all start as *little baby* stem cells. They all start the same. Nothing but potential.

She turns off the water.

—Like the babies you saw in that nursery.

She blinks.

—I'm not saying they *know* what they're doing. But if the guys at the top are saving cord blood for themselves to feed on, it's probably really, *really* good. I *mean*.

She licks her lips, frowns.

—The rich have a habit of saving the best for themselves. *I* ought to know.

She swallows.

—So if they like it so much, if it makes them feel so good, I mean, maybe it's the stem cells. All those.

She tries to smile, falls far short.

—All those babies.

She holds up a hand.

—Excuse me.

She throws up in the sink.

I watch as she rinses her mouth and spits it out.

—Sorry. *Gross*. I guess.

She splashes water in her face, blots with the bottom of her shirt.

—I guess.

She keeps her face covered.

—I guess.

She pulls her face out, smiling sick as she cries.

—I guess I'm not as tough as I think I am.

I take a drink.

—Here.

I offer her the bottle.

—Get tougher.

I stand behind her, looking at one of her monitors.

She taps on her keyboard, tears dried.

—This *fair*?

I shrug.

—There's no such thing as fair. But it's enough.

She hits Enter.

—Need me to write it down?

—I'll remember.

She looks up at me.

—I *mean*, how could you *forget*?

—Yeah. How could I forget.

She looks at her desk, moves a few papers.

—Fuck.

I look at a clock.

—Yeah, fuck.

I go to the chair and pick up my jacket.

—Guess you got some work to do.

She picks up several of the papers, shuffles them, drops them in a shredder, listens to it whine.

—Yeah. I *mean,* new priorities. I *mean,* Cure is still about a *cure,* but.

She looks at the floor, at the people on the floors below it.

—We'll need to start being a *whole* lot more selective.

I put on my jacket.

—And you'll need to buy guns.

She looks at me.

—Yeah. I mean, *so* many guns.

She comes around the desk and walks with me to the door.

—Thanks for, like, getting Sela *out of here* before you said anything. You were right about that. She would have *freaked* out. Sela, she's, I mean, *so* moral. Something like this, coming from you, she would have, I *mean,* she would have needed to *blame* someone. So. I mean, she *totally* would have killed you for not trying to save them. Or something. And that would have sucked.

I open the door and go out.

She grabs the tail of my jacket.

—It's not *your* fault, Joe. You couldn't save them by *yourself.*

I pull loose.

—Never crossed my mind to try.

Figure.

Figure it how you want. Figure it goes back. Way back. Don't lie to yourself about it. When Menace says, *You know where they come from,* he's right. I know where they come from. They come from that hole in the ground. Figure no one needs to stick a needle in their brain to make them dumb and docile. Figure they've been bred that way. Born in a hole, live in a hole, bleed in a hole, die in a hole. And when they're dead, figure their bones ground up with the gravel and mixed into cement.

Look at this city. Look at your city. Look at the sidewalk under your feet. Look at the foundations under the buildings.

You're walking on their bones. You're living in their skeletons.

Figure that's the story.

Figure that's the whole story and there's no changing it.

Figure life goes on and doesn't care.

That's how I figure it. Out the front door of the Cure house, down the steps and into the car Amanda called and has waiting for me. Staring out the window, not bothering to look for the tail I know is behind me. Looking at the streets where I live. Or do my little imitation of life. I figure it all the way down.

The advantage of one eye?

Brothers and sisters, you just fucking see less of what's going on.

Enough of a blessing to make a man think about putting out the other one.

I have a phone number.

It belongs to someone whose life I saved once. That might count for something, if she hadn't saved mine twice.

Borrowing the driver's cell, I call it. Not sure if I want it to still work. Not sure if I want anything but to be hung up on when my voice is recognized.

It still works.

And I'm not hung up on.

So in the spirit of poking out my remaining eye, I tell a story.

A story told, you can't untell it. It has to run its course to the end. The story I tell, it ends bloody. Or it will, anyhow.

Like I know any other kind of story.

Car lets me off well below Fourteenth.

Deep in Society turf. Far from the border. Far as possible from the blade that's coming for my head and all the things it now knows.

Moves to make.

People to see.

Stories to tell.

—'Lo, Joe. Long time no see.

I come up the tenement steps.

—Just saw you earlier tonight, Hurl.

He pushes up the brim of his hat.

—Sure, an' so it was. Still an all, seems some time ago. Funny dat, ain't it?

I put my hands in my pockets.

—Well, put it that way, does seem a long time. But I don't see anything funny in it.

He hooks a thumb in a suspender.

—Well, humor is a funny ting. Ta each his own.

I point at the door behind him.

—Terry in?

—Sure he is.

—Can I see him?

—Sure ya can, Joe. Nobody Terry'd like ta see more den yerself. C'mon in and be at home.

He raps hard on the door and it's pulled open.

Just inside are three skinny guys in faded fatigue jackets, light bouncing off their shaved heads and the barrels of their shotguns.

I look at Hurley.

—Not the kind of *we're all one* greeting I'm used to getting at a Society house.

He nods.

—Well, since dat last time.

He rubs his belly where the machine gun nearly cut him in two that last time.

—Since dat last time, Terry gave me charge of security.

I scratch my cheek.

—Gone back to the old-school ways, have you?

He shakes his head.

—It's a complicated world, Joe. I spend more of my life confused den clear. But some tings don't seem ta me ta need changin'. An bein' smart 'bout who ya let in yer house is one a dem.

I check out the three partisans and their guns.

—They itchy types?

He frowns.

—I'm a professional, Joe. Dese are my boys. Dey know how ta hold dere water and do as dere told.

I hold up a hand.

—Didn't mean to imply anything different.

He smiles.

—'Course ya didn't. Ya have some manners. Weren't born inna barn, was ya? Not dat dered be anyting wrong if ya had been.

He gives me a shot with his elbow, almost breaking a rib.

—Seein' as I was. Born inna barn. See.

He guffaws.

I rub my ribs.

—Sure, I see, Hurl. Real rib tickler.

He points at me and roars.

—Rib tickler! I get it, Joe! I get it! You go on in now. He'll be eager ta see ya, Terry will. Go on in.

I go in, leaving him to chuckle over the comic implications of our witty little exchange.

Hurley. Just when you start thinking he's maybe not as dumb as mud, he trips you up and sucks your shoe off and leaves you stuck in it.

The partisans eyeball me.

I flick a finger at the door at the end of the hall.

—Shall we?

One of them backs off and lifts his gun and points it at my face.

—Pat-down.

I raise my hands.

—Sure thing.

I turn to face the wall.

—Best make sure I don't got any nails on me. I go in there with a couple of those, and your boss is gonna be pissed as hell.

—I tell you, Joe, I didn't expect to see you so, I don't know, promptly.

I pick at some dry creek-scum on my pants.

—Everyone's so surprised with me being on time tonight. My reputation must be worse than I thought.

He fiddles his glasses.

—I just thought it might take you a little longer to work something out. Sure, the girl is fond of you and all, but I just thought you'd have to do something more nuanced than to walk in to her and ask for a bunch of money. Relationships, I've mostly found, are, I don't know, bruised by money talk. It's a shame really, that something as disconnected from real life as money, something that's just purely this monolithically theoretical concept that we've plastered onto life, that something fictional should be able to harsh our personal relationships the way it does.

He lifts his hands in surrender to market forces.

—But there it is. The stuff is everywhere. And people, they've, for better or worse, they've agreed we need it to get by.

I look at a poster on the wall. *The Concert for Bangladesh.*

—If it makes you feel any better, I had to use some nuance. Had to finesse it some, working the whole thing out.

He raises his eyebrows.

—I like that idea, I like the idea of you using some finesse. A quality like that, it could make all the difference for a person like you, Joe.

He lowers his eyebrows.

—A shame it, let's just say it, a shame it's too late for that kind of thing to change how we interact. Some of our conversations over the years, they would have benefited from a little finesse.

—So you say.

He takes off his glasses, folds and opens the arms a couple times.

—Yeah.

He puts them back on.

—So I say. For what it's worth, and all.

I point at the glasses.

—Something I wanted to ask.

—Yeah?

—Why do you wear those things?

He purses his lips.

—Um.

I nod.

—Yeah, *um*. Me, I never wore the things, but still I notice the Vyrus sharpened my eyes. Strange it didn't fix whatever's wrong with yours.

He takes them off again, looks at them.

—Yeah, well, yeah, sure. Honestly. These are just, you know, glass. Just. Well I'm not the only one with this, you know.

He puts them on.

—This affectation. I wore them before I was infected. Always felt weird without them. Even though they don't make me see any, I don't know, any more clearly.

—Hnuh.

He sits there, looking out from behind his play glasses. I look at the room some more. His little office. A bedroom squirreled away at the back of a tenement. Typical Society digs. Street-salvage furniture, rock and protest posters, books by Noam Chomsky.

Terry pushes a button on the oscillating fan that's moving the dead air around and it kicks up a gear.

—I try not to use it. The things burden the grid almost as much as an air conditioner. That's as much for our finances at this point as it is for the environment. So.

He watches me.

I let him.

He shakes his head.

—So, money. Joe.

—Not much finesse in that transition, Terry.

He leans forward, elbows on knees.

—Money. Joe.

I point at a coffee cup filled with pens that sits atop his press-wood desk.

—It's an account. You'll want to write down the number and password.

He picks up a pen and a piece of notepaper with a little circle of green arrows on it to let you know that no new trees were killed to make it.

—Shoot.

My hand twitches. But the partisans took my gun.

So instead of putting a bullet in him, I give him the numbers. I tell him how much Amanda put in the account.

He looks at the numbers on the sheet of paper.

—She must really care about you. No joking around, Joe. I may not like the idea of money as an expression of affection, and she may, I don't know, have it to spare, but this seems like someone trying to make a point about how much they value you. Not that I'm advocating using dollars to put a value on human or any other kind of life.

I wave a hand.

—Like I said, I used some nuance.

He looks at me over the lenses of those glasses that don't let him see any better.

—Tell you, man, I'd sure like to know what that was like.

—Well, Terry, seeing as this money is supposed to put me back on the map down here. Get me a place out of the way, some kind of privileges if I want to move around a little.

He nods.

—Sure, man, that was the deal.

I stand.

—Well seeing as that's the deal, and seeing as we're maybe on the way back to being on something like friendly terms, why don't I tell you what it was like.

He sets the paper and pen aside.

—Something on your mind, Joe?

I shake my head.

—Just like I said, just want to explain what it was like. Working some nuance for the girl.

I look at the floor between my feet, a long gash in the wood where something heavy was once dragged over it.

—What it was like was, it was like going down a hole and finding dozens of stupid, mute, starving kids with hoses stuck in their arms to make it easy to get their blood out. It was like going down that hole, and looking down it, and seeing a string of red lights, going deep, lights letting you know that there were hundreds more of them down there. And I'm wondering.

I look at him.

—That sound like something you might have seen at one time or another, Terry?

He takes off the glasses, looks at them, puts them aside.

—Yes.

He rubs his eyes.

—Yes it does.

I nod.

—Man. Were you smart.

He looks at me.

—How's that?

—Having your boys take my gun before I came in here. That just saved your life.

—It's interesting. In a way. Being able to talk about it. The terrible thing about a secret, it's that, I don't know, that pressure it creates. Right? That internal variance. Like with laws of diffusion, how a liquid or a gas is always seeking to spread itself evenly through a medium, yeah? So you exhale smoke, which I still wish you wouldn't do in here by the way, but you exhale, and rather than it doing what I wish it would do and just kind of cling to you, it gradually spreads, diffuses into the air. And like, I've thought this before, how a secret is kind of the same. It wants to, this is pretty spacey, one of my spacey ideas, but how it wants to spread itself. Like smoke. Diffuse into the atmosphere until it's evenly distributed. Yeah? And that, if the secret is bottled up in you, that creates pressure. Man, secrets, they just want out. Want to get everywhere. Especially, and this isn't always the case, but especially if the secret is the truth. Get me? 'Cause the truth wants to get out there, get into all the nooks and crannies, get into everyone's heads. The truth doesn't want to be bottled up, it wants to be free. And I'm down with that. You know I'm down with that. That's what the Society is about, getting the truth out.

He keeps rubbing his forehead, pressing his fingertips deep into his temples, eyes closed.

—But not all at once. Not like, you know, like when something is under extreme pressure and you release it, it just, man, it explodes out. Yeah? People get hurt. And, our life here, our life with the Vyrus, that's not like can-of-soda pressure. You release this truth you don't get some mess sprayed on the wall. The Vyrus, that's bomb pressure. That's, and I don't think this is hyperbole, but that's nuclear-device pressure. That's an explosion that rocks the world to its foundation. And.

He stops rubbing, rests his head in his hand, eyes still closed.

—And this, this secret we're talking about. That, that *instillation* in Queens, that's pressure on a whole different order. That's like, like, if the Vyrus is a nuke, that place is like a doomsday device.

He opens his eyes.

—That place, Joe.

He lifts his head, looks at me.

—That place is like a bomb that kills us all.

He points east, without looking there.

—People know about that, and there is nothing, nothing short of, man, nothing short of Jesus-Mohammed-Buddha-Gaia-Jehovah itself that saves us.

He wipes his mouth.

—So, to talk about it, man, something that exerts that kind of pressure, to talk about it for the first time in decades, that's just blowing my mind here. That's, the whole thing, it's like a mirror being held up, when you take something like that out of the box and look at it after so long. It's a, man, it's trip and a half.

He stares at his trembling hand.

—A trip and a half.

He moves his hand, reaches for his prop glasses, slips them on.

—But a thing like that, it belongs in its box.

I study that gash in the floor a little more.

—Well, I know you're no fool, Terry. Me the jury's still out on. Even so, I think I read this one pretty clear.

I lean down, pluck a stray splinter from the edge of the gash.

—This thing, it doesn't even need to get out in the *real* world for it to raise hell. This thing, it spreads in our community, our people will go berserk.

I roll the splinter between my fingers.

—Dog with a parasite, chewing at its own insides. Ugly. Ugly things will happen. Hard to keep a wrap on the whole deal once they start happening.

I look at the ceiling.

—Something like this gets out, like you say, people gonna start looking at themselves in the mirror.

I shrug.

—Lots of them, they're gonna figure, *in for a penny, may as well go for the whole pound. Been living off blood already, so why start worrying now about where some of it comes from.* Some others.

I shake my head.

—This would be the line. Down here especially. Types get drawn to your turf, they hear about this, they won't want to go on staying undercover. Not if it means that pit in Queens stays full of bleeding kids.

I poke the tip of my index finger with the splinter.

—So yeah, I get it. Something like this, it needs to stay a secret. I know the score. I've kept your secrets before. Your backdoor deals with the Coalition. That thing with the shamblers a couple years back. All those bodies I've put in the river. I can keep a secret. And I sure as shit know one that needs to be kept when I stumble into it.

I draw blood from myself.

—Something funny about it. Know what I mean?

He shakes his head.

—No, man, I don't know anything funny about it.

I lick the bead of blood from my fingertip. My own personal Vyrus.

—Funny thing is, for a while now, I've had it sussed that you're not just looking to find some kind of accord with the Coalition. Not just looking to get on an even footing so you could pressure them into going public alongside the Society. Use all those connections they have to smooth the way. Some time now, I've had it figured how you were never too happy about having to leave them in the first place. All your history with Predo, I've had it figured how maybe he leapfrogged you into running the enforcers and all that. How that was a bitter pill for you. How you went off and started your revolution. A *revolution,* you always call it. Not like you were looking to do your own thing and let bygones be bygones, but like you were looking to overthrow something. And it stands to figure, once something gets overthrown, someone's gonna have to step in and take control. Me, I've been figuring for a while now that that's what you're about, Terry. All that building a better world for everybody bullshit. I've had you figured for some time as Predo's flip side. Just looking to run the fucking show. Settle some scores. Like everyone else.

I point the sliver at him.

—But looking at the way you're trying to keep that hand from shaking, I'm figuring a little different now.

I lean toward him.

—You've been thinking about knocking off the Coalition alright. You've been thinking about sitting in Predo's chair. And not just *his* chair, but one of those chairs on the higher floors, where the show gets run. Not so you can teach Predo who's top man, and not so you can even past scores.

I lean back, pick something from between my teeth with the splinter.

—You, Terry Bird, you've been thinking about that hole in the ground. You've been thinking about what's in it. And you've been thinking about filling it in, stopping it up, and getting it out of the world. You've been thinking about being a savior.

I spit.

—And that only works if it stays a secret till you're in charge.

He presses the bridge of his glasses tight to his face.

—Only you, Joe, only you.

He shakes his head.

—Only you could describe a, you know, describe a man striving to do the right thing, and make it sound like he was, I don't know, like he was running the gas chambers at Auschwitz. Only you.

I flick the splinter away.

—Whatever.

I stand.

—Anyway, I get it. You need this thing to stay secret. The world isn't ready. Infecteds aren't ready. No one is ready. When they're ready, you'll tell them they're ready. And you'll march in and make everything OK. I get it. I get it. I know this is how it has to be. I get it. Motherfucker. I get it.

He studies me.

—I know you get it, Joe. When it all shakes out, you're pretty dependable in one way.

He slips the hand he's been trying to keep still from between his legs.

—You're no boat rocker. Truth is, and I don't want to say you don't get the job done in your own way, but the truth is, you're no revolutionary. If you'd been around in the early days, at the barricades, I have a feeling you'd have been on the other side, man. Your own back is all you've ever really been out there looking to take care of, and the best way to keep, I don't know, to keep safe, is to keep things the way they are. Just maintain that old status quo.

He holds up his hand, looks at its new steadiness.

—Just the old tried and true for you, man. Steady as she goes. Never any question that you can be trusted to keep a secret when the alternative would be, you know, bringing the whole world down around your head and changing everything.

I get a cigarette from my pocket.

—Yeah, keeping earth-shattering secrets, it's my specialty.

I put it in my mouth.

—Give me time to think about my own self-interest and I can be counted on to jump to that side of the room every time.

I light it.

—Too bad there was no one to spell it out for me this time around.

He stops looking at his hand.

I suck on my cigarette.

—I told the Horde girl, Ter.

His mouth hangs open in a way I've never seen before.

—What the hell, Joe?

—It's how I got your money. It's what she wanted. To know where all the blood comes from. So I found out. And I told her. And you got paid. Nice when everyone gets what they want.

—Oh. Jesus. Did you, Jesus, Joe, did you tell Sela?

—No.

—Thank Christ for that.

—But the girl will have told her by now.

He sits there, staring at me.

I blow smoke.

—Not that big a deal. Get your buddy Predo on the phone. You guys move fast, you can contain it. Cure has no contacts in the life. Horde can't spread the word. You can cap that one.

His eyes are scanning side to side, reading the immediate future.

—We'll need to. Yes. OK. I. OK. You should stay close, Joe. I may need you for something. And it goes without saying, you know, that this changes things, you stick here where you belong and we'll find a place for you again. A real place, not some corner to hide in. It'll take a few days to, you know, to contain this, but once that's done, once you've helped out with that effort, we'll have a spot for you down here.

I watch the smoke from my cigarette drift.

—Sure thing. Only you might want to wait on that until you talk it over with Lydia.

His eyes stop moving, draw a bead on my face.

I diffuse some smoke to his side of the room.

—I called her on my way over. Told her about the hole. Told her what I saw down there.

He doesn't move.

I shake my head.

—She didn't really believe me.

He licks his lips.

I nod.

—Yeah, funny, right?

I take a drag.

—But she started believing me more when I told her I found out while doing some special reconnaissance for you. Told her she was supposed to meet you over here. Told her how messed up you were when I told you. How you started immediately drafting a statement and an action plan. How you asked me to tell her to get together her bulls and come here so you can fill her in on the plans for dealing with this *monstrosity*.

I blow a smoke ring.

—Should be here soon. Her and her bulls. Fury and that bunch. Ready to hear how the Society is going to start changing the status quo. Today.

I flick some ash on the floor.

—No. No status quo this time around for any of us. The Horde girl, she was already talking about investing in some guns. Bright kid, that girl. She sees the writing on the wall. Everyone's gonna have to pick a side. Especially seeing all the bodies I left lying around Queens. Not that I was trying to make a point or sign my work or anything, but Predo's gonna know I was there. Figure he's already got his people arming up and closing the gates.

I wave some smoke from between us.

—No filling that hole in, Terry. No sealing it up like it was never there. It's there. And whether I walk out of here or not, too many people know now. I got no idea if the truth wants to be free, but it's out of the cage. And it's gonna kill some people. Anyway. You told me once there was a war coming. Looks like it's here.

I scratch my chin.

—So. You want to call those tough boys and Hurley into the room and make a mess of me and try to get me to change my tune when Lydia gets here?

I point at the door.

—Or you want me to get lost so you can start making a plan to change the world?

He looks around the room, a man suddenly across a border, not sure how he got there. Then he nods. Claps his hands once. Stands.

—Yeah. OK. You better take off.

He bounces his head up and down.

—Yeah, man. Brave new world. Brave new world. Change. Embrace it or get swept aside. That's the, you know, the deal. Like a wave, change is. This one, this one will be like a tsunami. And I think I need to have some alone time to get my balance for this.

He points at the door.

—Yeah, you do your thing, Joe. Probably better you're not here for this. I need to do some clear thinking. Look at myself in an unadorned light and come up with some truth.

I drop my smoke, grind it on the floor.

—Fine. You change your mind and want your boys to kill me, you got between here to the front door.

He reaches for me.

—You know, man, I'm just wondering. I'm just wondering if I shouldn't thank you for this. This is, you know, this is a unique opportunity for us all. And I'm not sure I shouldn't thank you for bringing it on.

He squeezes my shoulder.

—But you're gonna die for it, Joe. Not tonight. But, you know, pretty soon.

He lets go of me.

—As soon as someone has a second to spare, they're going to kill you.

I head out.

—Your hand is shaking again, Terry.

—An' how was it, Joe? All knitted up between the two a yas?

I stop on the stoop to light a fresh one.

—Well, you know how it is with old pals, Hurley. You have your fights and your disagreements, but in the end, you're too far under each other's skin to really hold a grudge.

—Glad ta hear it, Joe, glad to hear it.

He takes my gun, knuckles and razor from a pocket.

—An will ya be needin' dese?

I take them from his hands.

—Thanks. Hate to need them and be caught without.

I go down the steps.

—Keep the welcome mat out. Sounds like Lydia and some of her girls are coming by.

He raises a thick finger.

—Dem ladies, ya know dey don't like ta be called girls.

—So I hear. So I hear.

—Take care den, Joe.

—Thanks. And a piece of advice for you, if you like.

—Sure, an' why not?

—Think about rolling up your trouser.

—An why would dat be?

I walk down the street, trailing smoke.

—What I hear, there's high water on the way. And everyone's gonna get wet.

How you get what you want is, you make sure no one knows what it is you want.

Now, the world full of new hazards, everyone charting new courses to avoid collisions that are inevitable, I give in.

Pulled, I go west. To where forces draw me.

I have time now.

To take what I want.

But a new gravity catches me on Eighth Avenue. Catches me and smashes me down and drops me in an alley with my back to a wall and my ass in a pile of trash.

It bears down, rage distilled.

And stops, hovering over my head.

I cough up some of my own blood and spit it at his polished shoes.

—Christ, Predo, don't you have more to keep you busy right now?

The two enforcers make a move toward me, and something comes out of Predo's throat that makes them stand down and hang back at the mouth of the alley by the car that Predo burst out of to grab me and throw me into this pile of garbage.

I give him a look.

—Did you just growl?

He stands, rigid, sweep of bangs hanging over his lowered forehead, drops of my blood falling from the knuckles of one of his black leather-wrapped fists.

—I have no end of things to keep me busy, Pitt. No end of worries and concerns.

He bares his teeth.

—On the best of nights, I have an endless list of tasks that must be accomplished. And with each following sunset, it is replenished. And now.

He draws a finger across his forehead, pushing his bangs aside, leaving a smear of my blood on his skin.

—That list will be torn to bits. Rendered irrelevant. Those concerns and details relating to the security of the Coalition must now be cast aside for a matter more pressing. Wartime policy.

His head snaps back and he looks at the night sky above the alley.

—Do you know what concerns me most, Pitt?

I put a hand out and brace myself against a Dumpster and get myself to my feet, trying to figure what hurts me most.

—Got me. The health of your portfolio?

He points at the sky.

—Satellites. Antennae. Wireless signals.

He looks at the ground, points at the concrete.

—Fiber optics.

He looks at me.

—The wealth of data and information around us, that is what concerns me. The ease with which it is collected and transmitted. But most of all, Pitt, I am thinking about cellphones. And their little cameras.

He takes a step toward me, oblivious to a bottle underfoot and the glass that scatters about when it explodes.

—I am thinking of war between the Clans. Now. In an age when children scamper about with digital cameras in hand to snap pictures of their nannies sneaking drinks from the liquor cabinet. I am thinking about how long it will take before there is a visible confrontation between opposing Clan members. I am thinking of photographs and video of such an encounter, of men and women fatally shot, but still fighting, uploaded to the Internet. Aired on cable news. Analyzed by law enforcement and the military.

He takes another step, the shards of glass ground to powder.

—I am thinking of the brink. The final precipice I have used my influence and resources to steer us away from time and again for decades. I am thinking of the abyss we can all now clearly see between our feet as we stand at that brink with only our heels on the final edge of land.

He stops taking steps.

—Yes. I do have more to keep me busy. I have thousands of people, a way of life that goes back centuries, a culture threatened with extinction by self-immolation, I have all that to tend to and attempt to preserve. But none of it, I assure you, is so pressing that I cannot spare the moment it will take to kill the childish mercenary covered in years of blood who has pushed us all here because he caught sight of where his food comes from and he doesn't like the way the ranchers treat the cattle.

His fingers flex.

Keeper of secrets. Master of spies and murder.

Fed on infants' blood.

If he gets his hands on me, my bones will shatter like rotted wood. My flesh will tear. And my blood will wash across the alley like dirty water.

He's old and strong and fast and I cannot beat him.

But I don't care to die easily at his hands.

My hand flicks beneath the tail of my jacket and the gun appears in it like a magic trick. I raise my arm, inhaling, and in the space between inhaling and exhaling, everyone and everything in the alley frozen in that instant, I pull the trigger, the gun aimed at his face.

A drop of blood hanging from my eyebrow falls into my eye.

I blink.

And when I open my eye he is in front of me, the bullet meant for him has put a hole in the brick of the alley wall. His hand slaps mine down and away, the gun flying.

But I'm OK with that. That's OK by me. Because I may not have the gun anymore, but I do have the straight razor in my other hand. And he's close enough now for me to use it.

I cut, the blade cleaving the space between us, flaring in the shifting light cast by a TV in one of the windows overhead, arcing at his throat.

And then the razor isn't in my hand.

I flinch, looking for it between Predo's fingers, expecting to feel it across my own neck.

Down the alley, the brief flash of light on the straight razor's blade is echoed in twin blurs of white passing in front of the enforcers, leaving behind matched headless corpses, wavering before the final fall.

—You're in the wrong place to be settling your disputes.

The skeleton wrapped in its white shroud is next to us.

It places the blade of the razor under my chin.

—You should know that, Simon.

I don't move, not even to lodge my usual objection to being called by my real name.

Keeping the razor as close to the end of my life as possible, it turns its sunken eyes on Predo.

—You. Your Clan observes treaties and laws. Rules of behavior modeled on the ones those sheep out there follow. To humor you once, we looked at a line you drew on a map. We agreed it would be a very bad idea for any of you to cross that line. And here you are. On the wrong side of your line.

Predo licks his lips.

—I am a representative of the Coalition.

The skeleton shakes its head.

—You're a policeman outside his jurisdiction. You're where you don't belong.

The skeleton pushes his face close to Predo's.

—You're not Enclave.

He lifts the blade, forcing my chin higher.

—This one, what he is can be disputed.

The razor folds away from my skin.

The skeleton shows it to Predo.

—But you are meat. Ignorant and unclean and in need of purging.

Predo sweats.

—Killing me will be considered an act of utmost aggression.

The skeleton coughs laughter.

—Yes. And then? Will your Coalition send more of those to threaten us?

It waves a hand at the two headless corpses being loaded into the trunk of the car by another skeleton.

It shakes its head.

—Killing you would be a mercy. But there will be none of that for you tonight.

It points at the car.

—Go on.

Predo backs away, watching my eye.

—A final word, Pitt.

He smooths the length of his tie.

—Do you know you've tipped your hand?

I don't move.

Predo stops, hand on the open door of his car.

—I still don't know what it is you're after.

He waves an arm, taking in the neighborhood.

—But I know where it is.

He drops the arm.

—You'll be dead soon.

He gets into the car.

—But I'll be certain to find what it is you value so much. Before you die.

The door closes, the engine hums to life, and the car rolls away onto Eighth, not at all burdened by the dead it carries.

I look at the skeleton.

—Do I know you?

He offers me the razor.

—We've met, Simon.

I take the blade from his desiccated hand.

—Yeah, I wasn't sure, you guys all look alike to me.

I drop the razor in my pocket and take out a smoke.

—But seeing as you've met me, you maybe know my name's Joe.

The other skeleton joins us. This one, he's less of a skeleton than his boss, but he's on his way. All of them, all Enclave, they're all a bunch of withered tendon and bone held together by bleached skin. No surprise, that's what happens when you spend all your time starving yourself.

The first one shakes his head, looking like the gesture might snap his twig neck.

—Your name is what Daniel said your name is. Simon.

I walk a few steps, kick some garbage aside and find my gun.

—Daniel's dead.

He coughs that laugh of his.

—So you say, Simon. So you say.

He points at the mouth of the alley.

—You're wanted.

He starts to walk, I follow.

What's the point of running? If they want to, these guys can just pull my legs off and carry me.

Besides, they'll be taking me where I was headed in the first place.

It's not easy, but if you close your eyes, you can remember a time before the Meatpacking District became a vomitorium for clubbers and people with too much fucking money to spend on dinner for two anyplace that doesn't have a six-month waiting list for a reservation. A time when the cobbles here weren't quaint, when they were walked by tranny hookers and teenage hustlers, and cruised by limos looking for rough trade. 'Course the Enclave settled in their warehouse over here even before that scene. They settled here when those cobbles drained the blood of livestock, and white coats and meat hooks were the only fashion statements being made.

Still, the crowds waiting in line to get into the after-hours joints that are just now opening their doors are full of enough clowned posers that the all-white look the Enclave sport doesn't raise an eyebrow as we cut down Little West Twelfth to the final block before the water. Maybe a few club kids watch as we climb the steps to the loading dock and the door slides open to let us in, but none of them scurry over to find out what the scene inside is like. They know it's not for them. They can read it. The total lack of graffiti on the place, the silence, that chill that rises from it, the scraps of street rumor that adhere to it.

Bad shit goes down in there.

They know it. They feel it. So they stay in line like good little robots and wait their turn to flash a fake ID at the doorman so they can go inside some carefully padded pleasure dome and pretend they're living on the edge for a few hours.

Inside the Enclave warehouse, it's all edge.

A hundred-odd fanatics, weaning themselves from the blood the Vyrus demands, pushing their metabolisms to the crazed point Amanda Horde described, when memory T cells will stop reminding their own immune systems what not to attack.

The Vyrus, pushed to starvation, jacks their nervous systems. Desperate, it hammers on them to feed. At the edge of death, it empties its hosts of all resources, strengthening them for the kill.

Strong, fast, impervious to pain; blow a limb off one and they'll pick it up to beat you to death with it.

They vibrate with insanity.

That's what the kids on the street feel.

I feel it too. It goes to my guts, the madness in this place. The clattering of their bones striking one another as they endlessly spar, honing killing skills. The numb and complete silence that falls when they meditate on the Vyrus, focusing their wills to resist its hunger. The whisper of dry lips and tongues when they break their fasts and sip spoonfuls of blood to appease the Vyrus.

The fasting, it's not a rejection of the Vyrus' hunger, it's a supplication.

They are not its enemy. They are its acolytes.

Suggest to one of them that the Vyrus is a virus, an earthly thing, and they'll laugh in your face. Or chew it off.

Heresy is something they take pretty seriously around here. And rejecting the Vyrus as a supernatural agency of redemption is about as heretical as it gets for these guys.

All they want, all they starve for, is to be like the Vyrus, to let it gradually feed on them, creep into their bones and tissue, and transform them into something other, something that will stay in this world, while being entirely of another.

Fanatics to the ground, when they've found one who can complete that transformation, and he's taught the others to do the same, they think they'll become immune to sun and all the weapons of this world. And then, like all true believers, they'll go out and kill everyone not just like them.

It's weird shit.

I don't follow it.

And I don't like coming here.

But I used to be welcome all the same. The old boss, he had it in his head I was really one of them, that I just didn't know it yet.

But he died.

Daniel. Old man. Crazy old man.

I stop thinking about how he died, how the weight of his corpse was nothing in my arms, I put it away where you keep the things you don't want to think about. That place, it's goddamn crowded at this point.

I put it away so I can focus on the Enclave, mind myself so I don't end up dead.

The two that brought me inside leave me as soon as the door slides shut behind us and darkness' cover drops. I can hear more of them around me, breathing, barely breathing, meditating. I can hear others softly grunting, the whip of their limbs through space, the crack as they strike one another, a splinter of bones. I can smell their decaying flesh and the special taint of starving Vyrus that clings to them.

My pupils open, gathering light from candles scattered across the huge space. It looks the same as the last time I saw it. I figured that would be the very last time I'd see it at all. The last time I'd see it before I came back to burn it down.

But the best laid plans of mice and men and all that.

I had to come back without a torch.

I want to see my girl, after all.

—Simon.

I look at him, coming out of the gloom, wrapped in white like the other Enclave.

I nod.

—Nice suit.

He stops ten feet from me, fingers a lapel of the spotless white three-piece.

—Yeah-huh, right?

He tilts his head at the lines of squatting Enclave deep in meditation. Beyond them others spar, flickering, frozen for an occasional heartbeat as they study the other's defense, looking for a weakness before striking again.

—Like, I had no problem with the color scheme and all, but there was no way I was gonna be sporting a toga or a shawl or something.

I'm not paying attention to him, I'm paying attention to the others, watching them as my pupils widen and take in more light and the warehouse stretches and I see how many of them there are. More than a hundred. Many more. Twice that. At least.

I look at him.

He nods.

—Oh yeah, man, I been busy.

—Truth to an old friend, it ain't easy. This shit ain't easy at all. Like, let me tell you, man, that meditation shit, that is some boring-ass shit. Just sitting there, trying to get into the Vyrus and all that. And the sparring. At first I was so down with that. I wanted to get up and go kung fu. But that shit is hard work. And it fucking hurts, man. Enclave, there's no such thing as a pulled punch with Enclave. You have to, what you have to do is, here, let me show you. Punch me as hard as you can.

He comes close, crossing the small chamber he led me to in the lofts above the warehouse floor.

—Seriously, man, just hit me as hard as you can.

I look at the two Enclave sitting on the floor just outside the open door.

He waves a hand.

—No, man, don't worry about them, they won't do shit I don't tell them to do. They're cool. Just take a poke at me. You know you want to.

—Count, why the fuck would I hit you when you're expecting it?

He shakes his head.

—Same old Joe Pitt, no fun at all. Here I am, full of all this new knowledge, all these new skills, changed and wanting to share, and there you are, grumpy as ever, a total fucking drag.

He does a karate kick, pummeling the air with one of his bare feet, the one with the twisted bones jutting from it, the one I mangled for him.

He lowers the foot and smiles.

—But it's cool, it's cool. All I'm trying to do is say that this shit ain't easy. Being Enclave. I mean, sure, I understand that the Vyrus chooses you for this shit. You're either Enclave or you're not, that's what your boy Daniel used to say, yeah? Shit, but, I wouldn't even be here if that wasn't the case. Come to it, you wouldn't be here if that wasn't the case. Daniel hadn't given us both the Enclave stamp of approval, we couldn't come into this place except to get executed. But the point I'm weaving around here is, even if the Vyrus says you're Enclave, this shit is still damn tough. Like, I know this may come as a shock considering what you think of me, but like this shit is transformative. Really transformative.

He slaps a fist into his palm.

—OK, and I know that sounds redundant. Sure, like, because if the Vyrus doesn't transform you in the first place, then what the hell? But check it. 'Cause the Vyrus doesn't make you a different person. Yeah? So like me, I didn't suddenly stop being a spoiled-rotten, rich brat just because I needed to drink blood to live. More like, the fact I was already so self-absorbed just made it easier for me to make the transition. Like the rich already live off the fat of the land, so why not the blood as well, yeah? So, but, this stuff, to get it, to really get it, you have to work at it. Well, talk about new concepts for me. Work? Whoa! Not on my agenda.

He leans in.

—But being in charge here after Daniel cacked it, that *was* on my agenda.

He pushes his eyebrows way up.

—And that meant playing a role. Like, putting on the grave face, being all somber and talking in portentous sentences and shit, like so many of these guys do. It meant squatting in lines and pretending to think about the Vyrus. It meant learning that if someone was gonna swing at you, and really try to punch your rib cage out of your chest, that you needed to learn how to go with the punch.

He stretches his arms at me and points with both index fingers.

—Which you would have got to see I can do now if you'd taken a shot like I asked, man.

He drops his arms.

—But the point is, you start to do all that, even if it's a total front, even if you've made a life out of doing just enough work to get by, even if all you're really thinking about is how cool it's gonna be when you're in charge and get to call all the shots and cut this hard shit from the activities list, you keep doing it for all the wrong reasons, and it doesn't fucking matter. Because, dude, you are doing it.

He spreads his arms.

—I'm saying, *Look at me, man*.

I look at him. White skin to match the suit. Bald. His once skinny frame, now a coat hanger for the designer threads.

He claps.

—I was trying, I was trying to front, and the whole time, what was really happening was I was *becoming,* man. I'm saying, to play the role, I had starve the Vyrus, yeah? And that required some effort. So next thing, I'm in the meditation down there, and I'm really thinking about it. And all that shit I learned about it before, when I was studying it from the scientific angle, using my med-school chops to try and break it down, all that started to fade.

He puts his hands on his head.

—'Cause I'm telling you, if this shit can really change an asshole like me, then it is not of this earth. Hear what I'm saying?

His hands shoot over his head.

—I am a believer, man! I am in! And I love it!

He cocks a grin.

—And, Joe, all our shit, all our background and complication and all that shit, I am over it.

He reaches for me.

—And I want you to join us, man!

I punch him.

And he rolls with it. Falls away from the blow, tumbles backward, and comes to his feet still grinning, and points at me.

—I love you, man!

He comes at me faster than I can do anything about and wraps his arms around me.

—I love you, Joe Pitt!

Put a crazy man in an asylum, then lay your money on the odds he gets worse. Closest thing to a sure bet.

—It's not like I'm just filled with crazy Vyrus-love and I want everyone to feel it, yeah? This is about something more tangible. Take a look and see if you get it.

We stand at the rail of the lofts, looking down at the pairs sparring in the middle of a circle of kneeling Enclave.

I look at them. I don't say anything.

Why bother? You want to know what's on the Count's mind, you wait for him to inhale before he blows the next load of words at you.

—OK, so you're looking. And you're seeing it. There's way more of us.

He shows me five fingers, then shows me five more.

—We're doubling in size. It's crazy in here, all the new Enclave. We can barely find room for the new believers. Even with fasting as our primary tenet, we still have problems getting enough blood in here.

He points at a far corner where an Enclave has pulled the cover from a large sewage drain and another drops a sagging body down the exposed hole.

—Fast as we can drain one and toss it down there, we need another. Growth comes with costs, man. I learned that in school.

He shakes his head.

—But that's not the point, I'm getting off it again, the point. The point is all these new people we're getting in. This new belief and energy. These people who need something in their lives, what we can give them.

I find a crack to fit a word in.

—Thought the Vyrus did the choosing and the giving.

He looks around.

—Well, yeah, man, sure. But situations, they evolve. So in the past it was Daniel who saw when someone was Enclave or not, now someone else has to fill that role.

I look at him.

He gives a modest head shake.

—Hey, I didn't nominate myself. But like I said, I'm a changed dude, and I got some credibility around here. And, OK, I don't want to dis the big man's memory, and I'm not, but I'm saying that maybe in Daniel's case that when he was looking for the Enclave in someone and there was a shade of doubt, maybe he gave them a pass. And maybe me, maybe I'm more inclusive. Like I want these people to have what they need. Belief, change, newness. Transmutational experiences like mine.

He holds a hand parallel to the ground and waggles it.

—And maybe, OK, maybe some around here don't feel this is the way.

He makes a fist and pops his thumb out of it and at the sky.

—But there's more that do. Daniel, he was the man forever, and he was loved, still is, but he was on the conservative side. A lot of these brothers and sisters, they've been waiting to grow, they want change in their lifetimes. Sure they want to meditate and learn the nature of the Vyrus, but they also want to be here when it's time for the purge. When the world is remade to the Vyrus. They don't want to miss out. And I am down with that. It's a matter of how you come at your faith. I come at it like we need to spread it, we need to make it happen, that's what the Vyrus wants from us, that's why it makes us feeders, aggressors. It wants us to be aggressive. Yeah? So I say to these guys, *Let's fucking aggress, man*!

He points at the street door.

—Action like that tonight? Sending those hitters out to pick you up, giving them a weapons-free license to take care of any shit out there? That wouldn't have happened with Daniel. And they like that new attitude in here. They like that we stepped out and took care of some business on our own doorstep.

I raise a finger.

He bobs his head.

—Yeah, yeah, man, questions. Fire 'em up.

—Just wondering how you got wind of me.

—Easy, man. Had an eye out for you the whole last year. You hit downtown, that news got to me in a hurry.

I grind my teeth.

—Fucking Philip.

—Yeah, man, fucking Phil. That guy, again, there's a dude Daniel would never have had anything to do with, but me, having had a history with him, I was prepared to make use of his eyes on the street. He saw you, gave me a call. After that.

He leans his arms on the rail.

—Well shit, Joe, after that I knew it was a matter of time before you crossed no-man's-land to come here. Only thing I had trouble with was figuring out why it was taking you so long.

I watch another body go down the hole.

—I had some things to do.

—Hey, don't we all?

He puts a hot, dry hand on mine.

—But here you are, man. And that's good. That's good. That's really good.

I pull my hand away.

—How's that, Count?

He scoots closer, smiles.

—Wanting you to come inside with us, man, that's not just about spreading the joy. Like I said, yeah? Like, Daniel fingered you as Enclave. That means something. That's credibility. So, things are going on here. Like.

He frowns.

—Like, sure, most of us are down with expansion, down with action, down with bringing on the purge. Like, in my interpretation of everything, maybe the final transmutation we're supposed to make, maybe that's already happened. Maybe that's not supposed to be literal and physical like they've been thinking, maybe it's more a spiritual thing. And if that's the case, well, man, like I said, *I've* made that transmutation and then some.

He purses his lips.

—It's a puzzler, and I don't want to sound full of myself, but I may just be the Vyrus messiah.

He shakes his head.

—I don't know for sure. Have to meditate on that shit some more. Anyhoo.

He snaps his fingers.

—Some others, a few, they don't believe in a need for speed, they think we're going too fast. They think Daniel would disapprove. And that, that just causes all kinds of fucking problems. So having a guy like you, with Daniel-cred behind him, that's always a help. In this case, you can help big-time with a particular problem. But there's more to it. Like that's a surprise in our world, yeah?

He strokes his bald scalp, watching as one of the sparring Enclave below has his jaw shattered.

—These guys, when they go out as a force, once they start smelling the blood out there, they could go a little over the top. And that's not the point. We don't want a bunch of random spastics launching themselves into crowds and going off like bombs, rending folks limb from limb till the SWAT bullets take them down. The whole point is, this is a crusade; when Enclave kill, it's not like a retribution thing, it's a cleansing. And not just cleansing the world, but cleansing the people who get killed. So it needs to have some order to it. So to keep the warriors that go out in line, Joe.

He sidles very close.

—I'm gonna need a field general.

I poke the barrel of my gun into his ribs.

He looks at it.

I look at him.

And I ask the only thing that matters.

—Is she alive?

He looks up, rolls his eyes.

—*Is she alive?* Dude, have you been listening to me at all?

The hand of one of his bodyguards whisks between us and takes the gun from me.

The Count bugs his eyes.

—Whoops! Where'd that go?

He laughs.

—Yeah, so anyway, dude. *Is she alive?* Like, that's the whole point here. The tension I'm talking about. Old-school attitudes versus new-school attitudes.

He looks at me.

I look back.

He sighs.

—No comprehension at all, huh?

He takes my arm.

—Come here.

He pulls me to the corridor that runs the length of the loft, between rows of cubicles.

—The rest of this shit, the field-general gig and all that, we'll sort that out later. For now.

He points at the end of the corridor where four Enclave stand outside a closed door.

—For now, you go have your reunion.

He gives me a shove in the back.

—Do me a favor while you're at it and try and talk some sense into fucking Joan of Arc for me, will ya?

He turns, heads down the stairs to the floor below.

I look at the door.

Legs like stilts, holding me wobbly ten feet above the ground, I walk to the end of the hall.

These Enclave are a little on the beefy side. Looking like maybe they've only been in a concentration camp one year instead of five. They stand back from the door, one of them knocking before pushing it open.

I go in.

She's sitting on the floor, holding a little cup in her left hand, eyes gliding over the handwritten pages of a book lying open in her lap.

Her eyes stop moving.

Her finger marks a spot on the page.

And she looks up.

She's sitting on the floor, like the last time I saw her, but everything else is different. Then she'd just got over being about to die. Withered and hollowed out by AIDS and the chemo they'd pumped into her, red hair falling out in fistfuls. A fading ghost.

And look at her now.

All bones and alabaster skin, freckles bleached away, hairless.

Vibrant.

She looks back down at her book.

—Hey, Joe. Come to try and kill me again?

—It was hard. Of course. And I thought I was crazy. I thought they were all my hallucinations. This whole place. Like it was the pain medication. Then I thought, and it was probably all the white clothes they wear, I thought that maybe I was dead. And this was like a test or something. It took a long time.

She flips a couple pages in her book.

—That was why they started paying attention to me. Because I went so long before I tried it.

She shakes her head.

—Blood.

She bites her lower lip.

—It's funny to think how long I waited. 'Cause I was never religious. But I thought, *What if the second I try the blood I get sent to hell?* It was too weird to be real. But whatever I was thinking, they thought I was special, for fasting so long right after infection. And then I couldn't hold off anymore. I'd smell it when they all broke fast. And it smelled so damn good. And then I thought, *This is bullshit. This isn't real. I'm on a morphine drip and I'm never waking up and I'm gonna try some of that. I'm not going to hell.* And I tried it.

She shakes her head.

—And after that, I didn't care if I went to hell.

She looks into the cup in her left hand, the few tablespoonfuls of blood it bears.

—Do you think we're going to hell, Joe?

I take a drag, think about Queens.

—Yeah, seems that way to me.

She sighs.

—Yeah. I think maybe we are too.

She looks up.

—He thought about you. Daniel did.

—I doubt that.

—No, he did, a lot.

She flips a couple pages in the book, reads.

—*Simon. Again. An endless distraction, that young man. Adding up the time I've wasted trying to drill some kind of sense into his head. Pointless. No. Its not pointless. Simply tiring. My own shortcomings again. Impatient. Who was it that said it was my greatest weakness? Someone dead now. It could be the reason I keep trying with Simon is that it gives me an excuse to talk occasionally with someone different than the ones I've been talking to for so long. The Vyrus may be endlessly fascinating in and of itself, but talking about it all the time is boring as hell. Something interesting today. I feel hungry. Odd.*

She flips more pages.

—That's toward the end of this one. The last one. But there's lots more.

She points at the bracket-mounted shelves that cover two walls of the cubicle, every inch of every shelf lined with journals, notebooks, diaries.

—Lots more. I started just pulling them at random. Then I pulled one from toward the end and saw your name. Simon.

She nods at the door.

—A couple of them had used it when they were talking about you. So I knew who he meant. Also, the way he described you. Sullen. Childish. Temperamental. Funny. That all rang a bell. So I found the first one I could with your name.

She points at a red-spine notebook on the shelf.

—That one. From the late seventies.

She looks at me.

—How old are you?

I scuff the floor.

—Closing on fifty.

She nods.

—Funny. I'd never have picked you for the type to lie about your age.

I glance at the door.

—Look, baby, I want to get all caught up and all, but we should really think about getting out of this place as soon as possible.

She presses the tip of her index finger into the middle of her forehead and closes her eyes.

—You know what I hate?

She opens her eyes.

—What I hate is that I feel so stupid sometimes. I think about it. I think about you telling me you couldn't go out in the sun because of solar urticaria. That the blood bags and biohazard coolers were because you were an organ courier. That secret room in your basement.

She closes her eyes again.

—I think how it was so easy to convince you that I wouldn't fuck you because I didn't want to give you HIV. How you never argued with me about it. Never said it was a risk you would take.

She knuckles her eyes, pressing away a couple stray tears.

—Fuck.

She wipes her fingers on her white skirt.

—I think about all that, and think about all I know now, and I think, *How could I have been so stupid? How didn't I see that he was a fucking vampire?*

She makes a fist and hits the floor.

—And I hate that. Like I should have figured this shit out. Like somehow I should have put all the pieces of your weirdness and our fucked-up relationship together, mixed them up, and spilled them out and they should have come up *vampire*. Like that isn't utterly insane.

I lower myself to one knee.

—Baby.

She jabs a finger at me.

—Don't! Don't you call me baby.

I reach, put a finger on the sole of her bare foot.

—Baby.

She presses her lips together.

—Damn it! Damn you. You fucker!

I squeeze her foot.

—Baby.

She slaps the floor.

—You absolute fucking fucker!

I squeeze her foot a little tighter.

—Baby, listen, I know I got a lot to answer for. I know I. I know. But this isn't the time. We need to go now. Because in case you hadn't noticed, you're living in a madhouse.

She's on her feet, standing over me.

—*In case I hadn't noticed?* I noticed, you son of a bitch, I noticed that you fucking left me in this madhouse!

I look up at her.

—I'm back for you now.

She claps her hands together three times, slowly.

—Hail the hero, returned to rescue the damsel.

I stare at her foot. Beyond pale. Nails covered in chipped red polish.

—Look. I know. I know this is. Hard. I. I never told you. I thought. You'd think I was crazy. And you'd run. Or. I'd do something to prove it. And you'd be more scared. And you'd run. And I'd never see you again. And.

I paw the floor, looking for some kind of traction for my words.

—And so I didn't tell you. And. But there's no time now because all hell is going to hit the streets and we need to get gone before it does. We need to.

I look at her, lift my shoulders, drop them.

She puts her hands on her hips.

—Does it bother you the Count was the one infected me?

I look around the room, anyplace where she isn't.

—Yeah.

—Yeah. Me too.

I let myself look at her, see the anger, look away.

—My blood probably would have killed you. It's special, the way it works. Only some can infect some others. I don't know.

—Yeah. I read some stuff like that in Daniel's diary. But I didn't say I wish you'd been the one to infect me. I just said I wished it wasn't that prick.

I pull the smokes from my pocket, stare at the package.

—I know. I know this isn't what you wanted. To live like this. To be infected at all. I know. I tried to protect you from. I. I'm. Shit.

—You.

Half of an ugly laugh escapes her.

—You fucking idiot.

Her fist hits the side of my neck and I go down and my skull bounces off the floor.

—You think this bothers me?

She picks up the cup of blood.

—You actually think this bothers me?

She puts the cup to her lips and drains it.

—I was dying, Joe. I was really dying. It hurt so bad. And I was so scared. And I wanted to live. I prayed. I swore that if I could live I'd do anything. If I could just fucking live. If the pain would go away and I could not be scared and I could live. Anything. I swore I'd do anything.

She squats in front of me, grabs my chin.

—And I'm alive.

She forces my face up, my eyes to hers.

—And I don't ever want to die. I want to live forever, Joe. And I never want to be scared like that again.

She holds the cup in front of my face.

—And if this is what it takes, well, I swore I'd do anything.

She lets go of my face and rises.

I look at the pack of smokes I've crushed in my hand. I tear it open and pick a broken Lucky from the shreds. I put it between my lips. Take it out. Put it back. And take it out again.

—I didn't know.

She leans into the wall of books, presses her face into them.

—Joe. Why would you? How could you? If it's crazy for me to feel stupid for not knowing what you are, it's just as crazy for you to feel shitty for not knowing I'd want to be the same thing if it could save me. It's stupid. It's all crazy and stupid.

She looks at me.

—And it could get worse.

She splays her hands over several of the books.

—He had doubts, you know. He had doubts about what the Vyrus is. He had doubts about it all. And he was starting to think, toward the end, he was starting to think that the world didn't need to be remade in the image of the Vyrus, made so there are only Enclave. He had doubts. But that *asshole*. He's taking what Daniel believed, what was passed down for so long, and he's making it ugly and mean and dangerous.

I shake my head.

—You never met Daniel. You don't know what dangerous is.

She pulls one of the books down and opens it.

—He wanted a crusade. Of some kind. I know that. But he had doubts.

I get up.

—Baby, we should really.

She snaps the book closed.

—The Count, he doesn't have a doubt in his empty head. He's narrow and spoiled and, Joe, he's such a prick. And he's halfway to sending those fanatics of his into the streets to start it. All he needs is something to tilt out of balance and he'll do it. Then what? People will be killed. And this place.

She holds out her arms.

—It'll be destroyed.

She slides the book back onto the shelf.

—I don't want it destroyed. I don't want people killed. I don't want my friends here killed. I don't want to be killed, Joe.

She faces me.

—I just came back to life. I don't want to die.

She folds her arms.

—And some of them, they believe in me. Because I was the last Enclave Daniel found, they think I'm special. And because I fasted so long. And because I'm so fucking tough. Because I am tough. I can fast longer than anyone in here. I can take the pain. I can take the cravings and the cramps. I can go deep into the Vyrus and let it deep into me before I have to feed again. So thanks, AIDS and chemo, thanks for teaching me how to be tough. Because of that, there are enough Enclave who believe in me so that the Count can't just start a holy war whenever he wants.

I nod, shake my head, nod. I look up and down.

—Baby, that, all that, it doesn't. Matter anymore. What the Count wants, what these fuckers are all trying to get, power, whatever, it doesn't matter anymore. It's all going to hell no matter what they do now. And.

I look at her, I try to cross the room to her.

And stay where I am.

—I could. I don't know. If I had a chance, the things I did, or didn't do, I could make it up to you. I could. I want. Just.

I reach.

—Just come with me. Just. Now. Come with me.

A sound comes out of her, the kind of sound she made when she was dying in the hospital.

—Years. Years of my life. Years while I was *dying*. I spent them with you. And you, you weren't *who* you said you were. You weren't *what* you said you were. You. You. You.

Tendons jump in her neck.

—The rest of it. I could go! This place, I could leave this place. This life, I could live it with you. I could.

She grits her teeth.

—But you *lied* to me so much.

Drops are falling around her feet.

—I know what you are now.

Her fists clench, and a whiter shade shows at her knuckles.

—But I don't know who you are.

She points at the floor.

—Goddamn you, Joe Pitt. Goddamn you.

She charges me, slamming me into the wall, books raining down around us.

—Goddamn you, I don't know who you are.

I could say I struggle with that one, but it's not really a struggle. When there's only one thing to say, you just say it.

—Baby, I'm just the guy who loves you. Same as always.

She closes her eyes, leans her forehead against my chest, my heart stops beating.

—Well that counts for something, Joe.

She opens her eyes and looks up at me.

—But not enough.

She pushes away.

—Not now.

She kneels and starts to pick up the books.

—You better go.

I watch her, sorting the books, finding their places on the shelves, reordering Daniel's thoughts.

I think about the streets.

Piled high with bodies.

Back rooms crammed with them. Trucks hauling away the dead. I think about Coalition and Society and Hood and Cure at one another's throats. I think about it spreading to Brooklyn and the Bronx. I think about hunting parties of Van Helsings drawn by the chaos. And then organized hunting parities of soldiers and police.

I think about the future.

You can't hide from it. Dig a hole of your own, climb in, pull the dirt in over you, and the future will burrow up beneath you and pull you deeper.

You can't hide from the future.

But like most everything else, if you hate it enough, you can kill it.

And I hate it plenty right now.

I take off my jacket and go through the pockets, moving my few possessions to my pants.

—Yeah, I got to go.

She doesn't look away from the books.

—Yeah.

I hold out the jacket, the one she gave me on a fake birthday years ago.

—Hang onto this for me?

She looks at it.

—Seen better days.

I snap my Zippo open.

—I still like it.

She takes the jacket from me.

I light up.

—And I'll be back to get it.

She shakes her head.

—Joe, you shouldn't bother.

I blow smoke.

—Baby, you don't want me now, I'll go. But I'm coming back.

She shakes her head again.

—Joe.

Smoke gets in my eye, blinding me for an instant.

—Evie. I started a war so I could see you.

I rub the smoke from my eye.

—You being pissed at me isn't gonna keep me away.

She almost smiles. But doesn't, not really.

Instead she tears some of the lining from inside the jacket.

—Come here.

I go there.

She reaches up and ties the strip of black cloth so that it covers my dead eye.

—Now, go *Arrghh*.

—Arrghh.

She nods.

—There. You're a pirate.

And she kisses me.

Bitter.

But a kiss all the same.

—Whoa, whoa, that's it, you're just walking out?

I stop walking out and look at the Count.

—You want to make something of it, now's the time.

He points up at the lofts.

—After all the time you spent up there with her nibs, I thought you might have got her to see some realities.

I look up there.

—She sees the realities.

I shrug.

—She just doesn't like them.

He frowns.

—Then why doesn't she just get out?

I adjust the patch she put over my dead eye.

—Near as I can figure it, she thinks you're a psycho and she wants to stick around to make sure you don't do anything too fucked up.

He flexes his toes. One of the bones jutting from his bad foot scrapes the concrete floor.

—Make sure I don't do anything *too fucked up*. Bitch is begging to see some fucked-up shit she don't get out of my face in here.

I look at that ruined foot.

—Know what I think every time I see you, Count?

He puts his hands on his hips.

—What's that?

I scratch my head.

—I think to myself, *Why the hell haven't I killed this asshole already?* And then I remember, *Oh yeah, there's no rush, I can always do it another time.*

He nods, cocks his head, cups a hand to his ear.

—Hear that? You hear that, man? That ticking sound? Know what that is?

He takes his hand from his ear and starts swinging it back and forth like a metronome.

—That's your time running out.

He slows his finger.

—Now, I don't know exactly how much is left on it, but it's close. See, you got exactly two uses to me. Once those are done, so's your time.

He holds up his other index finger.

—One, you crapped out on. I mean, why the fuck do you think you're here, man? That crazy bitch is your chick. If *you* can't talk some sense into her, then I don't know what. So that's Use Number One down the shitter.

He holds up another finger.

—Use Number Two is what I said before, about a field general. Which, from what attitude I'm getting here, is a job you're clearly not interested in.

—Always quick on the uptake, that's you.

His finger stops swinging.

—*Ding!*

He shakes his head.

—Time's up.

I find a cigarette.

—Is that the sound it makes when your time is up? *Ding?* Talk about an anticlimax.

—You should have just collected your chick and got out, man.

I put flame to cigarette.

—Count.

I drop my voice to a whisper.

—You might want to stop talking shit before it gets you in too deep.

He puts his face in mine.

—You can't take me, man. Not anymore. I'll have your heart in my hand and be chewing on it before you stop breathing.

—No doubt, no doubt. But let me tell you a secret.

I put my mouth next to his ear.

—That girl up there, she still loves me.

I lean back and nod.

—Yeah, hard to believe, huh?

I raise a hand.

—Now I'm not saying she's all weak-kneed about me, but she still has the feeling. I can tell.

His eyes flick at the lofts.

I take a drag and nod.

—That's right. You kill me, she's likely to stop just sitting up there keeping an eye on things. She might decide that this is the right time to come down here and settle some shit.

If he had eyebrows, they'd be pulled together.

—Doesn't matter. She's only got a handful behind her.

I tap my forehead.

—You sure of that?

Our eyes meet up.

—What I'm asking is, *You sure when push and shove go at it that you got your supporters all locked down?* You sure some of them might not go over to the other side if things came to the big chop-sockey in here? Mean, when the limbs start flying, there's no telling which way some people might jump. And saying you carry it off, what do you lose? Daniel, he was top dog here for how long? Ever hear about internecine bloodshed on his watch? How long after that before serious doubts are raised about the quality of your leadership, O chosen one? Speaking of which?

I tap his chest with my fingertip.

—I ever tell you about how Daniel was always hinting that I might be the right guy to follow him?

I look over at the Enclave away in the shadows.

—Some of these guys know. Maybe, here's an idea.

I point at the stairs to the lofts.

—Maybe I should stay. Might be cozy. Me and her up there, you down here.

I drop my smoke on the floor between us.

—Or maybe you should back the fuck off.

I grind the cigarette under my boot.

—Before you embarrass yourself in front of your people, making threats you're not gonna move on just now.

I turn away and start for the door.

—Don't lose the suit, Count, it's you.

He starts after me.

—Uh-uh. Hang up, toughguy. You don't get last words in this place.

He raises an arm, circles it over his head.

—This is my house. And there are rules. And you need to be schooled in one of them.

He raises his voice, the sounds of sparring dying as his words echo.

—Like, OK, you don't want to make the scene. You don't want to stay and add your name to mine. You don't want to lead the troops when they hit the streets. Basically, you just don't want to help me. OK, cool. I'd be lying if I said I was surprised. Like, I thought you'd take your girl with you, but I know she's changed and so maybe she doesn't do it for you anymore. OK. But leaving here, that's not a casual thing. You're either Enclave, or you're not.

You're either in here with us, or you're not. The open-door policy, that is closed. No in-and-out privileges anymore. No one gets their hand stamped with a big E and gets to come and go as they please.

I'm at the door.

He arm-bars me.

—Like you got banished once, down the sewer, and how you got out I do not know, but this time it's final. You go out, you don't come back.

He shakes his head.

—Not for her. Not for no reason. Gone. And how we settle our differences in here, the chick and me, that will happen without your help either way.

I scratch the back of my neck.

—The way I know that girl, anyone's gonna need help in here, it's gonna be you.

We stare.

And he blinks first.

Which is a relief to me and my handful of bluff.

The last of the clubbers are inside. Daylight's trying to catch me out.

What the fuck now?

A rat rattles some trash cans and I sniff the humid air and smell the rat and kick the cans aside and pick it up by its scruff.

—Hey, Joe, what's up?

—Phil.

I let him go.

—Funny place to find you.

—Well, just a coincidence. I happened to be in the area to conduct some business.

I put an arm over his shoulder.

—Strange you should mention this *business* that you were conducting. It seems someone ratted me to the Count.

He shivers with outrage.

—What? A rat? Who, Joe? Tell me who it is and I'll take care of it for ya.

I pat his arm.

—It's a nice thought, but I wouldn't want you to go jumping in the river with your neck tied to a sewer grate on my account.

He flinches.

—Um, yeah, that, that's not my style. Um, Joe?

—Yeah, Phil?

He puts his palms together.

—There something I can do to get this over with quick? Like, can I just run in front of a cab and take my lumps and we call it even? As opposed to you cutting off my nose and all, I mean.

I give him a little shake. No old ladies' purses fall out of his pants legs, which is a bit of a shock.

—Cut you? Not gonna happen.

He wipes his forehead.

—Honest? No cutting?

—No cutting.

He smiles, pats me on the chest.

—Ah, that's great, that's just great.

He grins, skips a couple times.

—Well ain't that a beautiful thing.

He plucks a cigarette from the pack I offer him, winks.

—Ya mind me askin' what ya been up to, Joe? Not that I'm being nosy, just that I'm always curious about what my friends are up to.

I light his cigarette for him.

—I've been getting into trouble, Phil.

He laughs.

—So the usual, huh?

—Yeah, the usual.

He swallows.

—Say, Joe, ya don't mind me sayin', you're acting kind of weird. Like, not cutting me and all. Makes a man think that maybe you're waiting to lower the boom on him.

He bites the tip of his tongue.

—You sure we're OK here?

I pat his shoulder.

—Yeah, we're OK. See, you got something I need, Philip.

He clutches his throat.

—Aw no, Joe, not that.

I shake my head, curl my arm around him again.

—Easy, easy. All I'm talking about is your big fucking mouth.

His hand covers his mouth.

—Joe, no, I swear, I never sold you out, not once never.

—You sold me out so many times, Phil, you should be paying me royalties.

He makes to talk again and my razor flips open. I hold it across his mouth.

—Just hush a minute and listen.

I smoke.

—I'm going away, Phil. I came back, and now I'm going away.

I tap the middle of his forehead.

—And I want you to make sure everyone knows it. See, I made a mistake coming back. There's nothing for me here. Nothing but trouble. And I don't swing the weight I used to. Can't take the heat. So I'm going away. Joe Pitt is out of play. Gone. Crossing the water and taking his chances. Anyone has a score to settle, they missed their shot. Color me gone, Phil.

I take him by the ear.

—'Cause the only thing that will bring me back is if I hear you didn't do as I said. I'll come back and we'll assume this position again. And I'll make your big mouth a whole lot bigger.

He starts to nod, scrapes his lips on the blade, freezes.

I shake my head.

—Now I'm gonna hit you.

He rolls his eyes.

I nod.

—I'm doing it to knock you out so you don't see where I head off to. Not so hard that I'll break your jaw or any teeth, but I'm gonna put you to sleep.

I fold the razor away.

He wipes his mouth.

—Jesus, Joe, I could just close my eyes.

I flick my butt away.

—Shut the fuck up, Phil, you're getting off easy.

He covers his eyes with his hands.

—If you say so. Just get it over with.

I cock my fist.

—Hey, Phil, is that your dealer?

He uncovers his eyes.

—Where, where?

I punch him in the face and break his jaw and a couple teeth and he's down.

I wipe his blood from my fingers as I walk to the middle of the street and look to the next block. I see what I want and head that way.

I keep my feet moving, my eyes forward, fighting the draw of the building behind me, a force that drags on me, pulling open a wound as I move farther away.

Figure it's life. Figure we all got one. Figure how you gamble yours is nobody else's nevermind.

She says she doesn't know who I am.

Well I can't help her on that score.

Figure the wound is just as raw whoever I am.

Figure I could have said more. Told her where I came from.

Who birthed me. What I was like when I was a kid. What school I dropped out of. My whole curriculum vitae.

Figure I could have gone over all the years we had together. Cut open every one. Told her what I was thinking and when. Why I told every lie. What they cost me to tell. What I hoped they were buying me.

Who's got time to waste in that? A catalogue of lies.

Bottom line.

You want something to be safe, you pay a price.

And that's the deal in the end. She's safer in there than she is out here.

In there, she's got people who got her back. Out here, she's only got me. And once Predo starts sniffing after what I'm here for, he'll find her. He'll smell her like my blood in the water, and go straight to her.

And I won't be able to stop him.

She's safe inside. Safer, anyway. And anything I could have said to talk her into leaving would just have dragged her into the middle of something out of all control.

But that doesn't change a fact.

Letting her tear loose leaves a wound.

That wound don't close. No reason it should.

Wound like that, if you want to not feel it, you better have something planned to keep your mind off the pain.

I come to the next block and kneel in the street and work my fingers into the slots at the edges of a manhole cover and pull it free.

I look down the hole, and I think about the other hole.

A war.

Such a thing, you got to be on one side or the other. You got to know what you want, or get caught in the flames.

I smoke, kick a bottle to the gutter, spit, and smoke some more.

Kill the future.

Save the lost.

Choose a side.

I start down the hole. Burying myself. Away from what I want. But close enough. Close enough to protect it.

Close enough to feel it.

Love above me, shuttered away, pulling, pulling me still.

A gravity that can't be broken.

No matter who I am.

extras

about the author

Charlie Huston is the author of the Henry Thompson trilogy, the Joe Pitt casebooks, and the Los Angeles Times bestseller The Shotgun Rule. He is also the writer of the relaunched Moon Knight comic book. He lives with his family in Los Angeles.

Find out more about Charlie and other Orbit authors by registering for the free monthly newsletter at www.orbitbooks.net

if you enjoyed
EVERY LAST DROP

look out for

THE DEVIL YOU KNOW

by
Mike Carey

Normally I wear a Tsarist army greatcoat – the kind that sometimes gets called a paletot – with pockets sewn in for my tin
whistle, my notebook, a dagger and a chalice. Today I'd gone for
a green tuxedo with a fake wilting flower in the buttonhole, pink
patent-leather shoes and a painted-on moustache in the style of
Groucho Marx. From Bunhill Fields in the east I rode out
across London – the place of my strength. I have to admit,
though, that 'strong' wasn't exactly how I was feeling: when you
look like a pistachio-ice-cream sundae, it's no easy thing to hang
tough.

The economic geography of London has changed a lot in the
last few years, but Hampstead is always Hampstead. And on
this cold November afternoon, atoning for sins I couldn't even
count and probably looking about as cheerful as a *tricoteuse*

being told that the day's executions have been cancelled due to bad weather, Hampstead was where I was headed.

Number 17, Grosvenor Terrace, to be more precise: an unassuming little early-Victorian masterpiece knocked off by Sir Charles Barry in his lunch hours while he was doing the Reform Club. It's in the books, like it or not: the great man would moonlight for a grand in hand and borrow his materials from whatever else he was doing at the time. You can find his illegitimate architectural progeny everywhere from Ladbroke Grove to Highgate, and they always give you that same uneasy feeling of déjà vu, like seeing the milkman's nose on your own first-born.

I parked the car far enough away from the door to avoid any potential embarrassment to the household I was here to visit, and managed the last hundred yards or so burdened with four suitcases full of highly specialised equipment. The doorbell made a severe, functional buzzing sound like a dentist's drill sliding off recalcitrant enamel. While I waited for a response I checked out the rowan twig nailed up to the right of the porch. Black and white and red strings had been tied to it in the prescribed order, but still . . . a rowan twig in November wouldn't have much juice left in it. I concluded that this must be a quiet neighbourhood.

The man who opened the door to me was presumably James Dodson, the birthday boy's father. I took a strong dislike to him right then to save time and effort later. He was a solid-looking man, not big but hard-packed: grey eyes like two ball-bearings, salt-and-pepper hair adding its own echoes to the grey. In his forties, but probably as fit and trim now as he had been two decades ago: clearly, this was a man who recognised the importance of good diet, regular exercise and unremitting moral superiority. Pen had said he was a cop: chief constable in waiting, working out of Agar Street as one of the midwives to the government's new Serious and Organised Crime Agency. I think I would have guessed either a cop or a priest, and most priests gratefully let themselves go long before they hit forty: that's one of the perks of having a higher calling.

'You're the entertainer,' Dodson said, as you might say, 'You're a motherless piece of scum and you raped my dog.' He didn't make a move to help me with the cases, which I was carrying two in each hand.

'Felix Castor,' I agreed, my face set in an unentertaining deadpan. 'I roll the blues away.'

He nodded non-committally and opened the door wider to let me in. 'The living room,' he said, pointing. 'There'll be rather more children than we originally said. I hope that's okay.'

'The more the merrier,' I answered over my shoulder, walking on through. I sized the living room up with what I hoped looked like a professional eye, but it was just a room to me. 'This is fine. Everything I need. Great.'

'We were going to send Sebastian over to his father's, but the bloody man had some sort of work crisis on,' Dodson explained from behind me. 'Which makes one more. And a few extra friends . . .'

'Sebastian?' I inquired. Throwing out questions like that is a reflex with me, whether I want answers or not: it comes from the work I do. I mean, the work I used to do. Sometimes do. Can live *without* doing.

'Peter's stepbrother. He's from Barbara's previous marriage, just as Peter is from mine. They get along very well.'

'Of course.' I nodded solemnly, as if checking out the soundness of the familial support network was something I always did before I started in on the magic tricks and the wacky slapstick. Peter was the birthday boy: just turned fourteen. Too old, probably, for clowns and conjurors and parties of the cake-and-ice-cream variety. But then, that wasn't my call to make. They also serve who only pull endless strings of coloured ribbon out of a baked-bean tin.

'I'll leave you to set up, then,' Dodson said, sounding dubious. 'Please don't move any of the furniture without checking with me or Barbara first. And if you're setting up anything on the parquet that might scratch, ask us for pads.'

'Thanks,' I said. 'And mine's a beer whenever you're having one yourself. The term "beer" should not be taken to include the subset "lager".'

He was already heading for the door when I threw this out, and he kept right on going. I was about as likely to get a drink out of him as I was to get a French kiss.

So I got down to unpacking, a task which was made harder by the fact that these cases hadn't moved out of Pen's garage in the last ten years. There were all sorts of things in among the stage-magic gear that gave me a moment's – or more than a moment's – pause. A Swiss Army penknife (it had belonged to my old friend Rafi) with the main blade broken off short an inch from the tip; a home-made fetish rigged up out of the mummified body of a frog and three rusty nails; a feathered snood, looking a bit threadbare now but still carrying a faint whiff of perfume; and the camera.

Shit. The camera.

I turned it over in my hands, instantly submerged in a brief but powerful reverie. It was a Brownie Autographic No. 3, and all folded up as it was it looked more like a kid's lunchbox than anything else. But once I flipped the catches I could see that the red-leather bellows was still in place, the frosted viewfinder was intact, and (wonder of wonders) the hand-wheeled stops that extended the lens into its operating position still seemed to work. I'd found the thing in a flea market in Munich when I was backpacking through Europe: it was nearly a hundred years old, and I'd paid about a quid for it, which was the whole of the asking price because the lens was cracked right the way across. That didn't matter to me – not for what I principally had in mind at the time – so it counted as a bargain.

I had to put it to one side, though, because at that moment the first of the party guests were shepherded in by a very busty, very blonde, very beautiful woman who was obviously much too good for the likes of James Dodson. Or the likes of me, to be fair. She was wearing a white bloused top and a khaki skirt with an asymmetric hang which probably had a designer name attached to it somewhere and cost more than I earned in six months. For all that, though, she looked a touch worn and tired. Living with James Super-cop would do that to you, I speculated: or, possibly, living with Peter, assuming that Peter was the sullen streak of curdled sunlight hovering at her elbow. He had his father's air of blocky, aggressive solidity, with an adolescent's wary stubbornness grafted onto it: it made for a very unattractive combination, somehow.

The lady introduced herself as Barbara, in a voice that had enough natural warmth in it to make electric blankets irrelevant. She introduced Peter, too, and I offered him a smile and a nod. I tried to shake hands with him, out of some atavistic impulse probably brought on by being in Hampstead, but he'd already stomped away in the direction of a new arrival, with a loud bellow of greeting. Barbara watched him go with an unreadable, Zen-like smile which suggested prescription medication, but her gaze as she turned back to me was sharp and clear enough.

'So,' she said. 'Are you ready?'

For anything, I almost said – but I opted for a simple yes. All the same, I probably held the glance a half-moment too long. At any rate, Barbara suddenly remembered a bottle of mineral water that she was holding in her hand, and handed it to me with a slight blush and an apologetic grimace. 'You can have a beer in the kitchen with us afterwards,' she promised. 'If I give you one now, the kids will demand equal rights.'

I raised the bottle in a salute.

'So . . .' she said again. 'An hour's performance, then an hour off while we serve the food – and you come on again for half an hour at the end. Is that okay?'

'It's a valid strategy,' I allowed. 'Napoleon used it at Quatre Bras.'

This got a laugh, feeble as it was. 'We won't be able to stay for the show,' Barbara said, with a good facsimile of regret. 'There's quite a lot still to do behind the scenes – some of Peter's friends are staying over. But we might be able to sneak back in to catch the finale. If not, see you in the interval.' With a conspiratorial grin she beat her retreat and left me with my audience.

I let my gaze wander around the room, taking the measure of them. There was an in-group, clustered around Peter and engaged in a shouted conversation which colonised the entire room. There was an out-group, consisting of four or five temporary knots spread around the edges of the room, which periodically tried to attach themselves to the in-group in a sort of reversal of cellular fission. And then there was step-brother Sebastian.

It wasn't hard to spot him: I'd made a firm identification while I was still unfolding my trestle table and laying out my opening trick. He had the matrilineal blond hair, but his paler skin and watery blue eyes made him look as if someone had sketched him in pastels and then tried to erase him. He looked to be a lot smaller and slighter than Peter, too. Because he was the younger of the two? It was hard to tell, because his infolded, self-effaced posture probably took an inch or so off his height. He was the one on the fringes of the boisterous rabble, barely tolerated by the birthday boy and contemptuously ignored by the birthday boy's friends. He was the one left out of all the in-jokes, looking like he didn't belong and would rather be almost anywhere else: even with his real dad, perhaps, on a day when there was a work crisis on.

When I clapped my hands and shouted a two-minute warning, Sebastian filed up with the last of the rearguard and took up a position immediately behind Peter – a dead zone which nobody else seemed to want to lay claim to.

Then the show was on, and I had troubles of my own to attend to.

I'm not a bad stage-magician. It was how I paid my way through college, and when I'm in practice I'd go so far as to say I'm pretty sharp. Right then I was as rusty as hell, but I was still able to pull off some reasonably classy stuff – my own scaled-down versions of the great illusions I'd studied during my ill-spent youth. I made some kid's wristwatch disappear from a bag that he was holding, and turn up inside a box in someone else's pocket. I levitated the same kid's mobile phone around the room while Peter and the front-row elite stood up and waved their arms in the vain hope of tangling the wires they thought I was using. I even cut a deck of cards into pieces with garden shears and reconstituted them again, with a card that Peter had previously chosen and signed at the top of the deck.

But whatever the hell I did, I was dying on my feet. Peter sat stolidly at front and centre, arms folded in his lap, and glared at me all the while with paint-blistering contempt. He'd clearly reached his verdict, which was that being impressed by kids'-party magic could lose you a lot of status with your peers. And if the risk was there even for him, it was clearly unacceptable for his chosen guests. They watched him and took their cue from him, forming a block vote that I couldn't shift.

Sebastian seemed to be the only one who was actually interested in the show for its own sake – or perhaps the only one who had so little to lose that he could afford just to let himself get drawn in, without watching his back. It got him into trouble, though. When I finished the card trick and showed Peter his pristine eight of diamonds, Sebastian broke into a thin patter of applause, carried away for a moment by the excitement of the final reveal.

He stopped as soon as he realised that nobody else was joining in, but he'd already broken cover – forgetting what seemed otherwise to be very well-developed habits of camouflage and self-preservation. Annoyed, Peter stabbed backwards with his elbow, and I heard a *whoof* of air from Sebastian as he leaned suddenly forward, clutching his midriff. His head stayed bowed for a few moments, and when he came up he came up slowly. 'Fuckwit,' Peter snarled, *sotto voce*. 'He just used two decks. That's not even clever.'

I read a lot into this little exchange: a whole chronicle of casual cruelty and emotional oppression. You may think that's stretching an elbow in the ribs a touch too far – but I'm a younger brother myself, so the drill's not unfamiliar to me. And besides that, I knew one more thing about birthday boy than anybody else here knew.

I took a mental audit. Yes. I was letting myself get a little irritated, and that wasn't a good thing. I still had twenty minutes to run before the break and the cold beer in the kitchen. And I had one sure-fire winner, which I'd been meaning to save for the finale, but what the hell. You only live once, as people continue to say in the teeth of all the evidence.

I threw out my arms, squared my shoulders, tugged my cuffs – a pantomime display of preparation intended mainly to get Sebastian off the hook. It worked, as far as that went: all eyes turned to me. 'Watch very carefully,' I said, taking a new prop out of one of the cases and putting it on the table in front of me. 'An ordinary cereal box. Any of you eat this stuff? No, me neither. I tried them once, but I was mauled by a cartoon tiger.' Not a glimmer: not a sign of mercy in any of the forty or so eyes that were watching me.

'Nothing special about the box. No trapdoors. No false bottoms.' I rotated it through three dimensions, flicked it with a thumbnail to get a hollow *thwack* out of it, and held the open end up to Peter's face for him to take a look inside. He rolled his eyes as if he couldn't believe he was being asked to go along with this stuff, then gave me a wave that said he was as satisfied of the box's emptiness as he was ever going to be.

'Yeah, whatever,' he said, with a derisive snort. His friends laughed too: he was popular enough to get a choric echo whenever he spoke or snickered or made farting noises in his cheek. He had the touch, all right. Give him four, maybe five years and he was going to grow up into a right bastard.

Unless he took a walk down the Damascus Road one morning, and met something big and fast coming the other way.

'O-o-okay,' I said, sweeping the box around in a wide arc so that everyone else could see it. 'So it's an empty box. So who needs it, right? Boxes like this, they're just landfill waiting to happen.' I stood it on the ground, open end downwards, and trod it flat.

That got at least a widened eye and a shift of posture here and there around the room – kids leaning forward to watch, if only to check out how complete and convincing the damage was. I was thorough. You have to be. Like a dominatrix, you find that there's a direct relationship between the intensity of the stamping and trampling and the scale of the final effect.

When the box was comprehensively flattened, I picked it up and allowed it to dangle flaccidly from my left hand.

'But before you throw this stuff away,' I said, sweeping the cluster of stolid faces with a stern, schoolteacherly gaze, 'you've got to check for biohazards. Anyone up for that? Anyone want to be an environmental health inspector when they grow up?'

There was an awkward silence, but I let it lengthen. It was Peter's dime: I only had to entertain him, not pimp for him.

Finally, one of the front-row cronies shrugged and stood up. I stepped a little aside to welcome him into my performance space – broadly speaking, the area between the leather recliner and the running buffet.

'Give a big hand to the volunteer,' I suggested. They razzed him cordially instead: you find out who your friends are.

I straightened the box with a few well-practised tugs and tucks. This was the crucial part, so of course I kept my face as bland as school custard. The volunteer held his hand out for the box: instead, I caught his hand in my own and turned it palm up. 'And the other one,' I said. 'Make a cup. *Verstehen Sie* "cup"? Like this. Right. Excellent. Good luck, because you never know . . .'

I upended the box over his hands, and a large brown rat smacked right down into the makeshift basket of his fingers. He gurgled like a punctured water bed and jumped back, his hands flying convulsively apart, but I was ready and I caught the rat neatly before she could fall.

Then, because I knew her well, I added a small grace note to the trick by stroking her nipples with the ball of my thumb.

This made her arch her back and gape her mouth wide open, so that when I brandished her in the faces of the other kids I got a suitable set of jolts and starts. Of course, it wasn't a threat display – it was 'More, big boy, give me more' – but they couldn't be expected to know that look at their tender age. Any more than they knew that I'd dropped Rhona into the box when I pretended to straighten it after the trampling.

And bow. And acknowledge the applause. Which would have been fine if there'd been any. But Peter still sat like Patience on a monument, as the volunteer trudged back to his seat with his machismo at half-mast.

Peter's face said I'd have to do a damn sight more than that to impress him.

So I thought about the Damascus Road again. And, like the bastard I am, I reached for the camera.

This isn't my idea of how a grown man should go about keeping the wolf from the door, I'd like you to know: it was Pen who put me up to it. Pamela Elisa Bruckner: why that shortens to Pen rather than Pam I've never been sure, but she's an old friend of mine, and incidentally the rightful owner of Rhona the rat. She's also my landlady, for the moment at least, and since I wouldn't wish that fate on a rabid dog I count myself lucky that it's fallen to someone who's genuinely fond of me. It lets me get away with a hell of a lot.

I should also tell you that I do have a job – a real job, which pays the bills at least occasionally. But at the time currently under discussion, I was taking an extended holiday: not entirely voluntary, and not without its own attendant problems relating to cash flow, professional credibility and personal self-esteem. In any case, it left Pen with a vested interest in putting alternative work my way. Since she was still a good

Catholic girl (when she wasn't being a Wicca priestess), she went to Mass every Sunday, lit a candle to the Blessed Virgin and prayed to this tune: 'Please, Madonna, in your wisdom and mercy, intercede for my mother though she died with many carnal sins weighing on her soul; let the troubled nations of Earth find a road to peace and freedom; and make Castor solvent, amen.'

But usually she left it at that, which was a situation we could both live with. So it was an unpleasant surprise to me when she stopped counting on divine intervention and told me about the kids' party agency she was setting up with her crazy friend Leona – and the slimy sod of a street magician who'd given her an eleventh-hour stab in the back.

'But you could do this so *easily*, Fix,' she coaxed, over coffee laced with cognac in her subterranean sitting room. The smell was making me dizzy: not the smell of the brandy, but the smell of rats and earth and leaf mulch and droppings and Mrs Amelia Underwood roses, of things growing and things decaying. One of her two ravens – Arthur, I think – was clacking his beak against the top shelf of the bookcase, making it hard for me to stick to a train of thought. This was her den, her centre of gravity: the inverted penthouse underneath the three-storey monstrosity where her grandmother had lived and died in the days when mammoths still roamed the Earth. She had me at a disadvantage here, which was why she'd asked me in to start with.

'You can do real magic,' Pen pointed out sweetly, 'so fake magic ought to be a doddle.'

I blinked a couple of times to clear my eyes, blinded by candles, fuddled by incense. In a lot of ways, the way Pen lives is sort of reminiscent of Miss Havisham in *Great Expectations*: she only uses the basement, which means that the rest of the house apart from my bedsitter up in the roof space is frozen in the 1950s, never visited, never revised. Pen herself froze a fair bit later than that, but like Miss Haversham she wears her heart on her mantelpiece. I try not to look at it.

On this particular occasion I took refuge in righteous indignation. 'I can't do real magic, Pen, because there's no such animal. Not the way you mean it, anyway. What do I look like, eh? Just because I can talk to the dead – and whistle up a tune for them – that doesn't make me Gandalf the bastard Grey. And it doesn't mean that there are fairies at the bottom of the sodding garden.'

The crude language was a ploy, intended to derail the conversation. It didn't work, though. I got the impression that Pen had worked out her script in advance for this one.

'"What is now proved was once only imagined",' she said, primly – because she knows that Blake is my main man and I can't argue with him. 'Okay,' she went on, topping up my cup with about a half-pint of Janneau XO (it was going to be dirty pool on both sides, then), 'but you did all that stage-magic stuff when we were in college, didn't you? You were *wonderful* back then. I bet you could still do it. I bet you wouldn't even have to practise. And it's two hundred quid for a day's work, so you could pay me a bit off last month's chunk of what you owe me . . .'

It took a lot more persuasion, and a fair bit more brandy – so much brandy, in fact, that I made a pass at her on my unsteady way out of the door. She slapped off my right hand, steered my left onto the door handle and kissed me goodnight on the cheek without breaking stride.

I was profoundly grateful for that, when I woke up in the morning with my tongue stuck to my soft palate and my head full of unusable fuzz. Sexy, sweet, uninhibited nineteen-year-old Pen, with her autumn bonfire of hair, her pistachio eyes and her probably illegal smile, would have been one thing: thirty-something Earth Mother Pen in her Sibyl's cave, tended by rats and ravens and Christ only knew what other familiar spirits, and still waiting for her prince to come even though she knew exactly where he was and what he'd turned into . . . There was too much blood under the bridge, now. Leave it at that.

Then I remembered that I'd agreed to do the party, just before I made the pass, and I cursed like a longshoreman. Game, set and match to Pen and Monsieur Janneau. I hadn't even known we were playing doubles.

So there was a reason, anyway, even if it wasn't good or sufficient, why I now found myself facing down these arrogant little shits and prostituting my God-given talents for the paltry sum of two hundred quid. There was a reason why I'd put myself in the way of temptation. And there was a reason why I fell.

'Now,' I said, with a smile as wide as a Hallowe'en pumpkin, 'for my last and most ambitious trick before you all go off and feed your faces – I need another volunteer from the audience.' I pointed at Sebastian. 'You, sir, in the second row. Would you be so good?' Sebastian looked hangdog, intensely reluctant: stepping into the spotlight meant certain humiliation and possibly much worse. But the older boys were whistling and catcalling, and Peter was telling him to get the hell up there and do it. So he stood up and worked his way along the row, tripping a couple of times over the outstretched feet that were planted in his path.

This was going to be cruel, but not to stepbrother Sebastian: no, my un-birthday gift to him was a loaded gun, which he could use in any way he wanted to. And for

Peter . . . well, sometimes cruelty is kindness in disguise. Sometimes pain is the best teacher. Sometimes it does you no harm to realise that there's a limit to what you can get away with.

Sebastian had made his way around to my side of the trestle table now, and he was standing awkwardly next to me. I picked up the Autographic and slipped the hooks on either side, wheeling the bellows out fully into its working position. With its red leather and dark wood it looked like a pretty impressive piece of kit: when I gave it to Sebastian to hold, he took it gingerly.

'Please examine the camera,' I told him. 'Make sure it's okay. Fully functional, fully intact.' He glanced at it cursorily, without enthusiasm, nodded and tried to hand it back to me.

I didn't take it. 'Sorry,' I said, 'you're my cameraman now. You have to do the job properly because I'm relying on you.'

He looked again, and this time he noticed what was staring him in the face.

'Well – there's black tape,' he said. 'Over the lens.'

I affected to be surprised, and took a look for myself. 'Gentlemen,' I said to the room at large. 'Ladies.' A five-second pause for howls of mocking laughter, nudges and pointing fingers. 'My assistant has just brought something very alarming to my attention. This camera has black masking tape over the lens, and it can't therefore take photographs –' I let the pause lengthen '– in the normal way. We're going to have to try to take a *spirit* photo.'

Peter and Peter's friends looked pained and scornful at this suggestion: it sounded to them like a pretty lame finale.

'Spirit photographs are among the most difficult feats for the magician to encompass,' I told them gravely, paying no attention to the sounds of derision. 'Think of an escapologist freeing himself from a mailbag suspended upside down from a hook in a cage which has been dumped out of a jet plane flying about two miles up. Well, this trick is a little like that. Less visually spectacular, but just as flamboyantly pointless.'

I gestured to the birthday boy. 'We're going to take your picture, Peter,' I told him. 'So why don't you go and stand over there, by the wall. A plain background works best for this.'

Peter obeyed with a great show of heavy resignation.

'You have another brother?' I asked Sebastian, quietly.

He glanced up at me, startled. 'No,' he said.

'Or a cousin or something – someone your own age, who used to live here with you?'

He shook his head.

'You know how to use a camera?'

Sebastian was on firmer ground here, and he looked relieved. 'Yeah. I've got one upstairs. But it's just point and shoot, it doesn't have any . . . focus thing, or . . .'

I dismissed these objections with a shake of the head, giving him a reassuring half-smile. 'Doesn't matter,' I said. 'This one focuses manually, but we're not going to bother with that anyway. Because we're not using either the lens or ordinary light to form the image. But the thing you're going to be clicking is this.' I gave him the air bulb – sitting at the end of a coil of rubber tubing, it was the only part of the camera that I'd had to replace. 'You squeeze it hard and it opens the shutter. When I say, okay?'

I hadn't loaded the Autographic for more than a decade, but all the stuff I needed was right there in the box and my hands knew what to do. I lined up a new plate, peeled away one corner of the waxed cover sheet, then slammed it into place and tore the cover free in one smooth movement. It wasn't what a professional would have done: partly because there was bound to be some seepage of light if you loaded the camera like that in an ordinarily lit room – but mostly because I was loading print paper rather than negative film. We were cutting out one stage of the normal photographic process. Again, it didn't matter, but I noticed as I was tightening the screws up again that James and Barbara Dodson had wandered in and were standing at the back of the room. That was going to mean a louder eruption, but by this stage I didn't really give a monkey's chuff: Peter had gotten quite seriously under my skin.

I got Sebastian into position, steering him with my hand on his shoulders. Peter was getting bored and restive, but we were almost done. I could have ratcheted up the tension a bit more, but since the outcome was still in doubt I thought I might as well just suck it and see. Either it would work or it wouldn't. 'Okay, on my mark. Peter – smile. Nice try, but no. Kids in the front row, show Peter what a smile is. Sebastian – three, two, one, now!'

Sebastian pressed the bulb, and the shutter made a slow, arthritic *whuck-chunk* sound. Good. I'd been half-afraid that nothing would happen at all.

'Now, we don't have any fixative,' I announced, as my memory started to kick in again, piecemeal. 'So the image won't last for long. But we can make it clearer with a stop bath. Lemon juice will do, or vinegar, if you—?' I looked hopefully at the two grown-ups, and Barbara slipped out of the room again.

'What about developing fluid?' James asked, looking at me with vague but definite mistrust.

I shook my head. 'We're not using light,' I said again. 'We're photographing the spirit world, not the visible one, so the film doesn't have to develop: it has to translate.'

James's face showed very clearly what he thought of this explanation. There was an awkward silence, broken by Barbara as she came back in with a bottle of white-wine vinegar, a plastic bowl and an apologetic smile. 'This is going to stink,' she warned me as she retreated again to the back of the room.

She was right. The sweet-sour tang of the vinegar hit and held as I poured out about two-thirds of the bottle, which covered the bowl to half an inch or so deep. Then, with Sebastian still standing next to me, I slipped the plate out of the camera, very deliberately blocking with my body the audience's line of sight. 'Sebastian,' I said, 'you're still the cameraman here. That means you're the medium through which the spirits are working. Please, dip the print paper in the vinegar and slosh it around so that it's completely soaked. An image should form on the paper as you do this. Do you see an image, Sebastian?'

Peter hadn't even bothered to move from his place over by the wall: in fact, he was leaning against it now, looking more sullen and bored than ever. Sebastian stared first in consternation and then in amazement at the paper as he sluiced it round and round in the bowl.

'Do you see an image?' I repeated, knowing damn well that he did.

'Yeah!' he blurted. Everyone in the room was picking up on his tension and astonishment now: I didn't need to go for any verbal build-up.

'And what *is* that image?'

'A boy. It's – I think it's—!'

'Of course you can see a boy,' I interrupted. 'We just took

a photo of your brother, Peter. Is that who you can see, Sebastian?'

He shook his head, his wide eyes still staring down at the muddy photograph. 'No. Well, I mean, yeah but – there's somebody else, too. It's—'

I cut across him again. Everything in its place. 'Somebody you recognise?'

Sebastian nodded emphatically. 'Yeah.'

I like to see what I was doing here as siding with the underdog: but if there had been no element of sadism in it, I wouldn't have been looking at Peter as I said the next few words. 'And does he have a name, this other boy? What dark wonders from the spirit world have we captured and pinned to the wall, Sebastian? Tell us his name.'

Sebastian swallowed hard. It was genuine nerves rather than showmanship, but the strained pause was better than anything I could have choreographed myself.

'Davey Simmons,' Sebastian said, his voice a little too high.

The effect on Peter was electrifying. He yelled in what sounded like honest, naked terror, coming away from the wall with a jerk and then lurching across to the bowl in three staccato strides. But I was too quick for him. 'Thank you, Sebastian,' I said, whipping the print out of the bowl and waving it in the air as though to dry it – and as though keeping it out of Peter's reach was only accidental.

It had come out pretty well. In black and white, of course, and darkened around the edges where the light had got in at the paper, but nice and clear where it needed to be. It showed Peter as a sort of grainy blur, only recognisable by his posture and by the darker splodge of his hair. By contrast, the figure that stood at his elbow was very distinct indeed: sad, washed out, beaten down by time and loneliness and the fact of his own death, but not to be mistaken for marsh gas, cardboard cut-out or misapplied imagination.

'Davey Simmons,' I mused. 'Did you know him well, Peter?'

'I never fucking heard of him!' Peter yelled, throwing himself at me with desperate fury. 'Give me that!' I'm not hefty by any means, but for all his solidity Peter was just a kid: holding him off while I showed the print to his friends wasn't hard at all. They were all staring at it with expressions that ran the gamut from sick horror to bowel-loosening panic.

'And yet,' I mused, 'he stands beside you as you eat, and work, and sleep. In his death he watches you living, night into day into night. Why do you suppose that is?'

'I don't know,' Peter squealed, 'I don't know! Give it to me!'

Most of the audience were on their feet now, some surging forward to look at the print but most pulling back as if they wanted to get some distance from it. James Dodson waded through them like a battleship through shrimp boats, and it was he who took the print out of my hands. Peter immediately turned his attentions to his father, and tried again to snatch the photo, but James pushed him back roughly. He stared down at the print in perplexity, shaking his head slowly from side to side. Then, with his face flushing deep red, he tore it up, very deliberately, into two pieces, then four, then eight. Peter gave a whimper, caught somewhere between misery and the illusion of relief: but from where I was standing it looked like he'd be living with this for a while to come.

Dodson was working on thirty-two pieces when I turned to Sebastian and solemnly shook his hand.

'You've got a gift,' I said. He met my gaze, and understanding passed between us. What he had was a lever. Peter wasn't going to be as free in future with his elbows, or his fists, or his feet: not now that everyone had seen his guilt, and his weakness. There wasn't any extra charge for this: I work on a fixed rate.

I'd noticed the miserable little ghost hovering around Peter as soon as he'd come into the room. They're harder to spot in daylight, but I've got a lot of experience on top of a lot of natural sensitivity, and I know what to expect in a house where they don't keep their rowan sprigs up to date. I didn't know what the connection was, but unless Davey Simmons had no family at all there had to be a damn good reason why he was haunting this house rather than his own. He couldn't get away from Peter: his soul was tangled up in him like a bird in a briar patch. You could read that in any number of ways, but Peter's violent reaction had ruled out some of them, changed the odds on others.

Anyway, things got a bit confused after that. Dodson was yelling at me to pack up my things and get out, and spitting and spluttering about a lawsuit to follow. Peter had fled from the room, pursued by Barbara, and barricaded himself in somewhere upstairs to judge by the bangs and yells that I could hear. The party guests milled around like a decapitated squid: lots of appendages, no brain, faintly suspect smell. And Sebastian stood watching me with big, solemn eyes, and never said another word as long as I was there.

When I asked Dodson for the money he owed me for the performance, he punched me in the mouth. I took that in my stride: no teeth loosened, only a symbolic amount of blood-shed. I probably had that coming. He went for the camera next, though, and I went for it too: me and that Brownie went back a long way, and I didn't want to have to go looking for another machine with such sympathetic vibes. We tussled inconclusively for a few moments for control of it, then he seemed to remember where he was: in his own living room, watched by a gaggle of his son's best friends, whose fathers he also no doubt knew well in work or club circles.

'Get out,' he told me, his eyes still wild. 'Get out of my house, you irresponsible bastard, before I throw you out on your ear.'

I gave up on the money. It wouldn't be easy for me to argue that traumatising the birthday boy was within my remit. I packed everything up laboriously into the four cases, under James's glaring eyes and stertorous breathing. He was suffering a kind of anaphylactic reaction to me now, and if I didn't get out soon he might crash and burn as his immune system tore itself apart in its desire to remove the irritation.

Out into the hall, and I caught sight of Barbara on the upstairs landing. Her face was pale and tense, but I swear she threw me a nod. With four suitcases worth of heavy freight I was in no position to wave back – and it might have been tactless in any case.